JUAN

OF THE

DEAD

The Reanimated World Tour

Jacalyn Boggs

JUAN OF THE DEAD

For information contact :

http://www.erendi.com

Interior & Cover design by James Rock

ISBN: 978-1-950903-28-3

Second Edition: January 2022

ERENDI
PUBLISHING

DEDICATION

To LJ Idol for inspiring me and
the FXBG Wrimos who believed in me.

CHAPTER ONE

I never worried about time much, until time caught up with me. How was I to know time would show up looking like a giant Aztec calendar? Cliché, much? Or maybe that was Death taking on the appearance of the calendar? Like I know. You want to talk about putting a cramp in your social schedule, try taking death for a test drive.

It all started with an innocent cruise to Mexico. How can a girl pass that up?

Lounging on the deck of a ship working on your tan while pool boys service my every whim? Well, maybe not my every whim, but you know what I mean. I'm no dummy. When something like that was presented to you in your Christmas card from mom and dad it is run, do not walk to get your luggage packed! That's what I did, at least.

Along with lounging by the aforementioned pool, the cruise line prepared several day trips into Mexican towns and ancient Aztec-type cities. I think history and geography were my worst subjects in school, so I didn't see the attraction of visiting tiny towns. But, hey – when in Mexico, right?

Arriving in Chichen Itza, home of the death-dealing calendar, I noticed crumbly ruins and a huge pyramid alongside all the fun tourist-trap spots you could ever want. Take a tour or shop first? Oh, the choices, the choices.

Please, like that's hard? Crumbly ruins or shopping... DUH! I took my hot little buns in the direction of someplace to give my Amex a workout.

The main gift shop became the last store I ever entered-alive that is.

Too busy debating between spoons and shot glasses, all decorated with artistic representations of the Temple outside, I failed to notice the larger than life replica of an Aztec calendar suspended above my head. I picked up a shot glass just as the earthquake hit.

Maybe if I lived in California, I would know what to do in such an event, but guess what? In Virginia we didn't do earthquakes. Okay, like, there was that one earthquake, but it was a fluke and I wasn't even there for it, so it does not count. We mostly do humid, and there's really just no solution for that. Like any red-blooded American and fashion-conscious girl, I ducked in hopes of protecting my hair, my Coach purse, and my Jimmy Choos.

So, of course, that's how my life ended: protecting my fashion investments in the middle-of-nowhere, Mexico. Not high on the cool factor, but really, was death ever high on the cool factor? You can't blame a girl for trying. I didn't see the falling calendar but was told the weight of it broke my neck. In just the snap of a finger, dead. That would teach me that protecting my hair with my hands was not the best plan in an earthquake. In my defense, if you knew how long it took me to get my kinky hair to do anything in this humidity, you wouldn't blame me! Why waste all that work?

And then I was dead. Killed by the Aztec calendar. That was your Age of Aquarius right there. I always hated that sign on the zodiac.

I would like to tell you that I saw a great white light, or felt some sense of great peace, or whatever other mumbo-jumbo you want to give to the blissful darkness of death. Sorry. Mostly there was a whole lot of nothing. Nothing until I woke up, that is.

Pearly gates? Saint Peter waiting to assign me to Heaven or to Hell? Angels strumming on harps? Nope, not a one. Not even a glimpse of the other place, either. Unless you counted Mexico.

What did I see? A tall form, white coat covering a perfectly built body, and wire-rimmed glasses over chocolate eyes. He had shaggy black hair just the right length to run your fingers through and lips plump enough to kiss.

Mmm, tasty.

Who was this man leaning over me, and why was his hand on my chest?

Wait, my chest?

Now, I'm a modern girl, and no prude, but last I checked there was a serious lack of consent happening. What I had was a serious case of some guy copping a feel of my C-cups. What's with jumping straight to second base? While I was obviously unconscious, even? I don't think so!

I tried lifting my arm to bat his hand away, but unfortunately for me, his hand worked just fine while mine did not. In fact, nothing wanted to move. Except, of course, my eager little nipple which snapped to attention at the stranger's touch- traitor. Gotta love it when the body calls a mutiny.

When I caught a glimpse of those lips, all I could think about was kissing them. Forget that this guy could very well be some sort of perverted homicidal maniac; no, my mind

9

jumped to instant romance. I tried to tell him to stop, ask him who he was, say anything really, but all that escaped my mouth was a gurgle.

Gurgle? Oh, that is absolute hotness right there. Every man's gonna love that one. Cue immediate hand removal.

Except, he didn't remove his hand. In fact, I swore his thumb grazed almost absently over that pesky nipple, and I started to feel a warmth in my body. Up until then, my body was completely devoid of feeling, cold even.

I'm super glad for Mr. Grabby Hands. Insert sarcasm here.

Now, I could have been grateful that Doctor Feelgood came along to warm me right up, but nuh-uh. I don't do lack of consent. Was it too much to ask for a little wining and dining? Maybe a movie before you start in on a grope-fest?

If only I could have gotten my mouth to form some words, this jerk would have gotten the tongue lashing of a lifetime. I was just thinking about the many things I'd like to say to this jerk when he leaned down until I could feel his hot breath on my ear as he whispered to me.

"Just give it time."

And then there was his thumb, moving again.

Time? Time for what?

I'd show him time. I'd make sure he served time for assault! I thought hard, trying to remember how I got there-wherever 'there' was- while trying not to get distracted by that thumb of his. I needed to start building my case. The last thing I remembered was...

And then it all flooded back to me. Shopping. Shot glass. Earthquake. Protecting my...

Oh. My. GOD! My shoes!

I sat bolt upright, narrowly missing the guy in the white coat as he jumped backwards and looked down at my feet.

My bare feet. My toes wiggled as if to say, "Nope, no Choos here." Good thing he moved away from me.

This man stole my shoes. He better replace them or pony up some cash. I am on a tight budget since I maxed out my MasterCard last month buying clothing for this cruise. If I killed him for stealing my shoes, could I get off? Some crimes are completely justifiable.

Now that I had something to look at besides hot-but-creepy guy and a ceiling, I took in my surroundings. The only light came from candles spread throughout a room of stone walls. Come to think of it, the table I sat on was stone as well.

Who had a stone table? Fred Flintstone? What the hell? Where was I and how did I get here?

My next effort to talk did not end in a gurgle, but instead a raspy one-word question.

"How?"

Well, at least it wasn't 'gurgle'. My brain tried to convince my body to head towards standing, but my body replied 'no way'. I was too sluggish, like when you just weren't quite awake.

"Well it's all very complicated. You see, when I unearthed this book..."

The guy started babbling and I tuned him out. It sounded a lot like ramble, ramble, some kind of digging and Aztec and Mayan ruins, blah, blah.

Who cares?

My thoughts were more on the line of 'where the hell are my Jimmy Choos and Coach purse?'. I knew my priorities, and Geek Speak was at the bottom of the list. Like, six feet under, bottom of the list. Seriously, how hard was it to say something like 'I saw your hotness getting crushed by a giant calendar so I dug you out, gave you mouth to mouth, copped a feel, and now you aren't risking dying.'? See, that wasn't so hard. His eleventy-hundred-word answer surely had to end with something to that effect, right?

I had a bad case of the stiffs that I could not shake. I tried stretching and heard the sound of my bones crunching and cracking. Gross. Glad I could move and all but the stiffness thing had to go. I couldn't be pulling a snap, crackle, and pop every time I moved. That just was not sexy.

Maybe I just needed a good walk; through a department store. A walk through an expensive department store with a non-maxed out credit card. There was nothing like a good dose of retail therapy to wake up and invigorate a girl.

My thoughts wandered to the sales at Macy's back home, but around the time my brain entered the imaginary shoe department I noticed the man's ramblings stopped. He looked at me like he expected something. Maybe I should have listened a bit more carefully. I tried to focus, to remember what was said, but all my brain registered was a book. Digging, and a book and... nothing. I decided the blank look might be the best response.

"Do you see why this is so monumental?" he asked. I could tell he'd repeated himself.

Great, what was 'so monumental' and why did he look like a kid on Christmas morning?

I licked my dry lips, noticing just how cracked they were.

I hate this godforsaken country. I needed to get back to the cruise ship stat for some dire medical attention to my lips.

The ship store better have something good, none of that cheap drug store garbage.

I continued my stream of highly intellectual, one-word sentences, "What?"

"Too much? Maybe I went too fast? I never did this before." He pushed the glasses further up his nose and leafed through a fat notebook filled with handwritten pages.

"Where?"

We needed to move this forward and get right down to the bottom of things. I needed to shake the mental cobwebs, but for now one-word answers might move things along faster.

I knew where I was. I was in a tourist shop looking at shot glasses. Fast forward to now. Now I was here. My eyes looked again at the dark, stony room around me. I wanted to know where here was, and how I managed to end up on some creepy stone table.

"Where?" he asked, looking up from his weird notebook. "Oh, where are we? Well, after the earthquake... You see, I saw the replica fall on you. I cleared the debris away, but it was too late. No one would really help, it was chaos, so I brought you here. We're inside the Temple."

What the hell? No one noticed this guy carrying a hot babe so far out of his league to some creepy...

Oh. My. GAWD. I'm inside that nasty Temple that's like a zillion years old? Where some ancient primitive barbarians probably conducted sacrifices?

Did I wake up just moments before this guy tried to sacrifice me? Was he some sort of wanna-be nerd that thought if he recreated something from history that he'd be cool? And gross, was that table actually used for sacrifices? I was laying on it! My hair touched it!

The thought of centuries-old blood cooties did away with whatever stiffness still held me back. I leapt from the table in disgust. It rocked, and shifted about three inches, but I barely gave it notice. I was way too focused on the chance of blood creepiness possibly making its way to my personage. The whole thing managed to fix my speech impediment, too.

"You not gonna slice and dice me!"

Okay, the English was bad. Apparently, my speech still

needed some work. I'd rather speak in broken English than in one-word questions.

"What? No! I wanted to save you. It's why I brought you here," he said as he waved his hands in front of him while shaking his head like some flappy chicken. A cute flappy chicken. "You're safe! I swear."

I had to admit, the guy looked like a puppy dog in trouble for knocking over the trash can. I guess that's what happened when you're a beta male faced with an obvious, nine-point-five alpha gal such as myself. My heart softened. He was so pathetic it was cute. Maybe he didn't mean any ill while dragging me to Castle Creepy.

"Where's my purse? And my shoes? What the hell happened?"

I understood this guy seemed to think he was pulling a knight in shining armor. Save the girl from the fallen Aztec calendar. Fantabulous! How about saving the girl's Coach purse? Those things don't grow on trees.

He took a few steps back. "I'm so sorry. I didn't think to grab... I mean... I just wanted to save you. It might still be there. Under all that rubble. There was a second quake, after I got you out. And..."

Great. I went on some supposedly-fantastic trip out of the country and land in the middle of earthquake central. Just my luck. But, must I really sacrifice my Coach purse and everything inside.

Oh cripes, my Amex and Visa were in that thing. How's a girl supposed to survive without plastic? Impossible!

I stepped towards him and he stepped backwards, keeping the gap between us constant. I attempted to keep my voice even. "What are you saying?"

"Um, uh, that is..." His back hit the wall behind him. There was no escape, so I moved closer. "It... You see... the roof... it collapsed... and..."

"My purse is gone? Forever?" My purse, my credit cards, my makeup, that really gorgeous necklace I bought from some cute five-year-old girl near the docks. It was almost too much to bear. "And my shoes?"

"I removed those. I had to. For the ceremony. I told you that."

Hope! I might be out a necklace and whatever else was in my purse, but that could be replaced. One quick call to the bank and new cards would merrily wait in my mailbox for my return to civilization. And the cruise company better believe that 'they'd be doling out some major moolah for the loss of my purse and all this other craziness.

"What is this ceremony?"

Maybe I should have paid better attention when he rambled before, but if I found out he did some kind of wacky take-off-the-girl's-shoes-and- now-we-are-married garbage I was not going to be happy. A guy should at least take a girl out and maybe be on a first name (any name?) basis with her before engaging in some kind of ancient, ritualistic and insane marriage ceremony without any consent on her part. Call me old fashioned.

"Well, I told you," he continued. I noticed him licking his lips and fidgeting with his hands. A few more steps and I was right in front of him, nearly eye to eye. "I brought you back."

"Back from what?" I tried to be annoyed, but was it wrong that I wanted to kiss this guy? Something in me stirred, but I squashed it. Too weird. I couldn't give in to some sort of wacky attraction when there were too many questions in my muddled head. Annoyance.

Remember... Coach!

"From the dead. I reanimated you using this book I found while on a dig about twenty clicks from here."

And that's it. How my life began after my death. I was

one of the Reanimated Ones, though most might call us zombies. Just forget all that garbage from Hollywood about shuffling, drooling, brain-obsessed, homicidal corpses. Maybe that was how zombies rolled in the 1970's, but need I remind you that people also thought polyester was a good fashion statement? You cannot trust anything from those misguided times.

Besides, have you ever tried to remove dried brains out from underneath your fingernails? It's no fun and your manicurist really does not like it.

Juan of the Dead

CHAPTER TWO

Over the next few hours, my inner Libra weighed the changes between my old life and my new un-life. For example: as a newly dead woman, would my credit cards go into instant lock-down, denying me access to all things Prada, Gucci, and Chanel? Hmmm, hidden in there might be a well-dressed law firm that I might consider putting on retainer. Perhaps I could convince some jury to award me hefty reparations for this nightmare.

The scales of my zodiac sign groaned from the strain as my list grew, in an effort to find some sort of balance. I wanted only to ensure my continued existence in the manner I was accustomed to. Namely keeping myself stylishly dressed and on the VIP lists for all the great parties. Should it matter that I was dead? I could walk, I could talk, I could look great in Givenchy. Who could ask for anything more?

"Where are my shoes?" I asked again. If I got them and returned to the cruise ship, maybe the whole horrible experience would vanish. I was not afraid to pretend the whole thing never happened. No one needed to know, and I could get back to enjoying those cabana boys by the pool.

If my tone came off a little demanding, it served the guy right. Ok, maybe I should have considered being grateful since without him I'd be, well, dead but I needed shoes and needed them now. Denial was a beautiful thing.

"Let me get them for you. I put them... uh..." He cast about, a bit absentmindedly.

Oh, dear Lord, he lost my shoes.

These feet did not meet the great outdoors without something on them. I would never make it anywhere without protection for the soles of my feet. Did metabolically challenged folks need to worry about blood pressure?

"You said you only removed them for the ceremony. How far could they go without me in them?"

He blinked, maybe a little put off by my biting tone. Bully for him. Only an idiot would get between a girl and her shoes.

"I, uh, I took them off after bringing you here and... um.. . then..."

Oh geez.

He still refused to tell me exactly what he did? What on earth does it take to do some kind of Hocus-Pocus-Pretend-I'm-Merlin garbage anyway? I needed to take the fate of my toes in my own hand and find Jimmy myself.

"Hey, where did you put them? Maybe with your stuff? I assume you lit these candles with something? Or maybe..."

He snapped his fingers. Glad I could spark his brain to work by pointing out the glaringly obvious.

"Wait here. I'll be right back."

He ducked out of the musty, ancient room, leaving just me, and the cobwebs, and the table I woke up on. In disgust I looked at the table but saw no real signs of thousands of brutal ritualistic sacrifices. I hoped that meant I got lucky. Maybe this was just where the priests would come to have supper after a long day of those brutal ritualistic sacrifices. Carving up humans and chucking them to the gods must have worked up quite the appetite!

What did I know? I sure didn't pay attention to any of that history junk growing up. I had a life, so I focused on my clothes, my nails, and if Bobby McKearny liked me. (He did, we dated for nine weeks my senior year before I dumped him for a college guy I met at a party.)

Brutal ritualistic sacrifices... yech. I shuddered. I couldn't get the thought out of my head. It wanted to run around inside my brain, making me worry I might lose my mind. Then again, I was believing some crazy guy raised me from the dead. Did that mean it was too late to worry about my mind?

I edged towards the only escape from the room: a shadowy door frame. The dark tunnel he disappeared down looked rather foreboding. Did I really want to blunder down it? Barefoot? I squinted down the hallway mostly out of some sort of reflex or habit but realized the effort was completely unnecessary. No candles as far as I could see. How could I make things out?

No worries about premature wrinkling from squinting here! Killer perk! The future plastic surgeon in my life would probably mourn the loss of his new Audi. Worked for me, if not for the doctor. The idea brought a small grin to my face, and I stopped squinting. Laugh lines were okay. Crow's feet – not so much.

Did that mean I scored my glorious twenty-eight-year-old body forever? Okay, I claimed twenty-eight, even if I was really thirty-three. No one believed me when I said my real age anyway and I sometimes even got carded when ordering from the bar. No skin off my back if I got to stay young forever. If dying at thirty-three meant looking mid-twenties for eternity, how could one complain?

Really, at this point, downsides seemed scarce. Obviously, I was alive, so who could deny me use of my credit cards? Could they prove I was dead if I was walking around and talking to people? Corpses that walk and talk generally give off a non-corpse vibe to people, especially authorities dealing in death stuff. No way people could deny me my rights.

I wondered who to contact about discrimination towards the not-dead. This could be a whole new angle for civil rights lawyers.

What was I?

The question made me really think. I was dead, but not dead. No blood thirst and fangs, plus this guy totally did not seem vampy. That logic ruled out vampire.

The slim information he gave was this: I croaked, he performed some ceremony, and now here I stood. Un-croaked. I wasn't really alive. Undead? Re-alive? If you think you're confused, just imagine how I felt.

I needed to figure it out before crying foul. Undead discrimination people might not consider me undead. There's nothing like being dissed by your own people.

I needed to find out what this guy said and determine my new station in life and death. Why did it sound so boring? I planned on smiling pretty in hopes that nerd-boy might sum things up. Don't judge, sometimes flirting could really get the ball rolling.

My mental focus returned to the hallway. It was nothing more than a long corridor.

Where the hell did he hide my shoes?

You carried the hot dead girl from the crumbling building into the creepy Aztec Temple of Doom. You put her on a grody old stone table after hopefully making sure there's no gross, two thousand-year-old blood on it from barbaric sac-rifices. You removed shoes and put them underneath said table. You used crazy ritual, which once more, had better not mean we're married, to bring her back. You gave her back her shoes. End of story.

What part of this particular chain of events meant hiding my shoes in the next Mexican city over? Really, it wasn't a hard concept. How long ago did he leave? My impatience only grew.

I returned to the mental list for each category to hang on my scales. I needed to find balance, an equality between the two. Only then could I truly get on with my life; death; whatever.

On the side of being alive I added the usual goodness: Birthdays, parties, shopping, guys, shopping, family, guys, work, shopping, and guys.

On the side of being whatever I heaped on: Young and hot forever, oh can I celebrate my birthday and my death day? Double the presents! It was awful close to my birth-day, but still, little is perfect in this world.

That was as far as I got when my nerd in a lab coat re-turned. All praises to the shoe gods, his hands held my Jimmy Choos, albeit a little too carelessly. I raced to him, snatching my precious shoes for a tight embrace.

Ahhh, Jimmy Choo, how I missed you so!

A choice lay before me: sit on the dirty stone floor or perch myself on that nasty table. I Choos the road less trav-eled, attempting to balance myself on one foot while rein-troducing Jimmy to my feet. Worked fantastic for the first shoe, not so much for the second. I tottered a bit while struggling to put on lefty but managed to maintain my bal-ance.

My clothes didn't remember the better days of no earthquakes, but the shoes looked great. Order in my world reigned once more, if a bit weakly. Now, to get back to my cabin for some outerwear as well as a mojito, and I might just survive this insanity. Oh yeah, except I needed some more information.

"Thanks for my shoes. Think you could give me the Reader's Digest version this time of what the hell is going on?"

"Well it started four years ago when..." he began. I frowned.

Well, that's not going to work. I held a hand up, stopping his Sunday stroll down Memory Lane.

"I said Reader's Digest. You do understand Digest, right? Just the important stuff."

"It's all important. You need to know where it all began to understand what's going on now."

"No, see, that's where you're wrong. I really don't. Just tell me what you did in this ceremony thing."

"I reanimated you," he said. "I used a Mayan ceremony to bring you back from death."

He used the ceremony word again. I bet he thought I wouldn't notice. I did.

"Yeah, see, I don't get this ceremony thing. I know all about these creepy places out here in the back end of nowhere. All you do is accept an apple from someone and poof, you're married. You didn't marry us, did you? Cuz if so then let me tell you, I'll have it annulled so fast-"

"Married? No. What?" He looked taken aback. Apparently, he didn't watch the TV exposé's that featured all these crazy native cultures. I had the Travel Channel and I wasn't afraid to watch it!

"You better be glad. It takes more than some kind of re-animated- whatever that means- deal to get me, Mister."

Okay, it didn't take much more, but he did not need to know that. What can I say, I enjoyed a good time; even I had standards.

"Can I tell you more now so you can understand?" he sighed.

He wasn't going to give up, was he?

"Keep it short. I just need to know about this reanimation thing. I have a boat to catch, you know."

I was a little worried that I couldn't prove my identity sans purse. Another bone added to the scales. Balance appeared illusive for the time being. I bit back a growl in my throat. Where was the peace of normal life and would I find it again?

"A boat? Um, what do you mean?" He pushed the glasses up his nose again and then ran his hand through his hair. He still looked nervous.

"Do I seriously look like I am from around here? This was just a day trip for the cruise I am on."

What kind of nerd is seriously this clueless?

"There might be a problem then. See, it's been uh... a day and a half since the earthquake."

Well, that was definitely not news I wanted to hear. Not looking good for the reanimated side of things. If only I realized how much worse things would get. I might be hot and thirty-three forever, but it came at a price. No one liked having the dead walk amongst them. I thought life sucked having brown hair instead of blonde. I thought it was bad being a size 8 instead of a size 2. Forget whining about the race wars or the battle of the sexes.

Libras enjoyed balance. Their sign was the scales used by the modern judiciary system. I never understood what it felt like to be judged until I died and found myself resurrected by my very own geek guru. This was worse than being the pimply kid in eighth grade, worse than being a vegetarian in a steakhouse, worse than being a Republican in California!

Boggs

I saw the other side of the prejudice coin with crystal clarity. People walked on the other side of the street from me. It was like Julia Roberts in the beginning of Pretty Woman with the shopkeepers that won't help her because of the way she was dressed. Mothers kept their children from me.

And then there were The Hunters. At some point I needed to figure out how to grow eyes in the back of my head so those bastards didn't sneak up on me. I thought dying would be the end of my worrying about death, but no. There seemed to be those Shaun's of the world that wanted to fling their bad '45's in the lamest attempt to kill me. And then there were the serious ones, but we'll get to them later. Even after you die, you still needed to worry about taking a permanent dirt nap. Good grief, can't a girl rest in peace?

Juan of the Dead

CHAPTER THREE

There we stood: me in my Jimmy Choo's and not-dead, and he in his dusty clothes and entirely very-alive. It didn't take a degree in rocket science to figure out I was in one heck of a mess.

"You said it's been how long since the earthquake?" I repeated.

Maybe I heard him wrong. Maybe he was exaggerating. Maybe there was still a chance. My brain tried desperately to convince itself that there was no way what he said could be happening to me. It sounded more like a movie plot than real life.

"A day and a half."

Short, sweet, and to the point. Fine time for him to pick up that habit. I looked at him and sighed. No passport. No ID. Missing for more than a day after an earthquake. I was lucky enough that some weirdo decided to resurrect me from the dead, maybe my luck would hold out. Knock on...

uh... stone. Yeah, stone.

Maybe, just maybe, I Lady Luck was still on my side. Loads of us passengers came over from the ship for the day trip. I couldn't be the only missing person, could I? No way.

"Hey, look, things are still pretty messed up after the earthquake. Maybe your ship didn't leave," he offered. If it wasn't such an obvious problem, I might have thought he was a mind reader. All the same, it felt nice to hear my thoughts voiced by another person. Maybe my wish would come true.

"Yeah, but I also have no identification. That'll make it harder to get back on."

I wistfully thought about that darling Coach purse lying under the rubble of the shop and nervously bit my lip. Hey, I mourn the loss of good accessories. What girl doesn't?

"That might pose a problem. Uh, there's something else," he said in a tone that made me want to twitch. Coach purse forgotten, I returned my gaze to the man before me. What other problem could there be when you had no Amex or ID, not to mention the whole dead thing? Morbid much?

"Why do I get the feeling..."

"You might not like this? Yeah."

Oh great, he finished my thought. Talk about annoying.

"So, you see, the thing is..."

"Band-aid, dude. Rip it off- fast," I demanded. Guess he'd lost that short and sweet from before.

"What? Oh, right?" There went the finger pushing the glasses up his nose again. Was it bad that I started to find that endearing? Yech. Ever heard that 'be careful what you wish for' thing? Yeah, he decided to rip that band-aid off and he was right: I did not like what he said next. "The ceremony. It, um. Well, I don't know exactly how or what it does. I don't know if there are any side effects or..."

Side effects? Geeks performing this ritual may cause upset stomach, gas, bloating, headache, dehydration... that sort of side effects?

Well, I felt fine and a quick glance showed no bloating or swelling. I narrowed my eyes and glared at him.

"What. Do. You. Mean?" Breathe. I needed to breathe. Or wait, maybe I didn't. I could figure that out later. Right now, I had other scores to settle. Back to glaring.

"Well, I don't know how long the effects last. There was very little information. In fact, there was no information."

"Are you saying I might die? Again?"

No way. I was far too young (and hot) to die twice. Not an option. Moving on?

"I don't think so. I don't know. I don't know what it means for you. Like what can hurt you or what happens to any injuries or-"

"Well if I died from a roof caving in on me and I seem okay to walk what does that say?" I barked.

Oh, maybe I was like the vamps in movies!

No one beat the ability to survive accidents with hardly a scratch. Okay, the downside was a fascination with blood. Was that really such a bad price to pay for immortality and near invincibility? Then again, I didn't really like the idea of an all liquid diet. Well, liquid was fine, just not that liquid. I shuddered thinking that my next drink might literally be a Bloody Mary. Ewwwwwwww!

"True. But we have no real way of knowing what could happen. We should probably make sure you are um... really okay."

"And by really okay you mean..." I left the sentence unfinished on purpose. He looked thoughtful but remained silent. I cleared my throat. This was like pulling teeth. "You mean, what?"

"Well, you probably want to see how much you can do. How much energy you have? What your limits are."

"Look, I'm real thankful that you didn't leave me... dead. You know? I don't want to be your own personal lab rat."

Did he seriously think I'd be all like ready to hop into his maze and... well... whatever? Oh, thanks for saving me, let's go party? Not! Well, maybe. Depends on how happening the party is.

I noticed him shifting his weight from foot to foot. "Um, I'm sorry. It isn't like that. I mean..."

Now cut me some slack. I knew I needed to be nicer to my savior. Especially given the fact I also needed his help to get anywhere. Like back to civilization.

"Hey, this is a bit much to take in. We need to figure it out so we can get on with our lives, but that doesn't make it easy to accept." Yeah, I decided to settle down.

I guess he noticed because he nodded and swallowed. "Um, I'm sorry. I probably should have been better pre-pared. I just didn't think..."

Okay, I could buy that. Who really planed that in the event of an earthquake they'd just happen to resurrect some dead girl? Oh, that sort of thing happened every day, right? In real life? That's what I thought.

"What do we do now? Cuz it seems to me like things aren't cool right now. I'm trapped here with no passport, no ID, no Amex. I'm dead and you're clueless about what that means." I paused and licked my lips before muttering, "Some vacation this turned out to be."

My sarcasm was not lost on him. He raked his hand through his hair for about the millionth time and blinked. "We'll figure it out. We just need to-"

"We need to what?" I snarled. My temper wavered again. I'll admit it, patience was most definitely not my strong suit.

"First, we need to get out of here. Then we need to run some simple tests and we can probably find most of our answers out and go from there."

I totally got on board the get out of the creepy temple bandwagon about two seconds after I woke up. Not my idea of an ideal hang out spot. Dust, dirt, spiders, hundreds of years of creepy history. Looking back on it now, I shuddered thinking about that place. One word: creepy. Just in case you didn't get the picture before.

"Super. Let's jet." I looked around but had nothing to retrieve since all he grabbed out of the collapsing shop was the most important thing- me. "Hope you got some ideas because my knowledge is here, the bus ride to the harbor, and the ship."

"That's fine. I know a place." He turned toward the doorway leading to the long hallway and took a few steps towards it, but I stopped him.

"Hey, what about all the candles?" Guess this dude wasn't a Boy Scout. Abandoning lit candles? Sure, nothing here seemed likely to go up in flames, but still. People might notice something freaky deaky happened when affronted with burnt candles. Then again, maybe no one ever came in here. I know I could have gone on living without seeing the place. Or I guess I could have gone on in my death?

My brain hurt. It was just too much to try to figure out right now.

"Don't worry about them. They'll just burn out. Let's just go. It's gonna be morning soon and we probably need to be long gone by now."

This guy had a serious case of The Weirds going on. Then again, maybe the idea of whatever security busting our butts put him on edge. Mexican prison sounded like a bad place to be for anyone, alive or dead. I didn't know what the typical punishment for ancient and wacky raise the dead sacrifices might be, but I imagined it wasn't a good one. Weren't the people in these countries, like, really superstitious? We could be looking at a good old-fashioned burning at the stake. Yikes! Me and my Jimmy Choos didn't feel real flame retardant, so I followed him and high tailed it up a long hallway out of the Temple.

Standing at the precipice, I peered down into what should be the shadowy gloom of the middle of the night. Only it was not too shadowy or gloomy. Nifty night vision to the rescue! I always thought I had stellar vision, but this was fantastic. Yay for carrot eating as a teenager and adult. Go salads! Stay thin now, have great vision when dead. Healthy eating ad slogan for next year!

The steps leading down the side of the Temple were quite steep, but we clung to a chain running from top to bottom. From there we proceeded in silence to the base of the Temple and towards the nearby cover of trees. Once hidden in the safety of the tree line, we came to a halt.

He whispered to me, "Just follow me along the edge of the woods to my truck. Probably no one out here, but then again you never know. Looters like to take advantage of disasters."

Looters? What the heck was there to loot in the middle of nowhere Mexico? That nasty stone table I woke up on? Somehow, I didn't think so.

The truck was a rusty pile of junk, just the sort of thing you would expect to see in Mexico. Crooked bumper, peeling paint, and cracked vinyl seats greeted us when he unlocked the doors. I climbed into the cab to ride shotgun, glad no one could see me. I liked my cars low, fast and sporty. This did not fit the bill. Then again, there was a reason for vehicles like this in Mexico.

He popped the truck into gear, and we bounced off in silence. Hasta la vista, ruins. We eventually hit a dirt road that I would barely consider a path for wild animals and bumped our way along that for a while. The sky turned lighter with pre-dawn, and that was probably the first time I ever saw the sun rise. Sober that is. Anyone that spent more than a few weeks at college pulled an all-nighter at some point. An all-nighter with your good friend Absolut. Or maybe a high from risking-overdose-levels of caffeine to stay awake cramming. Pick your poison.

At long last we parked at a ramshackle house. I did not know where we were, but what could I do? I mean, he was it for my ability to get around and ever possibly making it back home. With options that slim, my main crankiness wore off. It morphed into a sense of a gloom.

I didn't even have the energy to worry that he might be some homicidal maniac anymore. Sure, he could have chains in the house and be planning to trap me forever for goodness knows what nefarious reasons, but I somehow doubted it. He'd already had that chance, if I believed his story.

"Come in," he said. "This is where I've been working and sleeping for the last eighteen months. Just excuse the mess."

Boy he wasn't kidding about the mess. He swung the door open to the shack, and I realized the truck was far better off than what lay before me. There were books and papers stacked haphazardly on any horizontal surface and a sink full of aged dishes. That was what welcomed me from the neatest areas. I hoped the earthquake caused the worst parts of the room. I wanted to call in FEMA, Mexico or not. Then again, FEMA might have run in fear. This was worse than the video footage from Hurricane Katrina.

Little paths ran through the mess of clothes, papers, books, and objects. I picked my way through the room, hoping I wouldn't knock anything over. He came in behind me and locked the door.

"You could single handedly wipe out unemployment in this country. Ever think about hiring a few dozen people to clean this place up?" I asked. It was de-scust-ing.

"I know it looks bad. But I swear, there's a method to the madness. It's awful, I start researching and then forget to do just about everything else. The mess sort of takes over and then..."

"And then what? Paper breeds like gerbils? Good grief. You are one man. What are you, some kind of hoarder?"

"Well it started with the first artifact I dug up. It's over there," he said, pointing to a chipped pot on the end of one counter. "And so, then it just kind of went from there. Before I knew it, I had this."

He spread his arms at the masterpiece of his mess. FYI, this was why God said Adam needed a woman. Could you imagine the pit Eden became in the short time under Adam's care? Anyone figure out why men can't organize anything? Born slobs. It was why I tried to keep men from sticking around my place long term. No way did I want to become some guy's maid.

"You couldn't, I don't know, get a notebook to put some of this paper in? There are really easy, and cheap things you can do. I'll bet you a taco that Lisa Frank has a low paying factory around here somewhere to make all that junk for pre-teen girls. Go raid it. Hit a salvage sale."

"Lisa Frank? Gah, my sister lived for that stuff," he chuckled, a sound low in his throat that sent a thrill up my spine.

"Get yourself some purple tiger notebook and boom, a little better organization. Though in this case, you might need a truck load."

I watched as he pushed aside three textbooks so thick they made War and Peace look like a teen novella. It took an awful lot of work just so I could sit in chair. I wondered how that was gonna impact his precious organizational system straight out of Pigsty Living Quarterly.

The chair became host to my butt, and he turned his attention to his own sitting space. Maybe he should have thought about things like that before he went about resurrecting girls from the dead and inviting them back home. Sometimes men just didn't think ahead. It really should have been right there on his To-Do list. 'Clean house – check; raise girl from dead – check; get milk – oops forgot to get the milk!'.

Once seated across from me, he dropped a book onto the mountain between us that, at one time, resembled a coffee table. Currently it looked like Everest. The book, older than any I had ever seen, teetered on the pile precariously. He flipped to a place roughly three-quarters of the way into the book and pointed to a picture. Upside-down, I could not tell what was before me. It looked like some sort of bad drawing on a cave wall or something equally ancient and nonsensical.

"I don't get it. What is that?" I asked. Simple question.

"These drawings are found near the site where I found... the instructions..." he faltered. I jumped on it.

"You mean this is related to whatever you did? But how? I don't get it, I'm sorry."

He sighed, more from weariness than anything else I thought. "It is. I think this shows someone performing the same ceremony. The next part of the story continued to a wall damaged by... well we don't know what. Might have been an earthquake, invading army, or just time. At any rate, this is the best we have."

"What about whatever it was that you found on how to do whatever." Oh yeah, that was clear and technical. So much for that A in English. His blank stare told me all I needed to know. He thought he resurrected a moron. "You know, wherever you got your instructions from. Surely it said something?"

Maybe it was just me, but if I was writing some sort of book about raising the dead, I would want to leave instructions. Something along the lines of: Becomes mindless zombie. Wants to eat brains. Becomes ruthless killer. Goes for the jugular. Turns to dust in sunlight. Don't feed after midnight. Will turn into evil monster. Things like that.

"Not really. It just said what to do and I did it and now here we are. It actually ended there."

"Let me get this straight. You found some crazy dude's instructions on how to do weird voodoo crap. The last entry is, 'Dear diary, this is how you raise someone from the dead.' Then there's nothing else. You didn't think maybe there was a reason?"

How stupid was this guy? He should have been glad I wasn't some sort of mindless freak or jumping his bones or goodness knows what else. There had to be a reason for no more information. Like the people got eaten by monsters from the forces of darkness or something. Hey, I was back from the dead. That sort of thing opens one's mind to a whole lot of options.

He cleared his throat and shifted his glasses back up his nose. "Well, no, I guess I didn't think about it. See, I found it, translated it, was trying to decide what it all meant, and then the earthquake happened. I figured why not and?"

"Let me guess. Now we're here," I groaned. "What the hell do you do?"

Seriously, what did this crackerjack do? Obviously, nothing involving common sense. Or he lived too sheltered a life to realize these things might not want to be messed with. Natural order getting mucked up and all that.

Note to me, buy this guy a whole lot of horror DVDs when I returned to civilization.

Sadly though, without this guy, life as I knew it would be kaput. I owed him big time for that, but boy was he ill prepared. Did he think it wasn't going to work or something? If not, how would he explain the dead chick he carried away? If it did work, what then? Ah, well, we saw that now, didn't we?

Some people just never learned to plan ahead. A hard lesson Fate decided to cram down our throats continuously over the next few days in each other's company.

CHAPTER
FOUR

I waited for an answer from my hapless savior hoping to learn more about him. He began his story, which thankfully only took about a million years in telling. Good thing I was already dead.

"Sorry to be so rude." He looked down at his feet while pushing his glasses up his nose again.

Note to self, offer to buy him some contacts as a thank you.

"I really should have introduced myself. Things just happened too fast."

Fast? You think?

Though I supposed Miss Manners lacked etiquette guidelines for properly hosting recently reanimated strangers. Someone should write her a letter. "I guess so. And you are probably right. I do need to know more about what is going on."

So, I could admit when I was wrong. Sue me. Besides,

with all my ID's and stuff missing, I couldn't do much of any-thing but listen to this guy anyway. I might as well hear it all. Every. Single. Detail.

He nodded. "I'm really sorry for the jolt. This probably isn't easy for you, having to take this all in."

Goody, his plan was hedge, hedge, hedge. And people say women take forever to get to a point.

"Yeah. This sort of thing happens to me every day. It's really no biggie," I droned. I rolled my eyes for effect, but he missed it.

"It all started when I arrived here. This is my first real thing on my own."

"First real what?" Nudge, prod, poke.

"I'm an anthropologist..."

"An anthro-what?" What kind of job has a name no sane person can pronounce? Or tells you anything about what it is?

"Anthropologist. I study civilizations, people," he clari-fied.

"What are you doing here in the middle of nowhere? No civilization here to study!" What was he studying? The soci-ety of trees? Dirt? It was just Mexico for crying out loud.

"Here? The Incan and the Aztecs and-"

"Oh. Yeah." Duh, I was just in one of their temples getting the voodoo smacked into me. "You study them? Like, they are dead. Isn't that more, um, archeology?"

"That falls into anthropology. The societies of ancient America are fascinating. I grew up in Phoenix and I remem-ber the first time I went to Montezuma's Castle. I wanted to know what it was like to live in those cliff dwellings."

"What is that?" I asked with full confusion on my voice. Okay, so, I knew what Montezuma's Revenge was, which was why I smuggled a bottle of water off the boat with me in my Coach handbag. Dang. Another reason to mourn the loss. Clean water.

"It's a series of cliff dwellings between Phoenix and Flagstaff. You look up the cliff wall and you can see all the entrances to the different rooms. It was the most interesting thing I'd ever seen. I remember thinking it was the Indian version of a high-rise apartment."

Indian high-rise apartments? Well that went against the wigwam's we learned about in elementary school. Kinda cool though. I never liked the idea of living in a tent. Go Indians in Arizona!

"And that brought you here?" I asked, looking around. "How? Phoenix has to be better than Mexico." I really was not a fan of history in school and now that flaw bit me in the butt.

"It's all that's here. I guess it's kind of a long story."

"Hey, it isn't like you could bore to death with it. Already hit the dead mark, ya know?"

What could I say? The guy grew on me like a bad fungus. How he ended up in the resurrecting hot girls in earthquakes biz interested me. Maybe the reasons were a tad bit selfish considering who he chose for a guinea pig. Nothing wrong with that! An impish grin graced his face.

Oh dear.

"I went to Montezuma's Castle in sixth grade. Some cousins from back east had come to visit and we piled into the car, planning a trip to see the Grand Canyon. Why not? They didn't make it out very often. My parents pulled off at Montezuma's Castle cuz I guess we were rowdy. I remember my mom yelling at us to be quiet for what had to be a half hour before we pulled over."

"Troublemaker, even then?" I held back on a snicker but arched my eyebrow.

"Yeah, I guess so," he breathed through a small laugh. "We pull over so we can do the whole stretch your legs thing. I guess they thought that would help. Three boys in the back of a car? Yeah, not really. I just remember looking up at those cliff dwellings. They were... awe inspiring."

"So, they made an impact, huh? More than the Grand Canyon?"

"Absolutely. We got home from the trip and I started reading everything I could. Fact, fiction, it didn't matter. That led me to other Native American tribes. At some point I ended up going south. The stories of the Aztecs and the Incas enthralled me. When I went to Arizona State, that's what I studied. I became an anthropologist and now here I am. It's fantastic. Like a dream come true."

Wow. Someone that actually liked their job. Talk about rare. Well, sort of. I liked my job. Who wouldn't like a job where you got to shop all day on someone else's dime? The creation of personal shoppers was the best move stores ever made. I got paid to read up on all the latest trends, to peruse the stores, to buy things. It was a girl's dream come true!

The only thing wrong with it was I didn't get to keep the stuff. Oh well. A small sacrifice. My Amex saw healthy usage, so it sure wasn't complaining.

Uh oh...he's still talking...

Sure enough, his gushing over ancient artifacts continued. "I love the stories of these people. From Quetzalcoatl to cities of gold. The temples and all the things that went into their architecture. The savagery of their sports."

Maybe I should have listened more to the tour guide. I just thought the Temple was a big huge building. Sure, totally magnificent considering people with no bulldozers or cranes or whatever built the thing. Hello, impressive back breaking labor? Yeah. What sports? Can you really get more savage than the Romans? To my savior's credit, he made it sound interesting; I wanted to hear about it. I guess

Chapter Four

rebirth in an ancient temple did that to a person.

"Really? I had no idea. Like what?" I prompted.

"Oh, well the Temple for instance. These people, they were fascinated with astronomy. You came at the wrong time of year. In less than six months we'll see the spring equinox. It's quite the sight. The way the sun hits the stairs makes it look like a giant snake is descending them."

"That's kinda creepy. Snakes are icky." I suppressed a shudder. Me and lizards did not mix. Ever.

"It's from their mythology. Fascinating story. I just find it amazing that they were able to build this temple to do that on the equinox. Their calendar system was far superior to ours."

"I guess so. Our calendar system is kind of confusing sometimes. All these leap days and the millennium years and stuff. Holidays that shift around."

"There's more," he continued. "There's one step for every day of the year. These guys even figured out how long it took the Earth to go around the Sun. No telescopes, no computerized star charts. They may have been primitive in some respects, but they were very far advanced in others."

"Geez. I was just impressed at how that temple stood there all these years. It must have killed them to build it all by hand or whatev."

"It's one of the wonders of the world," he explained. "I always thought so and now it's actually been named it. Man, that was a great day. My group here, we actually had a party when the word came out that Chichen Itza made the cut."

"Hey I remember! People were emailing out cuz everyone could vote on it. I never heard the results."

He grinned, a bit lopsidedly. "Well, here you are. You were just in one. The only thing I didn't like was that none of the ancient wonders made it."

"Yeah weren't they like the pyramids in Egypt and um... Okay. That's the only one I really knew."

"That's because the pyramids are about the only ones still remaining. Most of the others were destroyed completely or almost completely."

"Well that's kind of sad," I said in a total bummer kind of way.

"Yeah. I would give anything to see the Hanging Gardens of Babylon or the Lighthouse of Alexandria." He looked wistful.

"At least you get to work here. I was too busy going shopping to pay attention to any of this other stuff. Guess that's my biggest weakness... shopping."

"It did get you killed. That probably qualifies it for biggest weakness status," he grinned. I decided I liked his grin and matched it with my own

."No joke. Geez. This is taking those credit commercials a bit seriously. Who knew shopping was such a risky pursuit?"

It wasn't like Amex was your trusty neighborhood loan shark, ready to break your legs at the first missed payment. They wouldn't harass you unless you were an hour late with a payment. Who worked at 2 AM calling people for money? Bill collectors sucked.

"So that's how I ended up here. The rest, well that was a surprise. My crew, we found these records, and I was working on the translation and thought for sure I got something wrong."

"And these records? They gave you the secret to life and death? Or do all you anthro-whatevers know the secrets to raising the dead? I thought that was just like a Jesus thing to do."

Hmmm, while he was hunky in a nerdy sort of way, I don't think he could qualify as son of a god. The Rock on the other hand? Hummina hummina. There's a reason why that boy was cast as Hercules. Pardon my drool.

"I think I missed that class at the university. Sorry. No, these records. I don't know, it has no name, but it's like the American Book of the Dead. I did what it said and sure enough it worked. I had no idea..."

"But you thought, well I happen to have stumbled over a dead girl, let's give it a whirl? Who does that?"

"Uh, yeah..." The glasses went back up the nose. "It just sorta happened."

Maybe it was just me, but it seemed a little farfetched. Okay, so my sudden death-life also seemed out there, but hey. "You just happened to have whatever it was you needed, an empty temple, chaos, and a dead girl? Seems like you were planning."

"So, I went to Boy Scouts. You know the whole 'always be prepared' motto? Actually, it wasn't really like this ceremony called for much of anything out of the ordinary."

"Only about a zillion candles?" I remembered how many candles burned in that room. Did he really expect me to believe he happened to walk about with a crate of candles? If so, he probably had one happy candle supplier.

"Well, I love it here, but it is Mexico. I don't know what the deal is with the wiring. I lose power regularly. Candles are a way of life for me."

Summed up, I had before me one very nerdy dirt digger that stumbled upon a book detailing how to raise people from the dead. Maybe that was my cue to thank him for choosing to raise hot girls instead of an army of demon psychos bent on taking over the world.

The whole thing still just reeked of some kind of Twilight Zone episode. I kept waiting for the creepy dude in the suit to pop out of a corner. Maybe that one with the fallen stack of books as high as my waist.

"Okay, you happened upon a very dead me, and decided why not? What now? You have any more information?"

"That is why I wanted to come back here. Look, we only partially translated everything. And I think something happened because not a whole lot came after the details on raising the dead."

He rifled through some papers at his feet before pulling out some notes resembling chicken scratch. I leaned over to look, but decided chicken scratch was overly kind. Perdue chickens made more legible markings than what laid before me. Amazingly enough, he continued on.

"See, I was making these notes as I went along. And I've just got some words here or there, and a whole lot of questions. But with time, I know I can figure it out. And then there's you. Like this passage here, it says something about after you raise someone, but pretty much that's all I have. You can probably fill in all these blanks."

Wait... did he just raise me from the dead so he could have an easier time solving his little ancient mystery? That is most uncool. Sure, raise me cause I'm hot and you wanna party down with me. Don't raise me in some kind of creepy experiment.

"Look, I don't know what you think I can do–" I started.

"Oh no, no. I don't know that you can really do anything. At least not now. But just the fact that you are here and walking around and alive – uh..."

That's right, bozo. I'm not alive. I'm dead. Stupid earthquakes and stupid Mexico. The travel agent was never going to hear the end of this. Wonder who my parents used. Once I found a way back to the States, I planned some serious phone line burning.

"Look, here, Mister, I have no pulse. I think that classifies me as not alive. Thank you so much for the reminder."

Juan of the Dead

I was a little perturbed over the death thing. Almost as much as being trapped in this Godforsaken country with no purse, no id, and no credit cards.

"I'm really sorry. I didn't mean..." he trailed off, licking his lips. "And it's Jon."

"I don't really care... what? What's Jon?"

"My name. It's Jon. Jon Daniels. I realized I never told you."

I bet now he expected a thank you card. 'Dear Mr. Daniels. Thank you ever so much for raising me from the dead. Bea.' Just what did one say when thanking someone for that? I felt confident Hallmark did not make a card for this kind of circumstance. And was I supposed to give him a gift? I wondered if not sucking all his blood out or eating his brains might fall into the realm of 'gift'.

"Jon? Your name is Jon?" He nodded and looked down at the notes in front of him. Insert awkward silence here. "Yeah. Things kind of just happened fast and then I realized, I didn't tell you my name. I really am sorry."

I let my annoyance at the recent life events cool a bit. After all, it was not this guy's fault that a giant Aztec replica calendar fell on my head during an earthquake. That was my own bad luck and a lost hand at cards with Lady Luck. Darn her being like... lucky.

"Hey, you know. It's been kind of weird. I'm Bea."

"Like the letter?"

"Don't get me started. Yeah, like the letter."

Like I was gonna tell this guy my name was Bernadette? Hell, to the no. What kind of name was that anyway? Sometimes I hated my dad. There I was, this cute, innocent, defenseless baby. And he did that to me? Where was my mother, you ask? She was hopped up higher than a kite on baby-having meds. After giving birth to me she crashed like an eagle with two broken wings. While snoring away in the hospital, the nurse handed my dad the paperwork for naming me. He scrawled down Bernadette. Bernadette? Who, born in the last thirty-five years was named Bernadette?

My dad had a thing for Bernadette Peters. Lucky me. He waited till he could sneak it in and named me after the woman. Now don't get me wrong, I'm sure Bernadette Peters was a fine woman. But seriously? Worse yet, he liked to call me Bernie. What kind of name was Bernie for a woman? If anyone heard the name Bernie they thought of some kind of cigar-smoking, fifty-year-old pervert.

On the other side of things, like in Weekend at Bernie's, all the great parties happened after my death. I guess maybe dear old Dad had it right after all. I'd still rather be a Tiffany.

Juan of the Dead

CHAPTER
FIVE

After the exchange of names, we sat there for a few moments; staring at each other. That's when I learned I totally dominated in a staring contest. Don't even try. I'd beat you every time. Seems that the walking dead didn't have as much need for blinking as the living folk. Fantastic!

Hey, I was the living dead in Mexico with no Amex or anything. I had to find my perks somewhere, right?

"What now?" I asked, breaking that awkward silence. "You did your mumbo-jumbo and now I'm here and you say you don't know what else to do. I hate to ask..." Again. I hated to ask again. What was with this dork? "You really didn't have much more of a plan than this?"

Shrug. He shrugged at me. Nice that he was nonchalant. Then again, he didn't appear the sort that worried about things like missing luxuries from home. Or breathing.

"Just... no. I guess I shoulda figured this out better, huh?"

Boggs

Okay, I'd never understood the term sheepish before that moment. The face he gave me? Definitely sheepish.

"So, your book just ends? Like with no 'And we raised the dead and they ate us' sort of thing?" I know it sounded obsessive, but really the thought of brains as a permanent diet seemed rather vomitlicious to me. I wanted to prepare myself for any sudden and intense cravings. If ever there was a clueless look, he gave it to me.

"Um, if the dead ate them, who'd write that down?" he asked.

Was he serious? I rethought that DVD collection. This guy obviously needed even more of a life than horror flicks. Who didn't instinctively know that raised dead generally feasted happily on humans? Blood. Brain. Guts. Redrum! Redrum!

"Uh… ok, good point. So, partially translated incomplete book. Got that part of this crazy situation. What next?" I eyed the room again, wondering just how long I could not-live while he searched for a needle in a haystack. Scratch that, the needle would be easier to find.

He flipped to another page and studied it for a moment or two. I studied my nails, assessing the earthquake damage to my mani. Gah, I needed to get home and have these babies fixed. To say my polish was chipped would be like saying the bride of Frankenstein was having a bad hair day. What a shame. Jo just filed and polished my nails before I left on vacation.

"A-ha! This is what I wanted." He pointed at something in his book as he pushed it towards my face, but I couldn't make out anything on the page. Was this more of his untranslated stuff? It looked like more chicken scratch to me. My blank stare obviously clued him in. He cleared his throat and pushed on. "See, it talks about this reanimating. But the following bit seems not like a warning but like maybe a... prophecy almost. Like a warning, but a prophecy? That's part of what I wasn't sure about."

"You weren't sure about it, and you..."

"Well, it didn't seem like it was anything drastic. No end of the world or anything. It just seemed to be more of... I don't know how to explain it. The language is difficult. It could be the recipe for a tamale for all I know."

Nothing drastic, just a warning prophecy thing? This got more confusing the longer I talked to Jon. He could provoke a serious migraine.

"Okay, I really just don't get it. You need to explain better or something." Maybe if I was more direct he might get the picture.

"Well, see, here it says something about power and a warning." Sure, it did. Whatever he was pointing to looked like a bunch of nothing to me. He moved his hand to something else on his page. "And here it says something about dead."

"You got power plus warning plus dead? Nothing in the middle?"

Sure, seemed like he skipped a bunch of scratch in his jumping around. Then again it could be like one of those old Godzilla movies where the Japanese dude's mouth moved for like three minutes and all the dubbing said was "Help!"

"Well, that's the problem. Either it's something I don't know how to translate or it's missing part of the words. Translating is really hard to begin with just because of syntax structure and..."

Uh oh. Jon-boy was bordering on the edge of tune-out time again.

I didn't need gobbledegook about foreign languages. I took Spanish in school and got out being able to carry on a great conversation at... Taco Bell. Uno taco por favor!

Boggs

My glazed eyes must have clued him in again. Sometimes he was quick on the uptake, other times not. Guess I got lucky that time. "Um, I know it's really confusing. I thought the warning dealt with the power involved."

"Power? You said it didn't take much and if this is from some old Aztec group of people. What kind of power?" I didn't see any electric sockets in the Temple of Doom back there. Wasn't that why he used those candles?

"Well, that kind of confused me. I don't know what it meant. I think it meant some kind of will power or stamina. The length of time it took, wow. By the time I was done, I felt exhausted. But then you woke up and well, I think I'm on pure adrenaline now."

He did say a day and a half passed between the quake and that moment. How much of that time did he spend playing witchdoctor? He probably needed a siesta sooner rather than later. I looked over at him, but he didn't look any worse for wear. In fact, he looked yummy, and not in a next meal kind of way.

Jon licked his lips before continuing. "As a kid, I dreamt of being in one of these civilizations. Wondering how cool it would be to actually be able to go back and be in them. I would read the stories and try to picture myself there. I read all of this and just wanted to try it."

Oh great, somebody had on their King of the Aztecs under-roos today. Goodie for me.

Guess I should be grateful this guy had a hard-on the size of Texas for some ancient civilization since it meant I got a second shot at life on this ball of rock. Did I really need some half-crazy guy to accomplish this?

"So, are you playing that you're living like eight zillion years ago during the earthquake or what?"

"The Aztec civilization is not that old. They reached their peak only about five hundred years ago."

"Oh, I guess there's old and then there's ancient?" I wasn't sure about other people, but five hundred years seemed rather ancient to me. Then again, I thought thirty was ancient which was why I refused to acknowledge my own age.

"I suppose. I love all these old cultures. Even Egypt and Greece interest me. I just prefer this side of the world."

He didn't need to. I could see it in his eyes and hear it in his voice. His gushing sounded like a schoolboy with his first crush. He wasn't kidding around; he really dug this stuff. Pun intended.

"I get that, I guess. We all have our passions." Mine were more couture. Bring on the Fendi and Vuitton and I would sound just like Jon. Okay, there's no would about it. Just the thought made me want to dance in place.

"Yeah, I suppose we do." Aww, it was a Kodak moment. We could be kindred spirits. I saw it in his eyes. Obvious sign that bookworms were easy to please, socially speaking.

"So, go on. You partially translated this pile of chicken-scratch and..."

"I got stumped. I didn't know what to do next. I thought that surely this sort of thing was more likely to be done someplace like a temple. You wouldn't believe some of the things these people did."

I shuddered. Travel Channel gave away enough I'd like to not believe, thank you very much.

"Totally agree with that one. I am addicted to the Travel Channel. Besides, I don't know about you but if I was gonna be messing about with dead bodies, I wouldn't want to do it in my living room. My coffee table probably couldn't stand the weight and blood's a pain in the ass to get out of carpet."

He blanched. His skin was whiter than a bride's dress on

her wedding day. Since his skin was a natural looking tan from spending too much time outside, you can imagine the contrast.

"I don't think they worried about things like blood in carpet," he croaked.

Uh-oh...

Guess it was another clueless moment for him. How did someone miss out on such an obvious (and awesome, if I do say so myself) attempt at humor. Maybe if he got his head out of the dirt and spent time with humans that weren't skeletal, it would help him pick up social cues better. Scratch the humor.

"Maybe not," I continued. "But they did all sorts of weirdo human sacrifices and jazz, right? I'm thinking if you've got a guy wanting to raise the dead and a creepy Temple for sacrificing things-well it might make for a good place to do the raising the dead ceremony."

"Exactly what I thought. I took my notes and I headed for the Temple. I thought maybe if I studied some of the things around there, I might find a clue to translating the rest of this passage. You see, some stuff is easy. You can figure out things like altar or temple or house. Where it gets hard is when there are things you simply can't relate to because we just don't have those sorts of things. It's like in a recipe. Maybe they want to use a red berry growing locally and then a particular fruit. Only since you haven't a clue what's what, you think it's a root and some leaves."

"Yikes. That's way worse than just trying to convert from the metric system when measuring. I hate getting food ideas off of the net. I get these recipes from the UK and I'm trying to figure out how to measure out grams of butter or something."

Then again, I'm a terrible cook. I can't really translate American recipes into something edible either.

Chapter Five

"The Temple at Chichen Itza is the closest, and it seemed a likely spot. Though it's a trek on foot. Maybe the people wouldn't have used that Temple, but then again, maybe they would. I thought the most I'd lose was a day or two. If nothing came of it, oh well, I'd get back to work on things here. Maybe something more would turn up."

And something did turn up, apparently. Me and a life-ending earthquake. I guess this guy figured it out though, since I was standing around very much not too dead- like. Kudos for him, his translations weren't too far off. Unfortunately, there was a lot missing.

CHAPTER SIX

I looked at him with growing annoyance. "And that's when you ran into me, so to speak?"

"Well, I'd spent the morning inside the Temple. My team has an in, so we can get around when and where the tourists can't. I wasn't finding much, and I went to grab a bite to eat. All I had was granola bars and trail mix in my pack. That was when the earthquake hit."

"And you just saw me over in the shops? Cuz I'll tell you, they said we could take a tour of that Temple, but watching those people try to climb up the stairs? Didn't look good for me or my Jimmy Choos. I bagged that thought and went straight for the shops. I figured I might find some sort of cool trinket or two to take home for people."

He looked at my shoes again. "I don't know how you'd have done climbing the stairs in those things. They aren't very practical."

Did he insult Choo? I bristled.

"Excuse me? Practical? Who wears practical shoes? Old women who've lost all sense of fashion? Nurses? I don't think so. These are awesome shoes and they match my outfit. That's what matters!"

He looked me up and down. His gaze lingered over me in a way that sent a shiver up my spine. I sat up a little straighter, pushing the girls out a tad. He shifted in his chair and looked away. "I, um, didn't notice. I really don't know much about fashion."

Didn't take a neurosurgeon to figure that one out. His faded and mismatched clothes looked like something from a bad blue-light special. Oh boy.

I reminded myself that I was way outta this guy's league. I was the kind of girl geeks like him had wet dreams about. He was not the kind of guy I had dreams about. Normally.

"Uh huh. Well, just remember: Real women leave sensible behind when it comes to footwear. It's all about the hot factor." I could attest that Jimmy definitely worked in my favor when out at the clubs.

"I see."

No, he didn't. A blind person could see that much. Some people got it, some people didn't. Generally speaking, those that didn't ended up shopping at places like Goodwill and I avoided them like the plague. They can't be taught. You could lead a horse to Evian, but you can't make it drink.

"Well I think I get the next part. You went food searching. Big earthquake. I get crushed. You spirit me off to the Temple somehow managing to drag me up those steep stairs. And now we're sitting in your... um... living room."

"There was more to it than just that. I had to pull all that rubble off of you. And then once I got you into the Temple I had to go for my pack with the candles and search out the supplies and..." he said.

I was touched. That was a lot to go through for a

stranger. Even for weirdos starting out in some kind of raising the dead club founded by old dead Aztecs. Not everyone could join the in crowd. Others had to work really hard at it.

"All of that for me? Guess you got lucky with that earthquake. Bet you're glad it ended well."

"Um, really, I didn't think it would work. Or at least not do what it did. I don't know. It's cool though, I mean it did work! And wow did it work. I know that your neck and back had to be broken. Yet you can walk. You were absolutely dead. There's no rigor mortis, you can obviously access higher cognitive functions like speech and..."

Oh dear, the gushing returns and brought medical babble with it.

"I suppose," I interrupted. "Minus one Coach purse and a bad manicure, I guess I'm not the worse for wear." Really, I wasn't. Manicures could be fixed if one was somewhere civilized. This place wasn't civilized.

I held out my hands and my arms. No scratches or bruises to be seen. My clothes were ripped and dirty, probably with no salvation in sight. I felt my face and didn't notice anything like a crooked nose. Dr. Kricko back home would be happy to know that his pristine work survived death by shopping.

Two eyes, a nose, and a mouth full of teeth. Can I really complain? Maybe not. Besides, the newly improved eyesight seems a good tradeoff. Wonder if I should mention it to Jon.

"I noticed something," I started. "It is easier to see in the dark. When you left me in that creep-o room, I could see right down the dark hallway. That's pretty nice. Hey, no broken back and good eyes."

"Really?" He stood up and leaned down towards me. He looked me right in the eyes, his face very close to mine. I stared right back, glad I didn't need to blink. After his eyes opened and closed several times, he must have realized that development. "You aren't blinking?"

I arched an eyebrow at his statement turned question. "I guess not. It's kind of weird, but I don't feel the need to blink."

"Interesting." He kept his eyes on me while reaching behind him, trying to find a notebook without looking. I cleared my throat and looked away from him to see where his hand was. Like a spell broke, he turned towards his own hand and found just what he obviously wanted. Grasping the notebook, he pulled a pen from a pocket and scrawled something.

Grrr.

Apparently, against my wishes, I really was a lab rat. Something needed to change about that. I might look cute in a bow, but I was no Minnie Mouse. We needed to set some ground rules for this relationship. Did I think relationship? No. That was it. We definitely needed some ground rules. There would be absolutely no relationship with this guy.

"Excuse me. I don't know what you are thinking or writing there, but I got a big problem with you treating me like some kind of experiment for the tenth-grade science fair." I crossed my arms and pursed my lips.

He looked away from the paper and at me once more. "What?"

I sighed. As the breath escaped my lips, I worked to ensure an even tone. "I am not your personal lab rat. What are you writing?"

He fumbled with the paper and then pushed it towards me. "Here."

I stared at the page before me and felt my brows furrow. He really needed to go back for some penmanship lessons.

Geez, I'd seen children that wrote better than that in preschool. I made out the word 'eyes' and 'tear ducts' and everything else lost me. At least there was nothing that resembled 'subject' or 'patient.' I would need to rethink the whole not eating his brains thing if I saw that changed.

"What is this?" I asked, looking at him again.

"I told you, I just want to make sure we understand what's going on with you. To know what you can expect. You were dead, you know."

"Like I'm gonna forget something like that? Do you think I'm retarded?" This guy really pushed my buttons.

"No, no, no." His quick apology quieted my anger. "Really, no. I just, well, you see..."

I watched as he raked his hand through his hair again. I wondered if I should move that one lock of hair so it would go behind his ear. It seemed that one lock obscured his eyes and... wait... wasn't I supposed to be angry about something?

"Stop. It's okay." Not really. But I felt bad for him. If I wasn't careful, I'd end up adopting myself a puppy dog named Jon.

"I just want to understand what's happening to you. Don't you want to know?"

Hell, yeah I wanted to know. But I didn't want him to know that. What if there were some negative side effects to this deal? Okay, some might see eating brains and drinking blood and stuff as negative. I was thinking more along the lines of body part falling off and stuff. No one wants to hang out with a girl if she was going to be losing pieces of herself at random. I needed warning about things like that.

I was a live-in-the-moment kind of girl, but sometimes life came along and made you think about the future. Like giant things falling from the sky. Then, it was like you realized all the things you didn't do in life. See the last 007 movie, kiss the cute guy across the dinner table on the cruise even though he was obviously digging you, saying good-bye to your grandma before leaving on a trip. Those sorts of things.

For one brief second I even considered the children I'd never have before things went black. Yeah, kids! Never would have guessed that one. I'm allergic to children!

I really detested feeling like I was visiting a doctor's office. No needles, or poking, or prodding. Blah. There's a reason I avoided doctors like the plague they are. Did I have questions about my newly found situation? Yeah. Should I chill out and work with Jon on finding the answers? Proba- bly. Did I want to give in that easily? No, I was a stubborn girl.

"Maybe." That was as close as I would allow for him. He needed to work harder if he wanted to hang out with me more. Really.

"See. We can just talk about this some more. You al- ready told me about your eyes. If we start with things you've already noticed, that might help us out. This isn't the sort of thing I really know how to do."

"You mean to tell me you don't do this with all the girls you resurrect?" I cooed. Okay, a little shameless flirting might not be too bad. His ears turned red.

"I told you, I've never done this before."

"Yeah, I've heard that one before," I continued. I added a wink, and twisted until I faced him a little more.

He visibly relaxed, obviously cluing in that I was not seri- ous. "Oh."

I shifted my weight again, trying to get more comfort- able. Unfortunately for me, there didn't seem to be much room for me to move around for fear of knocking some- thing over and causing an avalanche of junk.

I thought about his request, trying to remember if I noticed anything out of the ordinary. Other than my sight, that was about it. It wasn't like we'd done much of anything. Got up off the table, walk down a zillion stairs, tromped through the dark, rode in the truck, arrived here. No marathons or leaping tall buildings in a single bound or deflecting bullets to make me suddenly go 'hey, that's not normal'.

Something nagged in the back of my head. I woke up... what was it?

"Oh!" That's right. I remembered those first few minutes. "When I first... came to... I was really stiff. It was hard to do anything like talk or move."

Oh yeah, the way sexy gurgling probably turned him on. Or maybe it was the cupping of my breast. Dr. GrabbyHands didn't seem phased by my bringing up those first few minutes.

"Stiff... hard to talk and move..." he muttered as he wrote.

"Feeling good now, though." I stretched. Some bones popped, relieving pressure in my back.

"That's good. What about when you moved that stone altar?"

"When I did what?"

"Uh... you got up. You came towards me..."

Oh yes. When I first debated decking the guy for his many crimes of shoe stealing and boob grabbing. I remembered it too well. It only happened like five seconds ago.

"What about it?" Maybe I should remember my anger at his copping a feel. With Choos intact and safely on my feet once more, I could deal with forgiving him of that particular felony.

"Do you know how you moved it?"

"What?"

"The altar. Were you trying to move it or was it just an

accident?" he persisted removing his glasses and rubbing them with his shirttail. Considering the shirt looked just as dusty as everything else, I wasn't sure his efforts would pay off.

I thought about what he said. At the time, my only thought was him. And figuring out what was going on. Did I move the altar? As I reflected, I remembered it shifting, but what was the big deal? He stuck me on a table, doesn't seem like a person leaping from it might be great on the sturdy staying in one place plan.

"I really wasn't thinking about it. I had other ideas on my mind."

Yeah, remember? SHOES!

How did he expect a girl to remember anything when shoes were on the line, anyway? And really, so what if I mucked up someone's feng shui in the process of locating my shoes? Totally expected and understandable, right? It was shoes, after all. I could lift a car off the adrenaline alone, as could any other woman.

"You probably moved it a good couple of feet. It was solid stone. Probably weighed a ton."

"Huh."

Really? Well that was kinda cool. Maybe my obsessed adrenaline pumped body turned me into Super-Bea. That wasn't just kinda cool, that rocked. I felt a smile creep onto my face.

"Maybe we should test that one. It really didn't seem like something... normal."

Was he trying to say I was a freak? No one calls me a freak and gets away with it!

"What?!" My screech probably hurt the ears of dogs for three miles. "Are you trying to say I'm not normal?"

I'd take above average, sure. His tone just didn't seem like that was his intent.

Chapter Six

"Well, you are dead and walking," Jon pointed out.

Good point.

"Uh. Maybe." I wasn't ready to admit that I might actually be a freak of nature. Cruise ticket up De Nile for one, please.

He asked me a few more questions that I had no clue how to answer. Like I knew that much about biology. Frankly, I was surprised Jon did. He dug in the ground for a living, why would he know anything about biology? I didn't pay much attention to course requirements in college. I took whatever Mickey Mouse course required to get me through distasteful things like science, math, and English. Mostly, I just hung out with my sisters in the sorority house and partied. That's what you went to college for, right? Forget the education garbage.

My answers satisfied him for the moment, but I got a nasty suspicion we'd be having a "lab" part of his science experiment gone psycho. Blah on that. Shouldn't we have focused on something more important? Like how to get me back to civilization?

The second time he yawned trying to ask the same question I put a stop to his game of Twenty Questions.

"Hey, you okay?" I asked. It wasn't that I cared, so much as I'd like to survive without third degree burns from his inquisition.

"I'll be okay. Just a bit tired," he yawned again. I could see the weariness in his eyes. I felt fine. Maybe death was the kind of power nap you got loads of energy from. What did I know? First time being resurrected from the dead and all.

"Why don't you go and get some rest. When was the last time you slept?"

"I dunno. Been a long day," he muttered.

You don't say. Try dying. That definitely makes for a long

day. Night. Uh… whatever. "Maybe you should rest."

"What about you?"

That better not be some sort of invitation. "I'll be fine."

Okay, maybe not fine, how could anyone be fine after the craziness my life dished up on a silver platter this week? But, really, his looking half asleep wasn't gonna help things. He was my ticket outta this Godforsaken hellhole of a country. I needed him fresh and ready to go. Surely, I could find something to entertain myself with. I looked around the shambles of a room.Or maybe not.

Juan of the Dead

CHAPTER
SEVEN

The fact that Jon was snoring in under two minutes without moving from his spot was sign enough for anyone to know he was tired. Who knew that a simple resurrection could drain you? The guy was beyond wasted.

I weighed the chances that standing might cause a landslide of garbage that would bury me versus staying put. I survived (with help) an earthquake and a falling ceramic monstrosity, but did I stand a chance fighting death by paper cut? Taking my chances, I stood. Carefully, I picked my way over scattered debris on the floor to look at the artifacts from Jon's dig. I marveled at the detailed work still evident on a broken cup that I picked up. These people took pride in their work, I'll give you that. Setting it back down, I continued my investigation.

I only hoped I wouldn't find more dead girls under all this stuff. Hey, he could claim "first time" all he wanted, but who knew. I bet Dahmer seemed like a great guy when you first met him, too. Then it was wham, bam, slash you ma'am. Except, everywhere I looked I saw books, papers, notebooks, half-chewed pencils, and broken items I assumed came from the dig. I returned to the seat Jon so kindly cleared for me and decided to look through the things he tried to show me. Maybe I could make sense of it. I gingerly took several papers from the pile between Jon and myself and began leafing through them. Silly me, thinking that I might be able to translate this gobbledegook into English. I shook my head. I hated studying. Why crack a book when I could be partying or shopping or anything infinitely more interesting?

Things had a nasty habit of changing.

I realized that with my newfound status in life or death, I might need to take the time to at least become familiar with the world at large. I wanted to fight against it with every fiber of my being, but what was a dead girl to do?

If I had my way, life would go back to the way it was. First, I would change my life status back to 'alive'. Then I'd be on my cruise ship. No more massacred manicure problem, and there'd be a nice cool beverage with copious amounts of alcohol. In a week, I'd be home at my job shopping on someone else's dime. I'd go out on many dates, and just be, well, normal.

For now, there was no way for that to happen, and I wanted to wallow. I wanted to throw myself on the ground in a fit. I needed to cry, kick, and scream. Times like this called for an indulgence of Double Brownie Fudge Chocolate ice cream. Smothered in chocolate sauce no less. But no. I was stuck in the back end of nowhere, armpit of Mexico. I had no way of getting home. There was a chance I would never see Double Brownie Fudge Chocolate ice cream again. Worse, there was a chance I would never see my shoe collection or designer clothes again.

It sucked. Not only because I liked my designer stuff, but you know what, just because I was the walking dead didn't mean I couldn't look good.

When I looked back, I realized how selfish I was at that moment. How vain and petty and shallow. Okay, like I grew that much? No, I'm still vain and petty and shallow. Maybe not as bad, but still.

It took me a few minutes to compose myself. I told myself I could not cry. I would not cry. My life was not over. It couldn't be over. I wouldn't let it be over. I had a second chance, and what was I going to do with it? I was going to get back to civilization, that's what I was going to do!

I made up my mind that, come hell or high water, I would find a way to get home. I'd return to my closet overstuffed with beautiful clothes and gorgeous shoes. I would not be stuck in a third world country for the rest of my... death.

Stubborn and determined when I wanted to be, yup, that's me!

What I needed was a plan. Jon could only take me so far. He could help me figure out the bigger part of this mess — understanding just what my newfound state of being entailed. After that? I needed to know.

I made a game plan. First up, I would actually start reading. Yuck, researching. I could feel the hives begging to come out. Gross. Which was worse? Researching or hives? I shuddered. Neither was desirable.

After that, we could run whatever those "tests" were that Jon wanted. After that? Well if it meant setting off in my Jimmy Choos, so be it. I could walk back to America. Didn't know what I'd tell the border patrol, but I could do it. Where there was a will, there was a way. Even without Amex. Right?

It was a light at the end of a miserable Mexican tunnel,

and I set about working. First up was trying to make sense of Jon's so-called organizational system. There was no way this was organized. Chaos looked in this pit and took off running, screaming in fear.

I began the lengthy process of sifting through the pile in front of me. The groan that escaped my lips didn't wake Jon. Poor guy. How could he sleep like that, all weird in a chair instead of in a proper bed? I was fairly sure chiropractors in Mexico were few and far between. I tried to figure out a method to the madness for reading. I didn't feel like I was accomplishing much, but at least it filled the time. After searching for forever, I thought I found some items that might be relevant to me and began reading.

The first text I read from was awful. Total snoozefest. Now I remembered why I hated studying in college. I stood corrected. It wasn't awful. It was abysmal. The person penning this should have been shot. No wait, that was too nice. Someone should force him to listen to a reading of this monstrosity. The words would daunt the SAT, and the text rivaled the Sahara in dryness. Sheesh.

I flicked through the pages anyway. Maybe there was something more my speed in this tome. Like a summary or some groovy pictures. What in the world was there a book about ancient peoples doing without photographs? Artists renderings? If nothing else, snap a photo of some people digging in the ground. Low on excitement? Do a bit of breaking up the humdrum.

Giving up on that book, I moved on. I could waste my time on some other nine-zillion page book, thank you. One that didn't make me want to claw my eyeballs out with a spork. Jon must have been certifiable for reading something like that. Then again, he did decide to attempt to resurrect someone from the dead based on some writings that were five hundred years old. I think we passed certifiable long ago.

The next thing I looked at was a notebook filled with Jon's scrawl. I know, I should've felt some sort of guilt for snooping, right? Hey, it wasn't like it was his most secret diary. No schoolyard crushes or whining because a bully robbed him of milk money. Not even any dirty sketches to pass away the boredom inflicted upon one's self by hideous dusty bricks passing for books.

Deciphering Jon's handwriting should've been paid work. I squinted, turned the book from side to side, and even debated turning it upside down. When I got back to the States, I definitely needed to buy him a personal recorder to thank him for his efforts. What he needed was an assistant to write for him.

I slowly got used to the way he formed his letters, if forming letters was what you wanted to call his handwriting, I began to make out more and more words. His notes followed a stream of consciousness guaranteed to spark a migraine.

Piecing together the events leading up to my resurrection wasn't hard, if I used patience translating everything from scrawl to geek to English. Unfortunately for me, more questions came up from my reading than were answered. Nice. Looked like me and Jon-boy needed to have more chat time. Wonder if he could at least provide some coffee. A good latte would make up for this.

Thinking of my favorite yummy drink from Starbucks for a minute, I realized something: I wasn't thirsty. In this oppressive environment, how was I not thirsty? For that matter, I wasn't hungry, and I didn't need to visit the little hottie's room.

It'd been hours, more than a day's worth, since I'd eaten or had a drink. And let me tell you, the cruise food was beyond scrumptious but hideously fattening. If I'd known breakfast would be my last meal, I probably would have made time for it and gorged myself in manners simply vile for civil company. The snap at the top of my shorts may have popped open, but at least I would have died with a happy belly. What did nearly two days with no food or drink mean? Or no bathroom needs?

Oh well, there's always bathroom needs. A girl's gotta look her best at all times. But you know what I mean by bathroom needs. I paused in my own thoughts and realized I had not taken a look in a mirror since I woke up in my living nightmare.

I moved the notebook out of my lap and stood up. Jon's scraggly stubble showed signs he generally kept himself groomed. An earthquake and spending a day raising moi from the dead really didn't aid in his ability to shave. Once he took care of that ten-hours-past-five-o-clock shadow, I bet he'd be hot.

Oh wait, I'm not thinking about him, I'm thinking about me. What do I look like, that's what's important!

It only took five minutes of tripping over the crap scattered across the floor to find what passed for a bathroom. It made me instantly grateful for no nature calling my name. Egads, scratch Montezuma's Revenge being a stomach ailment. This was it, right here. The bathroom of one Jon 'the Raiser of the Dead' Daniels. It was time to breathe through my mouth to keep the stench from entering my nostrils and gagging me.

A broken bottle sat on the back of the sink. And by 'sink,' I meant a little bowl on a pedestal. I could see the rusty pipes leading to the toilet and the sink. I tried not to look towards the toilet for fear of finding the monster causing the hideous odor. Instead, I looked into the mirror shard and gulped. I should have left well enough alone. Oh, don't get me wrong, everything was intact. I didn't have any giant gashes marring my face. But the grime! Oh, lords the grime! And my hair! I needed a brush and some shampoo, conditioner, mousse, and my flat iron to tame the snarly rat's nest on top of my head.

I opened my mouth and pulled back my lips, reassuring myself that my dental work was intact (and not horribly mutated by new non-alive status). I checked myself over as best I could in the cramped bathroom. Didn't look like anything was amiss, though my clothes definitely needed to be chucked. Blast it. I really liked this outfit. And I didn't think I would be finding a Macy's or Saks anywhere nearby. This was a little far off 5th Avenue.

What was I going to do? No makeup, no brush, no clothes. No way could I be seen looking like this! Even in the back end of nowhere, Mexico. I would scare little children. Then again, if they knew what I was, shouldn't they be scared? It kind of scared me.

Nothing more I could do standing around in the bathroom staring at my ghastly reflection. I needed to get back to what I was doing. I was just turning to go back into the main room of the house when there was a loud knock.

"Señor Juan? Señor Juan?" The voice on the other side of the door sounded suspiciously female to me. I wasn't sure I wanted to get into the middle of any possible domestic squabble. I froze, debating answering the door and kicking Jon outta his not-so-comfy seat.

The knob turned and the door opened with me standing frozen, looking like I'd gone for quite the romp to hell in a hand basket. Glancing at Jon, who looked the same, I tried to wake him up with willpower alone. Too bad groovy psychic powers didn't come with this whole life after death shindig.

"Señor Juan?" A young Hispanic woman entered just as Jon woke up, snorting on a light snore.

"What?"

Boy did he sound groggy when he woke up. Kind of cute, too. Lucky for me I was behind him and didn't have to worry about unsightly drool ruining the nice picture in my head. Sometimes that was nice.

The woman looked at him and then at me. Taking us both in, her mouth formed a little 'o'. Oh boy.

Juan of the Dead

CHAPTER
EIGHT

"Leahonia?"

Jon's voice sounded groggy. I saw him lift his hands to his eyes, probably to rub the sleep from them. The way he sawed those logs, I'd take any bet that his eyes felt like they were glued shut.

"Señor Juan, I no mean to..." the woman said, stumbling over her words a bit before trailing off.

"It's okay. What time is it?" He seemed to wake up quick, even stood up without issue. He also had no trouble navigating the mess in the small room, crossing it in no time to where Leahonia stood. I remained in place rather than risk drawing attention to myself by stumbling on something.

"It's lunchtime, Señor. I bring you lunch and you laundry."

Seriously? She brought him lunch and she did his laundry? What on Earth was I standing in the middle of?

"I not know you have... company."

I didn't like the way her eyes slid to me. I leveled a cool gaze on her. My basic game plan for situations such as this was cool and aloof. Look uninterested and gave no responses to people, and they'd leave you alone. Half of what people did, they did it hoping for a reaction. Besides, when you knew you lead the polls in hotness, it was easy to relax in mixed company.

Juan, er Jon, took something the new arrival had just outside the door. He turned and I saw a large basket of folded clothes. Huh, she really did his laundry and hand delivered them. That was service for you. Service that you got from someone you were close to. I fought the urge to arch an eyebrow.

His eyes flickered, glancing around the room. He was out of his ever-lovin' mind if he thought that basket was going anywhere in there. Not if he wanted the contents to stay intact. Maybe he should get Leahonia to clean up so he would have a place for special deliveries. He stood there holding the basket rather impotently.

"Thanks," he mumbled. I didn't know how I could hear, let alone understand him. "Um, sorry, I forgot what day it was. Uh..."

The woman rolled her eyes. Eh, not surprised. Something told me that she dealt with this sort of absentmindedness from Jon often. It gave me more information though, like she came by at regular intervals. What did that mean?

"Señor Juan, I clean kitchen now or you want me wait till," she paused and looked my way again, "company leaves?"

Oh gods in heaven, clean! For the love of everything in Mexico, clean this dump! Don't stop at the kitchen!

I wished I had my purse; I'd shove every last dollar and peso I could find at her if it meant she'd stick around and bring some order to this poor shack.

"Uh, um," Jon looked my way as well and rubbed his jaw. I knew instantly what went through his head. The same thing that would go through mine: time to weigh the pros and cons of this woman hanging around cleaning things up.

Sure, this place was a dump, and needed her ministrations like no tomorrow, but then again, he might not want her to take a guess at his most recent hobby of raising the dead. It could cause some confusion and then, of course, there was the screaming factor. Would Leahonia dig the idea of hanging out mere feet from the walking dead?

I think the scales weighed in favor of cleaning. Sorry, but terrorizing someone seemed rather inconsequential when you compared it to the state of this crazy place. Just me.

Not sure where Jon weighed in on this, I studied him hoping for a clue, but he just stood there like some kind of dope. Nice. Maybe two women in his house blew his little nerd mind. There was a reason why geeks didn't get the girl, I guess. More than their brain could process.

"Jon?" I needed a big stick to poke this guy. Maybe he was a turtle in a previous life. Just plodding along or hiding in his shell.

His attention snapped to me. Quickly, he turned back to Leahonia. "Um, okay. I haven't been here the last few days, but it could use some work I'm sure."

Oh, I was sure. This guy needed help. Then again, if this gal came and cleaned with any regularity, she was falling down on her job. Or she needed to come more. I was kind of thinking she needed to take over even where she wasn't invited. Drastic times called for drastic measures.

They stood in place for a few moments until she cleared her throat.

"Pardon, Señor Juan?"

"I'm sorry." He shuffled about in the classic dance of

awkward apology before finally realizing that he could just come back towards me to move out of Leahonia's way. He went back to his seat, nodding in its direction. Okie dokie, I can go sit back down. What else was I gonna do anyway? I definitely wasn't going to go help Leahonia unearth what was apparently supposed to be a kitchen. I was barely functional at cleaning my apartment, which stayed clean mostly because I never ate there. If I did, it tended more towards the takeaway variety. When you lived out of Styrofoam cartons and used plastic silverware, your kitchen stayed remarkably clean. Good tip I'd pass on to Jon, if he lived close enough to such luxuries. Too bad for him.

Carefully, I made my way back to my seat. By some small measure of luck, I managed to not knock anything over on my way. I guess it wasn't so hard moving around hoardertopia. Don't get me wrong, I was fully in support of good organizational practices, but I supposed it wasn't near as bad to live in as I imagined. Then again, I knew what I was like in the middle of the night. I'd probably kill myself (again) trying to navigate this place in the dark and half asleep. Maybe that was the key to Jon's ability to waking up quickly. It was a survival tactic.

While waiting for me, Jon juggled the basket of laundry from Leahonia. He finally used a foot to move some things to the side on the floor near his seat and placed the basket there. I watched, but amazingly nothing fell over.

Jon waited for me to sit before sitting himself. What a gentleman. Where was that gentlemanly nature when he was copping some feels? I didn't even want to contemplate what he did to my corpse. Yikes.

He leaned forward in his seat, elbows on his knees and rested his face in the palms of his hands. He must still be tired. He cleared his throat and looked up. "Sorry I was just tired. Are you okay?"

I felt great. Better and better by the minute really. I couldn't remember a time when I felt this good. Just wished my appearance matched how good I felt. A shiver went through me at the thought of my reflection in the mirror. "I'm fine. Just wishing that I could, you know, change clothes and stuff."

"Not tired then?"

"Nope." I hadn't felt this awake in years. Probably since before I met my good friends Jack and Absolut. I don't think I'd slept eight hours straight since learning the great art of partying. A party sounded really good about now. A night of dancing at the clubs. I was up for it. I was just itchy with desire to get moving. Sitting around the piles of dusty books was obviously getting to me.

"Hmmm." He fidgeted for a few moments. I let him think about things while drumming my fingers on my leg. "Well, okay. Uh... Well..."

And I'd thought we'd made some progress. Tongue-tied again already?

"Yes?" He looked embarrassed.

"I gotta admit, I don't really know what to do next. Guess I've always been better at research than theoretical lab stuff."

"Really," I droned. Given his amount of social ineptitude, I wondered how he'd survive in real world settings, let alone in a lab. I wondered if the sarcasm dripping from my voice even registered with him. The notebook I'd leafed through earlier still rested where I left it. I picked it up and offered it to him. "I hope you don't mind. I was trying to figure things out and looked at this."

"Um, no, that's okay." He took the book from me and I offered him the large (hideously boring) book, too. "You looked at this?"

His incredulous look made me wonder if he found it just

as dull as I did. "Yeah, I looked. I didn't do much else, it was awful."

"It is a bit dry. I only open it for pure research. Thank God there's an index in it. I think I'd pull my hair out if I had to actually read it for any length of time."

Oh good, it wasn't just me. But how sad was it when someone in the field the book centered around said the book was bad? Sheesh, that's one for the Amazon ratings- negative one zillion stars.

"Your stuff didn't really help any. I don't know anything more than when I woke up after... everything. Don't get me wrong, I'm not ungrateful, but maybe you shoulda done some more research before doing the whizzbang action or whatever."

"Maybe, but you know sometimes circumstances just... happen."

"Like random earthquakes giving you the perfect chance?"

"Well, yeah. I don't know. I just got caught up in the mo- ment."

Oh, like a girl hadn't heard that line before. Or used that line before. Yeah, right. Caught up in the moment my big toe. Men really liked to recycle lines. The sad thing was they were dumb enough to think we women didn't catch on.

"Really? I think most people would have been too busy doing the duck and cover for fear of earthquake damage to be all 'caught up in the moment'. You? You think, 'Hey what if I just totally take advantage of this-"

He cut me off. "Hey, cut me a break. I really don't know what possessed me. I guess I wasn't really thinking, just re- acting."

Reacting to what? Probably Little Jon, knowing how men

are. Eh, not like it would be the first time a guy had that reaction around me.

"Okay, okay. So, I looked through this stuff hoping to get some kind of answers to what you did or what happened to me. I got a big fat nada."

"It's still hard to believe it worked. But it has and here we are."

"Yeah. Wherever that is," I sighed. My topsy turvy life summed up. I lowered my voice and leaned in closer to Jon. "And who is she?"

His eyes flicked to Leahonia and back to me. He continued in the same hushed tone, "My maid. She comes in once a week and takes care of things here. In case you couldn't tell, I'm a bit disorderly."

A bit? Understatement of the Year had an award waiting with his name on it. I snickered. "Well, that's nice."

Though I wasn't surprised with what I'd heard about Mexico and the job market.

"I guess. She takes care of things that I forget about. Like eating or doing my laundry or taking care of the kitchen."

"You should think about having her take care of things in here, too. Maybe you could rediscover the floor."

He looked around. "But I wouldn't be able to find anything."

He could find things? I'd believe it when I saw it. "Right. What next? See if I can leap tall buildings in a single bound? How do you plan to determine how much your whatsiwhosit did to me? Aside from me being your lab rat."

"That's about it. We're just trying to determine anything out of the ordinary off the bat, which would be great."

Great for him, but I was the one needing to deal with it in life or death or whatever. "Yeah like what? I don't know what you're looking for."

"That makes two of us," he chuckled. Maybe he could find the humor since he wasn't the dead girl.

"Yeah, so you say. I still think you do this with all the girls," I smiled at Jon. Harmless flirting, didn't mean a thing...except helping me get what I wanted.

His face flushed. "I guess we just have to figure out what's changed. Do you feel any different?"

"Not really. Didn't I already tell you that? Just the lack of the many things that should be wrong with me after that kind of accident. Like you know, broken bones or lack of breathing or whatever."

Then again, did I really need to breathe? Seriously, some things you didn't think about. You just did them because you'd done them your entire life. Breathing happened to be one of those things. No one tried to go without it since then you got the rather predictable end of death. However, I'd already met that particular end. Was I breathing? If so, did I need to?

For that matter, what about my heart? You didn't normally feel things like your blood flowing, your heart beating, your stomach digesting, your spleen doing whatever it was spleens did, and so on. You just went through life taking for granted that your body was behaving and doing its thing. What was mine doing? Wouldn't we really need a hospital to truly determine most of that? Well some things, no. How hard was it to purposefully try to hold one's breath? Take a pulse? We could do stuff without the wonders of civilized science. And I supposed since I didn't know what a spleen did normally, it wouldn't bother me to know if it was or wasn't working now. If it wasn't, I wouldn't know what to look for and what's the worse that would happen? It'd kill me? Ha! I laughed in the face of possible death by malfunctioning spleen! Do your worst, it couldn't match an earthquake!

"You were kinda messed up," Jon said into my stream of inner dialogue.

"Kinda messed up?" A giant calendar fell on me. I'll took his word since I was, you know, dead, but really? I'd say dead was more than kinda messed up. "You think?"

He just looked at me. He seemed to expect me to have a better sense of humor about the fact that I died like, two days ago, but that was just not gonna happen. Death had a way of doing that to a girl.

I stared back at him and said, "So what do you suggest first? I can tell you I looked at myself, scary as that was. Egads. But I've got a reflection, right? I figure that's a good start."

"What does a reflection have to do with anything?"

"Hello?! It means that, first of all, I can keep myself looking good. I just need to find some good product and make up and clothes and whatnot. Probably scarce her in the back end of nowhere. But more importantly it means that maybe I won't go on a drinking binge, if you get my drift."

"Huh? Drinking?"

Slow on the uptake again? You betcha. Nice.

"Uh, duh much? You need to read more. Something besides that dusty pile of slice my wrists boring there. Or at least take in a movie." I motioned towards that one book I'd made the mistake of picking up.

Yech, don't want to contemplate how many minutes of my life (or death) that I'll never get back thanks to those books.

Hope my death was kinda long and eternal like vampires or whatever. That would rock. Guess if that were the case, I could totally not mind losing time reading to that piece of junk. Not minding is not the same as raring to do it again.

"Why?"

"You aren't near up to date enough on lore, man. Did

you grow up under a rock before coming here? It didn't sound like I could be going in that direction, but hey, I watched Buffy. I read Stoker. I know what happens to one sect of people in my situation. It's not pretty. Not the sort of lifestyle I wanna live, you know? Sure, they're all sexy smoking hot in the movies, but that diet leaves a lot to be desired."

And there it was. The giant light bulb went off over his head. "Oh."

"Yeah. I got a reflection going on so I can keep myself looking good and hopefully not on an all liquid diet. Since none of those sorts were involved, probably cuz they don't exist, figured it wasn't the case, but who knows. Of course, who knows what exists anymore."

"True. Reality has changed in the last two days, hasn't it?"

I'd say so.

I went from a nice world where there was a definite line between fantasy and fact. Things in the movies and books you knew couldn't happen, just didn't. Now, who knew; I shouldn't have been there. What else was out there? I really didn't want to contemplate that. I was monster enough to deal with, thank you very much.

Facing a world that might have all sorts of crazy things like werewolves and vampires and witches and whatnot really freaked me out. Thankfully I had new and improved night vision. Hopefully that meant I could see whatever went bump in the night. I suppose you could say I was what went bump in the night.

I wasn't really a monster, but then again, I was. I liked to consider myself cute and cuddly like the monsters on Sesame Street. Hey, I've got a soft spot for Cookie Monster, what could I say. He's blue, he's got googly eyes, and he liked cookies. That was cool, and we forgave him being a monster, right?

Why not me?

CHAPTER NINE

Those first few days I spent a lot of time attempting to convince myself life could be normal. That I could be normal. Things didn't have to change, did they? I could only dream, except it didn't take me long to realize I no longer needed sleep. So much for dreams.

My voice was quiet when I spoke. "Yeah, things have changed."

I wondered if he could hear the melancholy in my voice. It was more than just the loss of my Amex, my ID, my appearance. Somewhere deep inside I knew there was a loss of a life I'd expected to have. A loss of a life I currently enjoyed. That was a lot of change to deal with.

There's supposed to be these stages of grief people go through. I probably didn't experience them in the right order, but I definitely went through each one. I never paid attention to all that psychology stuff. I just knew I wasn't really ready to accept all the changes even though they kept smacking me in the face.

"Are you okay?" he asked. He sounded really concerned about me. Maybe he was. I took a deep breath, trying to calm my nerves. I felt like letting myself unravel. Crying sounded like a good idea. I fought back a sniffle. I survived death; surely, I could survive the ramifications of surviving not-death. I took another breath.

"For now," I nodded.

"I'm sorry. Maybe I did the wrong thing..." Now it was his voice that was soft. Wait, no, if he did the wrong thing, then that meant he should have left me for dead. I didn't know about anyone else, but that seemed like a bad idea to me. This way I got another shot at the world.

"No, no, no. It wasn't wrong. I just gotta figure things out. People go through major life changing events all the time. They survive. I'll be good," I assured him.

People found their life in shambles all the time, and they made do. I thought this whole thing proved I was a survivor. Bring it on. I could totally buck myself up. Sometimes it paid off when I was having a bad hair day or something. But this was way past bad hair day. No way was I melting down over this. I banned flipping out and going psycho while there were witnesses.

Maybe now would be a good point in time to bring up the lack of the sleepiness, hunger, and thirst. Seemed as good a time as any. He beat me to the punch, though.

"If you are sure you don't need to rest, what about food?"

"Nope, feeling chipper as anything. Not hungry, or thirsty either. You'd think I'd be feeling something like that, though."

He steepled his hands. "Yeah. I'm starving."

He eyed the basket at his feet. On top of the clothes rested a towel wrapped item that smelled quite tasty. Not tasty enough to make my stomach grumble, though. I'd never been a huge Mexican food fan, just a good taco now and again.

"Why don't you eat?" I motioned towards the basket. "Shame for Leahonia's hard work to go to waste."

He took the towel and unwrapped it. Something in a tortilla shell greeted him. The flour tortilla was the greatest thing the Mexican people gave us. I would take a wrap for lunch any day. At least, I would before I died. Anything put inside a flour tortilla shell was a winner. Mmmmm.

Jon didn't even sniff it, just bit into it. And bit into it again. If I blinked, I probably would've missed him finishing the thing, he ate it so fast. Guess he was hungry. Rescuing a girl from earthquake rubble and reviving her must work up quite the appetite. While he ate, I tried to take my pulse without looking too obvious about it. I never was good at that sort of thing. I remembered in gym the teacher would make us try after we ran. I was either dead then, too, or I couldn't find my pulse.

Finding nothing, I figured it could be a sign of no more heartbeat or a sign that in the fifteen odd years since leaving high school, I still didn't know how to take my pulse. I gave up and paid attention to my breathing instead. Was I breathing?

Actually, I was. Vaguely, I remembered a science lesson regarding air over vocal cords equals talking. At least, that's how I remembered the lesson ending. Surely there was some sort of scientific principle I was missing out on, but it really wasn't necessary for me to know. If it ain't broke, why fix it.

It begged the question though: did I need to breathe to talk or did I need to breathe to function? I didn't want to make a big show of sucking in a breath and just holding it, so I decided to let it go unless Jon pushed it. Really, I spoke enough that I'd probably never go without breathing.

While he ate, I learned nothing. Wasn't that just nice? I remembered now why I got a C in my science classes. Too much work and I never got the hang of experimenting. I could do all of that or I could flirt with cute lab partners. He watched me while eating. I shrugged to let him know that my pulse-reading attempt failed. He wiped his hands on the towel after taking the last bite and reached towards my wrist.

"Let me try."

I held out my hand. He expertly placed his fingers on my wrist, and I knew instantly he'd hit his mark. Talk about making it look easy. A thrill went up my arm at his touch. That'd get my heart beating in my chest. Yowzas. Watching his lips move as he counted might do it, too. I tried to distract myself from thinking about those lips moving in other ways.

Something nagged at me, but I was too distracted to consider it. My thoughts carried me away to places I'd rather not mention. Instead, I forced myself back to the present when he released my wrist, fingers lingering on my hand. I reminded myself that he wasn't my type and tried to ignore the losing battle my mind was fighting with my body. Maybe I could treat Mexico like Vegas. What happened in Mexico stayed in Mexico! Sounded good. Sure, would like to leave my untimely demise behind. Hey, it could work. Settle down the whatever hormones raging through me and then leave that and my death behind. Sure, I could totally do that!

"Twenty."

What was he saying?

"Huh?"

Get a grip, girl. Pay attention again.

"Your heart rate. It's twenty beats per minute."

Okay, now, I avoided doctors like the plague. I wanted nothing to do with a snot nosed, brat filled doctor's office. They were the breeding ground for various creepy diseases that I wanted nothing to do with. And we'd already seen my stellar ability to take my own pulse. Twenty sounded odd, but heck if I knew why.

"Is that good?" Hey, maybe it could be like looking your age: lower the better. No woman wanted to look her age. Obviously, you didn't want to go too low, but 20 was a nice number. Could it work for heart rates like that?

"Uh, well, it's good in that you have a heartbeat. Bad in that it's seriously below normal. I'm guessing you don't know your normal heart rate?"

"As if."

Now I knew that the gym has those swanky machines you hold onto while you are working out and it will tell you your heart rate. But since I wasn't currently on the stairmaster, that wouldn't help much. Plus, I never touched those things. People sweat on them. Gross!

"Well, normal should be more like around one-hundred probably. Really depends on your health and your weight and your age, but yeah. You're at like a fifth of that."

Hmmm, well, uh... "So that means?"

"I don't know. It means your heart is beating really slow. That could be good or bad. But it is a difference"'

"Okay then. I have a mysterious and weird heartbeat. Now what?"

"I think we need to go back to your strength. I don't think you should have been able to move that altar. I don't think I could move that altar. Yet you did and didn't even notice it. What else do you think you can do?"

Like I sat around checking what I could and could not bench press? I dated a guy obsessed with weightlifting once. What a meathead. As long as I could lift my purse, what more did I need? Then again, if there was a giant stone thing and I moved it, that was kind of crazy on the strength level. Maybe I could pick up a car single handedly. I could be like Supergirl. Maybe I could even fly!

I figured I couldn't fly and picking up a car with one hand seemed a bit of a useless talent. I'd be happy with getting the lid off the pickle jar. I hated those things.

"It sucks being a girl sometimes," I shrugged. "Well, not when there's a cute guy around or anything. Guys like to rescue girls from the greater evils of the world like spaghetti sauce bottles that won't open. But, when you're home alone and want a sandwich and can't get the jam open, you're cursing life. Some extra strength is something I could get behind."

He grinned at me. "Girls like to play they can't open bottles? Or they really can't? You're letting me in on all the deep dark secrets of womankind here."

Oh my gosh. That bordered on flirting. I winked at him. "I'll never tell. You gotta keep guessing."

He groaned. Oh, how I liked the sound of that.

"You're gonna kill me!"

"Too bad I can't read your scrawl there or I would know the secrets to eternal torment! I could bring you back and you could suffer more!"

Maybe joking about my situation wasn't such a great thing. Especially with someone else around. I'd actually forgotten about Leahonia while we'd been talking. Pretty much after he'd touched my wrist, I'd forgotten about everyone else in the world. Something clattered in her direction and Jon and I snapped our heads that way. Leahonia stood, staring at us, a cast iron skillet at her feet wobbling to a standstill.

She looked at me and at Jon with eyes opened wide. What was her problem, I wondered? We were kidding around, but I didn't think we'd actually said anything someone could take seriously. Especially someone that spoke in broken English. But she had been listening. And she understood far more than we could have guessed. I never wanted to frighten her, but in that moment, she looked like she'd seen her own ghost.

CHAPTER
TEN

"Lea? Are you okay?" Jon asked the simple question. I merely sat there, not knowing what to do or think.

Leahonia took a moment to regain her composure. "I sorry, Señor Juan. I so sorry, I no mean to cause problem. I no mean to listen you two talk."

It didn't matter if she meant to eavesdrop, she had. Anyone caught listening in on a conversation quickly learned they got more than they bargained for. Without knowing the full context of what people were talking about lead to a lot of misunderstanding. Maybe we could brush this off as a misunderstanding.

"It's okay."

No, it wasn't. How could Jon say that? People should mind their own business.

"Are you okay?" he asked again.

"No. Yes. No." She couldn't make up her mind.

"Lea?"

Boggs

She stooped to pick up the skillet, and I noticed her hand trembled. Was she upset from causing a ruckus, upset for being caught listening to us, or was it the topic of conversation? Her hand grasped the handle of the skillet and she held it before her as though it were a club she wanted to keep between her and us.

"You no making sense. You no joke about those kinds of things. Bad stuff happens when you go against nature!" Her voice sounded a few octaves higher than before.

"Calm down. We were just talking." Jon kept his voice soothing. Probably a good thing since she sounded fairly superstitious. Normally, I'd question someone so concerned about obvious fictional poppycock, but things had changed in that regard. Could be this woman's superstitions were founded in reality? Like my reality?

If her superstitions had any bearing on my new status, how on earth were we to bring it up? You couldn't just walk up to someone and say, "Hey so you know, I died. You got any legends on that? Like am I going to become a homicidal maniac bent on destroying the world?"

There was simply no way to tactfully bring it up to a woman who was little more than a stranger. At least Jon had some sort of working relationship with her.

"You don't know what you joke about, Señor Juan. There are stories of things people do. Wrong things. Evil things. It no funny stuff."

I tried not to roll my eyes. You want to talk not funny? Not funny was my current sitch: Lost in Mexico with no ID, and a bit of a health crisis. Not many could find the humor in that. Me being one of the 'not many'.

I could have seen Jon perk up a mile away. "Stories about what?"

"I no want to say. They told to scare children. No good come from the things happen in the stories."

Her broken English through a thick Spanish accent didn't deter Jon's interest. Or mine, I just happened to play cool better. I looked at her, hoping my best poker face was up to par. Jon all but lapped at her feet.

"Leahonia, you know how I love hearing the stories about the people here. Will you tell us?" Okay, I had to give him credit. He played to his strengths. What better way to get someone to tell you legends than to express an interest? Fessing up to nefarious acts typically came off a little mad-scientisty.

Leahonia lowered her pan. "I not sure that a good idea, Señor Juan. People, they hear stories. They think stories stupid and laugh or they think stories worth looking at. History speaks of people giving lives in search for gold city."

Jon waved his hands. "Oh now, none of that. You know that's why I'm here. I want to study this area, the culture that once lived here, how it influenced the culture today. Please share with us the story."

Dang, was he good. Even I believed him, and I knew why he was asking. It was more than idle curiosity. He'd probably already done whatever she was afraid of and here I was to prove it. I was just surprised she spoke such broken English but seemed okay with all those words he said.

"Please put down the pot and come over. We really didn't mean to upset you." I flashed her a winning smile. Maybe I could try to take her anxiety down a notch or two with some old-fashioned friendliness. Besides, I bet that would come off very not- monster-like.

"Okay." She put the pot down and came closer to us, but still held onto a safe distance from us. Did she suspect anything? Surely not.

"What you want to know?" Her question's simplicity in form held almost no information, but she took the initiative to clear a spot to sit down.

Holy cow there really was a table under this giant pile of stuff between Jon and myself. And her speed at straightening up books and properly stacking paper was nothing short of superhuman.

Within minutes she seated herself on the edge of the table in her freshly cleaned space. Jon just stared at her, probably in shock. I bet he didn't know what to make of her quick tidy of his so-called system. I bet it was eating at him somewhere deep inside.

"See, Bea. This is what I'm talking about. This is why I'm here. I love learning about these cultures. Leahonia, tell us anything. Like what upset you." Looking back and forth between Leahonia and myself, he urged her to open up.

And so, she began. What a way to fill in some gaps. Hindsight is 20/20, they say. By the time she finished, I would take any bet that he regretted giving me the wakeup juju. I was kind of questioning his raising me, even if it did mean saving me from becoming moldy worm food. Ick!

Like any other indigenous story, it of course started a long time ago on a dark and stormy night. Okay maybe not a dark and stormy night, but you need your mood to come from somewhere, right?

As it turned out, her story included a relative from way back in her family tree. But of course, who didn't want to tell a story like that and not include a relative? Dearly departed Great whatever Grandpa was quite the rabble raiser. Someone at the high point of this area's civilization thought it would be a fantastic idea to wake the dead. Nice, sound familiar? I tried very hard to not look at Jon when she brought up that particular nugget. Instead, I tried the lay low play, and that meant no suspicious shared glances. As long as I drew no attention to myself, things would work out well.

This guy tried really hard to find a way to sucker punch

death in the face. Find a way around it. It turned out his wife died in childbirth and he couldn't cope.

Sometimes people were like that, and they just didn't take death well. Not many went around trying to raise their dead wife from the grave, though. Didn't they have wine back in the dark ages? I'm not sure who told this guy that he could haggle with the devil, but he tried it. 'A' for effort but things went bad so fast I he eventually scored a big fat 'F'.

The description Leahonia gave of what happened to this guy's wife was the stuff nightmares were made of. Horror movie villains with masks and axes had nothing on this stuff. At the time I thought the shivers up and down my spine might never stop. I was glad that Jon's efforts on my behalf didn't turn out that way. Yeesh. The wife came back but, let's just say she didn't stop at eating her husband's brains. Oh, it was much worse. She didn't survive for long after rending him limb from limb, so there was a happy ending. To his part of the story at least.

Of course, it didn't end there. Who thought it would? Turned out there were others in the tribe from many hundreds of years ago that kept the research going. I guess they were all a little touched in the head. Hopefully that particular gene was watered down and lost in the generations between then and now.

Leahonia told us that even after the unfortunate attempts of the man, the leaders wanted to continue the efforts. The idea was to bring back fallen warriors, then they would hold the power to truly reap revenge on enemies. Still others liked the idea of resurrecting loved ones. Didn't some people deserve second chances at life? Apart from me?

Apparently, the idea of a necropolis of undead became the hot idea of the area. Boy, aren't you glad you didn't live here like a thousand years ago? Made you want to double check your locks at night.

Attempts still ended with a lot of death and destruction at the hands of those returned from death. Guess scary movie ideas came from somewhere. It didn't matter whose folklore you read or watched, those that crossed the line between life and death liked the idea of bringing more people across that threshold.

Leahonia told us of whole tribes wiped out overnight. Whole civilizations like the one Jon enjoyed studying. It made me think of his mysterious recipe he found with no information after it. I bet it was from one of those civilizations taken out by hordes of zombies. Leahonia concluded that at long last attempts to raise the dead were halted.

The nightmare brought to life needed to end, and I couldn't agree more. I wasn't a fan of the grisly.

When the Spaniards came to the Americas and began to really intermingle with the indigenous population, things changed in this area of the world. By then, many of the early American tribes were gone in this area of the world. They mingled with the Colonists, becoming like them while losing a great deal of what they were. But some legends would never fade.

Thank goodness for those legends. I was glad that Leahonia's family still told them. I'm sure others would choose to abandon them, maybe only bringing them out for scary campfire tales.

It sounded bad, but it couldn't have anything to do with my circumstances. I wasn't going all homicidal and taking out innocent women and children. I felt very much like my old self. Just more alert and with better eyesight. And apparently a slower heartbeat. Jon still lived and I didn't see any reason to hurt Leahonia.

Maybe her legends dealt with something else. Goodness knew there were enough legends to go around out there. Vampires, werewolves, zombies. Everyone had a story and every tale was different. Sure, her story came from the right part of the world, but I bore no resemblance to anything she spoke of. I looked at Jon. He pulled out that book, the really boring one, the one that might have killed me a second time over. Flipping through the pages, he found something and turned the book towards Leahonia.

"Was this what you were talking about?" I stretched to see what he was showing her and noticed a small picture of a dig site. Leahonia turned pale. Hard to do with her lovely natural tan coloring. No amount of tanning beds or sun worshipping ever gave me such a lovely hue. What could cause her to go pale?

"Si, Señor Juan. That it."

A nice mysterious answer. I cleared my throat. A little fill in for the dead girl would be nice. Especially if it means warning me when I might go all hack and slashy on people.

"That is most interesting. I didn't know you kept those stories going all this time." While his tone sounded thoughtful, it didn't give me much insight.

"Hey, what is that?" I asked. Pointing at the book I tried to give him my best 'help me understand, too' look.

He turned his attention to me. "Oh, there's just this picture of a rubbing taken from a site in South America." He brought the book my way. I took in what was on the bottom of the page, but it meant nothing to me.

"And what does that mean? And are we close to South America?" Actual geography of Mexico was a bit fuzzy to me past the whole Mexico is between the US and South America. For all I knew a good hour in Jon's beater pick-up truck, and we could be finding our way into South America. Or it could be a six-day drive.

He looked at me and sighed. "We are on the Yucatan

peninsula, Bea."

"The yuckawhat?"

Yuck was right. Someone probably landed here and said, "Where the hell am I? Yuck! There's nothing here but sand and grossness." Named it Yucatan and beat feet for home. Sounded like what I'd do, quite frankly. Kind of wish I had, now.

"The Yucatan peninsula. You didn't bother to look to see where you were going before leaving on your trip?"

"Um, it said 'cruise' and 'Mexico'. What more did I need to know? I wasn't navigating the ship. It was supposed to be a vacation, not a get lost and set up a new home sort of trip. A day here, a day there, but mostly a whole lotta lounging on the deck of a really big boat."

"I see."

Why did I get the feeling that was his way of dismissing me as stupid? I wasn't stupid. I just didn't happen to be up on geography of somewhere I did not live. Was there something wrong with that?

"Okay, fine. Yucatan. I get it. I take it we're not that close to South America?"

"Well we're closer than the States are, but eh, not particularly close. We can't just run over there for a taco if that's what you are asking."

Actually, it was, but I wasn't about to let on. Not when he was talking down to me. Jerk.

"Okay, fine. How far away is this place the rubbing thing is from?"

"Pretty far, really. I find it interesting that the tales are the same," Jon said.

"Señor Juan? It is these stories; this is why we have celebration this week. Honor the dead so that the dead no come back for us."

Say what? They are gonna do what with the dead?

Jon smacked himself in the head. "I totally forgot that this week was Day of the Dead. Yikes."

"What the hell is Day of the Dead?" I asked. It sounded to me like today was Day of the Dead since here I was, dead girl walking and talking in the day. Somehow, I didn't think that's what he meant.

"Si, Señor Juan. Tomorrow we all celebrate Dia de los Muertos. We remember the bad times and hope for better times. We honor our dead. My family travel far to where we once from. We must honor the dead, so they honor us."

"Hello? Clueless here! Day of the Dead? What is that?"

"Sorry, Bea. It's a celebration here. It is the first of November. Their way of celebrating the Halloween time. It comes from the ancient Aztec civilization's traditions of honoring the dead. It's actually really interesting. They choose to honor their dead."

"Spooky. Guess it fits with Halloween."

"Yeah, it coincides with All Saints Day which is the way the Catholic Church decided to accept ancient pagan rituals at this time of year. I could go into more detail-"

"Naw, that's good. I got the basic gist. You said it's like now?" I said, interrupting him.

"November 1st. I was here last year and travelled with Leahonia and her family for their celebration. It was really great. Thanks again for inviting me, Lea."

"Is no problem, Señor Juan. You come again or you busy?" With her last word she looked at me. I wondered if that was an invitation or not.

"No, not busy. In fact, I think I should go. Bea, you up for a trek?"

Was I? Depends on how much walking me and Jimmy Choo would have to do. And what I could do to make myself a little more presentable. This was ridiculous. But, yeah, why not. Some celebration for dead folk? I liked to party, and I was technically in some sort of dead-like state.

"I guess. But what about my problem...?"

"No worries. This will help us in trying to figure out your problem."

Oh, the beauty of code. How do you go about saying someone is dead and you wanna find out what that means without actually saying those words? Yeah, that's always fun. Lucky for us, Leahonia here wasn't fully fluent in English. Maybe she'd just rack up her confusion on the language barrier.

"Yeah well there's my other problem." Oh yeah, lets confound the code some more.

He looked at me with a question in his eyes. "There is?"

I rolled my eyes. "Hello? Do I really look presentable? How can I go anywhere looking like this."

Leahonia, ever helpful, piped up. "Oh señorita, I take and wash your clothes if you want. I maybe fix, too?"

Just what would I wear if she did that? It was warm in Mexico for this time of year but running about in my birthday suit might draw a little too much attention for my comfort.

"I had an accident in the earthquake. This is all I have. Thanks for the offer, but I don't think I can really take you up on it." Not a lie in there at all, right? Good. I wasn't real hot on telling lies. Unless it meant getting into a party that's rumored to be high on the legendary scale. Her mouth formed an 'o' again, just like before. No doubt her mind was all sorts of places I didn't want to contemplate.

"I can maybe help, señorita. I bring you some clean clothes I have. You wear those and I see what I can do with these."

That was awful sweet of Leahonia. Given her fear over our previous topic of conversation I wondered if she'd be as kind if she knew my secret. Probably not. She'd most likely take off screaming and we'd never see her again. Or she'd return with villagers with torches and pitchforks.

"Thank you." Until I got a handle on things, I needed to rely on the kindness of strangers. Though Jon hardly felt like a stranger anymore, even though it'd only been a few hours since I first woke up on that altar.

"My pleasure. You friend of Juan's. I want to help. He good to my family. I good to his friends."

Well, I guess you could call me a friend of Jon's. Whatever worked. He did save my life in a way.

I mumbled another thank you and contemplated her kindness. Would I be as willing to help some stranger? I couldn't be sure.

"Leahonia, that is very kind of you. Why don't you go ahead and go take care of that? You didn't have much more here, did you?" If I didn't know better, I'd think that Jon was trying to get rid of her. Then again, I did know better. I bet he was trying to get rid of her.

"Si, Señor. I go now. I finish here later." Leahonia stood and made her way for the door. Jon followed her while I decided to sit like a lump.

How awkward. I didn't mean to disrupt everyone's life. She had a job to do and now she was going to have to go and find me clothes. He probably needed to do far more interesting things than try to give me a crash course in an ancient people doing crazy voodoo crap. And me? I longed for the simplicity of my life.

Everything would be okay. Then I'd straighten up. No more drinking binges, no more partying all night, no more spending all my paychecks on fabulous shoes and handbags and clothes. I'd give back to the world. Hey, wasn't bargaining one of those steps of grief? If I could bargain my way out of this mess, you better believe I'd go for it.

CHAPTER ELEVEN

There I sat, on the verge of tears, when Jon returned. Leahonia, off to find ways to help me that I didn't deserve, was no longer in earshot. We could speak freely once more, and he didn't waste any time. Which was fine, I relished the distraction that would help me keep the tears at bay. He had a new book in his hand when he sat down, and didn't take his eyes off it as he leafed through the pages.

"When she mentioned Day of the Dead, it reminded me of something. There are many ancient legends from before the Spaniards arrived. Many of the ancient American cultures seem to relate to this one core legend... armies of undead used to cause terror and greater swaths of destruction."

He paused then and thumbed through a few more pages before he found what he wanted. He spun the book towards me and pointed at a large drawing of natives. Whatever they were doing went right over my head, but not before I noticed the skulls they held in their hands. It looked almost like they might be dancing about holding the skulls. Now that was downright creepy.

"What is this? Doesn't look like anyone raising undead armies from the depths of Hell or anything."

"This was found on a dig on the northern half of South America. The general consensus is that it predates the Spanish settlers' arrival and it shows an unaffected Day of the Dead celebration. The Spaniards came to the Americas and were settling here at the same time as their Inquisition in Europe. They had a definite religious agenda. You can only imagine the things they did here."

"Really? I gotta admit, history is not my strong suit. What happened? Did they force everyone to become Christian or something?"

"Pretty much. Maybe not right away, but over time as the Spanish settlers gained more and more of a foothold in the Americas, they slowly pushed out the native population. Or they brought the population in by marriage. It was an interesting time, but it is also sad because of how the way of life changed. The natives were worshiping a new god, eating different foods, and speaking a new language. You name it. Not much was the same at all."

"Wow. Just like in America. I remember that from History. What was it, the trail of whatever.."

"Trail of Tears. Thank goodness the Spanish don't have any sort of persecution quite like that, but they have their own negative stories."

"Nobody expects a Spanish Inquisition!"

He grinned. "Exactly. They came here and they plundered the land. They searched high and low for some famed city of gold. They killed people for being in the way. Brutal."

I shook my head. "I guess so. Wow. What happened to

Day of the Dead that's changed?"

"See, I'm not altogether sure. This passage and picture make it look like quite the festival, but the Spaniards wouldn't let anything remotely pagan occur. We know they morphed the Catholic holiday, All Saints Day, and that made it easier for the population to bite. It's still a celebration, it just honors the deceased. I want to learn about what it was before that, and that's part of why I wanted to travel with Leahonia. Maybe we'll get more insight at the festival."

"Do you think there's really any hints for helping me out? Most of what I know at this time of year is kids in costume begging for candy."

Color me still confused. I liked a good party. I was more than ready to go along for the ride. Put my name on the guest list and all that but what did it have to do with costumes and candy?

"There's people who think that maybe part of the Day of the Dead went well beyond just honoring your deceased. Maybe it went into these tales, like what Leahonia spoke of. But it looks like maybe it was more. Maybe it was to celebrate the successful attempts at raising the dead."

"Well it seems to me if armies of psycho undead were marching the countryside wiping out people, that would be pretty successful. Destructive, but successful."

He nodded. "True, but that's not it. Successful as in, like you. Where the person appears to truly return. Intact cognitively, as opposed to being mindless, or death dealers."

Oh, that's a joyful way to consider myself. A success because I'm not mindless and shambling.

Don't get me wrong, I'd rather not be mindless and shambling, but still. What a sucker-punch to the self-esteem.

"You're saying that maybe there were those that created the things that nightmares are made of. And then there were some that kept it more... on the up and up?"

"Yes. My plan is that we head out to the Day of the Dead ceremony. Given the proximity of Leahonia's family to my dig site, and the obvious proof that people in this area were able to raise the dead with non-destructive tendencies, there might be something we can learn. It would be ridiculous to pass up this opportunity."

I thought for a moment. "So, do you think she is just in the dark to the possibility that maybe... well... I could exist? She seemed awful nervous."

"Oh no. I trust her. She's genuine. It may not even be a cover up on the part of her ancestors so much as they may have left things behind. Maybe that's for the best. If her people did know how to do this sort of stuff and left it behind, there's probably a reason."

"Um, except it kind of affects me. What reason could possibly be even remotely good about abandoning this?"

For real, did I want to know that I might suddenly go all homicidal cannibal on people?

"Well, uh, true." He ran his hand through his hair. "But I think that even if there was a good reason, it doesn't pertain to you. Which is why I thought it safe to even try this."

Or maybe you kinda liked the idea of being the mad scientist. "Okay, what's our next move?"

"Well, we can see what else we can find out on our own. When Leahonia returns, you can get cleaned up. And then? We go to Day of the Dead."

Well, it sounded like I could get myself back to looking decent and then we got to go party. Sounded good to me. The quicker we got started, the happier I'd be sitting in my home back in Virginia.

"Let's get rolling. Once I get myself back to looking decent, I'm not gonna want to muck about doing whatever it is you wanna do."

Jon stood. "Come this way. Let's just try the testing on the ridiculous first. You already said your eyesight was better. Let's check your other senses."

I didn't know how he expected to do that, but I followed him. Over the next half hour, we ran through some simple games to test my senses. I couldn't hear through walls, meaning no hearing things miles away. Guess I'd not be running off like Superman to save cats stuck in trees on the other side of town. My sense of smell was not any better than when I was alive, which I was thankful for, given the pungent things Jon managed to find to test me on.

My sense of balance was no better or worse than before I died. Sometimes I could be really graceful, and other times trip on my own two feet for no particular reason. I could move about easily enough but kept that wonderful propensity for random balance issues. Bummer, because the loss of my not-so-inner-klutz would have been fantastic. Well, couldn't have everything.

The last thing we tried was a basic strength check. A winner, finally. Turned out that while I wouldn't be flinging cars about like they were made of paper, I could actually lift the back end of Jon's truck with one hand. I didn't even break a sweat. That was when Leahonia returned with the promised clothes and some beauty supplies in the form of a hunk of homemade soap that smelled of lavender. Divine!

"Leahonia, wow, I don't know what to say!" Really, that soap smelled absolutely heavenly. The crazy in my life faded away as the soap hypnotized me. Using that soap meant rejoining the human race. "This soap, it's delicious!"

"I made it," she said, her voice soft, almost shy.

"You made this?" Wow, she made this? Like without getting it at some sort of market? "Leahonia, you are a woman of many talents."

I needed to ensure a lifetime supply of this stuff before I

left Mexico. I tried not to wonder what a lifetime would be for me.

"Gracias, Señorita. You look like you needed it. I hope you like."

"Oh, there's no question. I like this already."

Jon snickered. I thought I overheard him mutter something about women.

"Wanna share with the class, Jon?" I shot him a dirty look. Let him get killed in an earthquake and see how he felt. He'd probably be ready to go all homicidal just for a sliver of this soap, too.

He cleared his throat. "Um, no. But if you want, the bathroom is that way." He pointed towards the skeezy bathroom I'd found before. I didn't need a mirror in the nasty room to know how that affected my already pale skin tone.

"Señorita, you no want to use that room. He no let me clean."

No news there. The science experiment growing in that room would probably take over the world someday. What on earth possessed him to have someone come and do his laundry and clean his little kitchen area and not go near the bathroom?

"I already made the mistake of going in there. It's disgusting. Jon, why the hell don't you let her clean in there?"

"I... uh... well..." He stumbled for a few minutes, before finally answering. "I really don't know. No real reason."

I'll never understand men. If I should live to be a thousand, I'll never ever understand men. They are weird creatures that defy the law of common sense and nature. That author was right, men really are from Mars.

Now I had a dilemma. In my hand I held the yummiest smelling soap on the planet and wanted nothing more than to head off and get myself cleaned up and human looking.

Juan of the Dead

It might be Day of the Dead, but I didn't need to look like death walking. In order to do said cleaning up, I needed to go into the scuzziest bathroom of all time.

I knew Mexico wasn't a rich nation or anything, but I'd expect a nicer bathroom in the poorest of third world countries. Did we have any fifth world countries? That sounded about right.

I should've been happy he had running water. Given the state of this place, and the lack of anything remotely nearby, we could easily be in a shack that wouldn't see running water for another hundred years.

"You come to my house. You can take care of things there. I also have place you can sleep. Señor Juan no have that. I not sure what Señor Juan does with himself!"

I wasn't sure what Señor Juan did with himself, either. Maybe he slept in his truck. There definitely wasn't much of a place here to stretch out like a normal human being for some shut eye. No way could he survive sleeping in that chair for any length of time.

Of course, I still wasn't any closer to being tired. Maybe I no longer needed to worry about sleep. That could pay off after a late night on the town when I needed to work in the morning. Sometimes, no amount of coffee could make me functional enough. If I didn't need sleep, what was I going to do at her house? I didn't relish the thought of counting little stucco-peaks in the ceiling until dawn. That might pass for late night entertainment in some parts of the world, but not for me.

In the end, the thought of a nice bath won out over anything else and I took Leahonia up on her offer. How could I resist the call of cleanliness? I wanted to clean up the rats' nest taking up residence on my head. I really wanted to change into the clothes Leahonia gave me and burn the remnants of post-apocalypse couture I currently wore.

In return, I'd try to control any sudden urges to murder and eat her, should they come up out of the blue. Leahonia might have been unwittingly taking her life into her hands welcoming me into her home so it was the least I could do. Of course, I hadn't gone after brains yet. No insatiable longing for a beverage most warm, either. Was I going to ever do it?

Jon tried to protest but I stopped him short. I wanted to hear nothing more until I was human again. Once I looked decent for society, he could blather on about whatever he wanted and maybe I'd listen. If it didn't get too boring again.

CHAPTER TWELVE

We followed a dirt path to Leahonia's place. It was far enough to impress upon me that my feet didn't hurt- yet. I loved my Choos, but Jon was right. They were high on the sensible list if you wanted to look good and do a lot of sitting, but not so much if your plans involved long strolls through the Mexican countryside. As if one normally planned for such a thing. You could break a heel on the sidewalk, so some pitted dirt path probably didn't leave shoes with a long life expectancy. What a shame. Shoes could be so pretty. Lucky for me and my Choos, we arrived intact.

I understood that Mexico was an economically disad-vantaged country, probably due to their lack of high-end de-partment stores, but Leahonia's modest home with a little garden surprised me with its charm.

We entered the house and I saw Leahonia enjoyed dec-orating and had a good eye. Was there nothing this woman couldn't do? Splashes of bright color everywhere gave a sense of joy and excitement while soft touches of blankets and pillows gave a feeling of comfort to the home. Some sort of local art hung on the walls, and not the touristy crap by the docks people haggled over.

Hand woven baskets scattered the room and the floor. No mess here, it was all contained. A place for everything and everything in its place. After the pit of despair back at Jon's, this was a welcome relief.

The furniture appeared worn, but Leahonia obviously took meticulous care with the need of it to last. I bet there was no nearby Ethan Allen for her to go jaunting off to just because she decided to paint the walls a color that would clash with her furniture.

Just off the sitting room was a small dining area. Obviously where Leahonia's family dined, though the table looked almost too large for the space. That led right into a cramped, but tidy, kitchen.

With signs of children, I wondered how many people lived here. It didn't look large enough for a family, but then again, what would a family do here? In America there'd be a zillion remotes in a basket! And a huge television and every gaming console in existence. A mountain of DVDs and the Tivo recording away.

Not here. No TV in sight. Probably couldn't get anything to come in anyway. Did cable reach out this far? No TV meant no gaming consoles, and there was no computer in sight. Did that mean no social networks or online shopping? I'd die.

"Leahonia, your home is... beautiful." The words didn't seem to do the place justice. This went beyond beautiful, even if it was foreign. My apartment back home still had the same white walls as the day I moved in. I liked it, but it wasn't a home like this place.

"Thank you, Señorita. I try to make nice." She was too modest. There was no simple "try" here. Or "nice" for that matter.

"Call me Bea. It's okay. And this is so much more than nice. This is... I don't even know if there's a word for this."

"This way, Señorita."

Hey, didn't I just tell her to stop with the señorita crap? It seems so formal. And old. I'm not old.

"Really. Bea. Please." I followed her down a short hallway to a door. She opened it and revealed a tiny bathroom with a gleaming tub, toilet, sink, and mirror. Now that's what I was talking about.

"Here, I leave you. You take what you need. Get cleaned up. No more big mess." She smiled softly at me. I could tell she didn't mean anything mean by calling me a big mess. I'd looked in a mirror and could think of far worse ways to describe my current appearance.

"Thank you so much, Leahonia. I don't know how I can ever repay your kindness. I never planned to get stuck in a crazy earthquake and end up stuck here with nothing. It's been just so... crazy." I wanted to just unload on her, but I held back. It wasn't like she needed to hear all the problems of the undead girl, after all. Not that she could relate or anything, anyway.

I went into the bathroom and closed the door. I drew a bath, shed my clothes, and grabbed my lump of soap. The water wasn't steaming when I climbed into the tub, but still felt warm to me. Almost like it should be steaming. I laid back in the tub for a few minutes, luxuriating in the water. My muscles relaxed and I just let the tension slide out of me. Lump of lavender soap, take me away!

I scoured myself with the aromatic soap. This was not like the cheap bars of soap you bought at the drug store. I needed more of this stuff. A lifetime supply would do just nicely. The dirt, the dust, the grime, it came right off. And with it my mood improved. I worked on everything, too. Even between my toes. I wanted to be clean again. I went over every inch of my body three times.

I saw no shampoo or conditioner, let alone any of the other products I used religiously. All I had was the bar of soap. I slid under the water without even thinking about it, to get my hair wet. Anything was better than nothing at this point.

Submerged, I realized I never thought to take a breath. If I was holding my breath, it was a completely involuntary reaction to my thought to submerge. I remained underwater, contemplating my possible need for air. We really hadn't tested my lung power at all at Jon's. This was a perfect way to see what my newly dead body did as far as breathing went.

Maybe I wasn't so disgusted with the lab rat experimentations after all. I remained under the water. Actually, it felt good. The pressure of the water against my ears, gave me a sense of calm. And then I was crying. I don't know how I knew, but I was.

That's what finally forced me above water. Not a need for air, but a need to get a handle on myself. I surfaced and wiped at my face with my wet hands. That was super helpful. I'd set my stack of clothes and towel on the floor by the side of the tub.

Through teary eyes, I looked over the side of the tub and managed to find the towel. I wiped my face with the towel, but the tears continued to flow. I gave up. I let the tears come, quietly sobbing. Something snapped inside of me with the release of the tears. I sat in the tub, hair dripping, crying until I could cry no more. I cried for the loss of my purse and my belongings on the ship. I cried for the loss of identification, making it hard to function in the world. I cried for the loss of my life, robbed from me at such an early age.

I cried for the life I'd never known I wanted and now never would. I was living on borrowed time and something inside of me knew that more than just a slower heart and fantastic eyesight changed inside of me. I somehow knew that the things I'd avoided in an attempt to remain young, footloose, and fancy free were no longer options.

Not that I wanted to be a mother now or anything, but I'd always thought I would be. Same with settling down. I'd put off for tomorrow so many things. Why had I not thought about things? Like most people, I assumed there'd still be time for that.

Who dies in their 20's anyway? Or in their 30's?

Now that I was dead, I realized how much I wanted to be alive. I wanted to travel the world and I wanted to make a name for myself. Right now, my tombstone would read: Here Lies Bea- Biggest Party Girl of the Century. That was not exactly how I wanted to be remembered for time and all eternity.

It was through those tears that I realized that through borrowed time or undead eternity, nothing would stop me. If my body stopped working tomorrow, I'd make sure that today I did

all I could to make the best of it. If I had eternity, then I guess I could catch up on that bucket list and then some. But no more procrastinating.

Oh, there was a list. Everyone has that list of things they'd like to do. Learn a foreign language, see Europe, read War and Peace. So, I didn't want to learn a foreign language or read War and Peace, but I had my own list of things I wanted to do before I died. Now I'd just have to deal with a kicked bucket list. It could work.

Now I knew what I wanted to do with my life after

death. Did it stop me from being shallow or kill the insane need to enter a shoe store because I saw a sale sign? Absolutely not. Even the dead needed to look good. But, I could do more.

Once the tears stopped flowing, I slid back under the water. This time, I purposefully didn't take a breath. I wanted to see how long I could stay under, how long I could go without breathing. Working on my hair was just a bonus. I kept my face underwater but used my hands to work at my hair. Not an easy task laying in a bathtub, let me tell you. Mostly I tried to ensure anything foul like dirt clods or whatever came out before I soaped up.

That task done, I was no closer to needing air than before. The answer seemed obvious to me. How long could I hold my breath? A really long time. I gave up waiting. I surfaced and grabbed the soap. Rubbing it in my hand, I worked up a good lather that I used to begin washing my hair. When I ran out of lather, I went back to the bar of soap. I worked through my hair, hoping to get it at least somewhat clean.

I liked the idea of lavender scenting my hair, surrounding my head with the yummy garden scent. I was a little worried about not having proper hair products, but hoped the soap would treat my tresses well. You did what you had to in times of dire need, but I still wanted to avoid split ends.

My hair would just have to realize it was as clean as it was going to get. I slipped back under the water with eyes clamped shut. My fingers kept up their task under the water, attempting to get as much of the soap out of my locks as I could.

At long last I finished. I set the tub to drain and grabbed for that towel once more. Bending over as I stood, I allowed my hair to hang away from my body and wrung it out. I used the towel to dry off as best I could before I wrapped it around my wet hair. I stretched and winced as my body popped more. Nice. If that kept up much longer, I might get really cranky again.

I grabbed the clothes that Leahonia picked out for me and unfolded them. Very Mexican in fashion, and I actually liked the look. "What did you do on your vacation? I died in Mexico and went native!" At least the bright colors might give my skin some semblance of life.

I towel dried my hair as best I could. It promised ultimate frizziness upon drying. I glanced around the bathroom but saw no product to tame my crazy locks. Anything was better than the ultra-wild woman hair I sported before. Picking up my thrashed clothing, I tried to fold it somewhat for ease in carrying and slung the towel over my arm. With one last glance in the mirror, I decided I looked a million times better. Now the simple sight of me wouldn't make people quake in fear or turn to stone.

I opened the door and left the bathroom. I followed the sounds from the common area of the house and sure enough I found Leahonia in the kitchen. I cleared my throat.

"Excuse me? Leahonia?"

She turned towards me with a smile on her face. "Señorita, you look better."

"I feel better. Thank you like a million times over." I really wished I could do something to show her how great she was. Instead I just stood there awkwardly holding my torn up and filthy clothes, unsure what to do next.

"Is nothing. Glad to help." She seemed so sincere and warm. I couldn't say that I'd be so brave as to let someone I didn't know into my home. Or generous. I guess that was the difference in America. We looked at everyone as a possible serial killer. You never knew when your charity case could end up being someone who enjoyed slicing and dicing people for an afternoon snack. So instead you just kept your charity to safe check-writing to your organization of choice.

She held out her hands, so I passed her the wet towel. She beckoned for my clothes as well and I handed them over. She disappeared with the items and I remained where I was, not sure what to do.

She returned. "I clean those later. See if I get them better. You hungry?"

No, I wasn't hungry. Which was kind of starting to worry me. How long since she brought Jon that food he ate? Surely, it was time for another meal and how was I to turn away her food? Normal living folk ate, and if I didn't eat would that offend her? Or would it clue her in to my peculiar situation?

I shook my head. "No, I'm not hungry. I'm fine." Maybe I'd get off lucky and she'd think I was just anorexic. How sick was my life if I actually wanted someone thinking my worst problem was anorexia?

At some point I needed to figure out what to do about this whole no hunger thing. And prepare for when my body did need something. I understood the basic principles of biology. You ate and that got turned into energy to help you keep going. Sure, was a nutshell summary, but it's just the way it was. What was powering my body if it wasn't regular food?

At some point my avoidance of food would become a lot more obvious. Eventually,

Leahonia was going to start putting two and two together. She already had legends on her side.

"You not hungry? You sure?" She looked more than a little worried.

I definitely needed to work on an explanation. Maybe

Jon would have some pearls of wisdom. Again, the lack of not thinking ahead. Coming up with a believable reason for me to not eat instead of playing mad scientist.

"No, I'm fine. Maybe I'll be hungry later." I tried really hard to not make that into a question. It could happen, and when I did, I prayed for something palatable.

She looked a bit skeptical but bought it. For now. This would become a problem in another few hours. It was pretty obvious that I didn't eat at Jon's. Did he even have food at his place? How often did she bring him food?

She turned back to her work in the kitchen leaving me with nothing to do. There was no way I could find my way back to Jon's on my own. I know we followed a path of sorts, but I also knew that my inner navigation system was only equipped with the useless geography of a mall.

I just stood there, wondering what to do next. Did I offer to help out Leahonia?

Ask about returning to Jon's? I know she offered me a place to crash for the night, but the day was fairly early still. While I could get sleepy at any time, I wasn't betting on it coming soon. I'd prefer to go back to Jon's where I could discuss a game plan with him. Namely a game plan for getting me home.

"Excuse me? Leahonia?"

"Si, Señorita?" She didn't turn to look at me.

"Um, it's still early. How do I get back to Jon's? I think I need to talk to him some more." I couldn't think what to say next. There was no real tie between Jon and myself, and I felt we'd made that pretty clear earlier. We needed a better cover story.

"I take you back."

She looked busy with her household chores. "Are you sure?"

"Is no problem."

Boggs

So, we returned, following the rough path towards Jon's. I tried to pay attention to the turns and branches, but it didn't stick in my head. I needed to get back to the city where I could use the nice grid system when walking in town.

The walk through the warm afternoon didn't feel like end of October weather to me. Being from Virginia, I was used to a little more chill in the air. It was pleasant, nice weather for a walk. I'd never been much for walking, unless it was through a parking lot. Blame my new post-death enlightenment for actually enjoying the whole nature walk thing.

CHAPTER
THIRTEEN

We knocked on Jon's door. From inside we heard a muffled sound that could pass for a "Come in." Leahonia opened the door. Jon squatted in one corner of room, sifting through things. I wasn't sure what he was doing, other than enacting tornado fury on his poor residence.

"Jon?"

He sounded rather distracted when he answered me. "Yes?"

"What the hell have you been doing?" Why bother beating around the bush, especially if it meant getting any details he may have stumbled upon?

"Research..."

All I ever wanted! One-word answers that smacked of the obvious and told me nothing! Research? And here, I thought he was having square dancing lessons.

I grumbled something rude under my breath and heard a quiet snicker from Leahonia. Obviously, she felt the same way and wasn't too surprised by our little absent-minded professor. "I leave now. I be back later for you?" I'm sure she didn't want to stick around here. Given the neatness of her home, I bet this place made her toes sweat.

"Thank you, again." I still felt like no amount of words would let her know just how I felt about her charity. She slipped out the door, closing it behind her. I waded through the piles of papers and books littering the former walkways to stand over Jon.

"Hey, Earth to Jon. What's the story?" I said.

He peered up from the papers he held in both hands. "Oh, yeah, hi. Sorry."

He stood and looked me in the eye. There was a thrill that he finally recognized my presence, but something in the way he looked at me put me on edge as well.

"So, I repeat. What's the story?" I continued. Details! A girl needs some details!

"I thought to look up Day of the Dead histories and myths. I had already looked at most everything I knew of for the ceremony before, well, performing it. But I hadn't thought about Day of the Dead traditions."

Ramble, ramble, ramble. "Got it. Day of the Dead. Did you find weird and freaky stuff that could resemble my little scenario here or what?"

"Yes and no. It seems that each indigenous tribe had their own personal views on exactly how to honor their dead. There were a lot of commonalities, but each little cluster kind of went their own way with it."

Did he just say the same thing twice? "Same basics, differing practices? So..."

He pushed his glasses up his nose and swallowed. "Right. So, you have one tribe that thought that if they honored their dead, those that went before them would protect them. Another believed that the spirits of those gone would bless their tribe with a good crop or prosperity for the next year. So, you see, they would be slightly similar, but slightly different."

"Right, cuz protection from starvation is always good. Kind of the same thought at any rate – the dead spirits would totally take care of your needs. Rock on. What about, like, bringing them back?"

"There was a story of someone who successfully reanimated the dead. Not like warriors or legions, but the details were really sketchy. The person may not have really been dead. It seems unclear."

"The story was the person supposedly died but then came back?"

"Pretty much. Of course, this was like 800 years ago. So, with no real coroner or medical death certificate, it could be argued that the person was maybe in a coma or something. The people may have thought he was dead when really, he wasn't. There are enough things that mimic death that could have happened."

"Like you know, you're like dying, but get CPR so you're saved. But I guess they didn't have CPR back then, so people would think it was like raising the dead?"

"Exactly. You don't need magic, just science that hadn't been discovered yet. The story is this guy was dead for three days. And then he rose and was supposedly back from the dead, reanimated by a shaman type person."

Three days? Sounds awful biblical to me. "Uh huh, three days dead? Well I wasn't down and out for three days."

Now look, I liked my fellow man. Sometimes. I'm not so proud to think that I could give them eternal salvation or any of that other Bible thumping type stuff. Of course, the thought did make me wonder: if I was now not-dead what did that mean for my soul? Of course, there was the big black nothing I experienced between the quake and the time I woke up in Ye Olde Temple too. Not a thought I'd like to think about, so I shoved it to the back of my head where it could just nag me later.

"No, you weren't," he continued. "There wasn't much information after that. I guess the record was incomplete or they just figured not to include more."

Rather rude of them, if you asked me. How could they not plan for giving me information? Humph. That's the thoughtlessness you got from these ancient people. They just never thought about future generations needing information.

"So, nothing like he raised the dead, healed the sick, any of that Jesus stuff? Cuz you know..."

"I know. There's definitely an interesting history with ancient cultures and numerology. Three pops up in a lot of places, as does seven and forty. Not just in the Bible. Across various regions and histories. Fascinating. Even in modern America, do you know how many people think seven is their lucky number?"

"No idea. Everyone I know thinks it is their lucky number, so I'd bet a lot."

"Exactly."

We both grew quiet. We still didn't know any more than we did earlier. This might've just been one of those learn the ropes as you go along situations. Old legends came from somewhere. The tales of many undead soldiers really didn't do it for me., It was so hard to believe. If you could send troops of dead folk out instead of sacrificing your living kin, who on earth would really stop it?

If the undead soldiers took out whole villages, isn't that considered collateral damage in a war? There's no compassion in war.

It kind of creeped me out that anyone might have that sort of power. What if that had been passed down through the centuries? Could someone today actually do this? How would anyone survive? Note to self, don't say a cross word to anyone in Central America lest I become responsible for the legions of zombies rising and declaring war on America. Undead illegal aliens sounded like a pretty bad problem.

"Well, I have something for you." I planned to tell him about holding my breath in the bath.

"Hmmm?" He seemed distracted still as he looked back at the papers in his hands.

"While I was bathing, I went under the water and I'm not sure how long I was under there, but I didn't feel like... like I needed to breathe. What do you make of that?"

He peered at me over the rims of his glasses. "What?"

"I said that I'm not so sure that I need to breathe. Or at least not as much as before."

"Interesting." He shuffled his papers into one hand and went to where we'd previously sat. Now both seats were completely covered with things. He put the papers onto a pile and looked about, almost confused.

"What?" I asked. I was getting tired of that, honestly.

"Well, I thought I had something around here, but I'm not sure where I put it. It was here. Or, I thought it was here...."

"Again, organization. That's what you need. Maybe you could find things easier."

"I told you," Jon shrugged. "I can find things. It's crazy, but it works."

"Except now you can't find something. You know, books on a bookcase, that sort of thing. Really easy to find things in a library you know. And you could do the same with all these notes."

"Maybe, but usually this works for me. I've just looked at so much while you were gone, and now I've forgotten..." He sort of trailed off and I wondered if he thought of what it was he wanted. Since he didn't move, I guessed not.

"Anything I can do to help?" Like hit you upside the head and knock some sense into you? Hire an army of home organizers?

"I don't know. Maybe it'll come to me." He clapped his hands together. "Well, let's see what we can do with the whole breathing thing. You breathing now?"

Was I breathing now? I don't know, it's not like I walk around thinking, 'breathe in, breathe out' all the time. "I'm talking. So, I guess air is getting to my vocal cords. Anything more..." I shrugged.

"True. I guess the bath thing made it easier for noticing. I'm pretty sure you'd notice if you were trying to breathe underwater."

"You think? What would be my first clue? The water choking me or..."

He grimaced at my sarcasm. "Hey, I'm just saying."

"Look, it's just something you do. I haven't consciously thought about it. Frankly I've tried to pay attention but it's kind of weird to focus on. Eventually you make yourself nuts going 'am I breathing because I'm forcing myself to or because I need to?'"

He nodded. "Point taken. We could just have you hold your breath till you turn blue. It sounds childish, but it would answer the question."

"Oh, that sounds like a barrel of fun. Let me get in line for that."

"Probably not important to know how long you can go without oxygen. I mean, it could be forever. Or until you needed to talk again, as you pointed out the need of air over the larynx. Unless, of course, you are planning to go somewhere without air."

I was more a lay on the side of the pool than a get into the water gal. And since I was pretty sure personal shoppers were low on the list for a ticket into outer space, I was probably good. What need would I have for holding my breath for an indeterminate length of time? I shrugged again.

"Not particularly in my plans. But hey, what part of this week has gone according to my plans? If I get bored, I'll check it out. I just thought I'd mention it."

He stepped towards me. "No other problems that you've encountered?"

"Not really, just that one. And that I'm still not hungry or thirsty."

Another step closer to me and then his voice was soft, almost shy. "I see that the bath water did you no harm. You look... well... amazing."

My stomach flip-flopped. It felt good to hear that. Especially since I might be clean, but I was still running the natural look with no makeup, hair product, or any accessories. Best I had was my trusty Jimmy Choos. Thank goodness for Jimmy! I'd hate to think what this would do to my cred.

My voice came out rather throaty in my response. "Thanks."

He reached for me, and touched my arm lightly, running his fingers down it to my hand. His skin felt so warm against mine, the touch so soft. Despite myself, I knew I was one step closer to falling for this guy who was so not my type. Maybe it was some sort of Nightingale effect.

I might have been dead, I might have not looked my best without my usual accouterments, but he still thought I looked great. How many people could say that when they were dead? The slightly romantic side of me wondered why I had to die to meet a guy like this. Where was he when I was alive?

We stood there for a few minutes, his hand touching mine. Neither of us seemed to want to break the spell encircling itself around us. I peered up through my eyelashes and saw him looking at me, as though he could see right to my soul. A shiver ran up my spine at the intimacy.

He let out a breath and pulled his hand away. His movement broke the spell and the world rushed in on us once more. I told myself it could never work. We came from two different worlds, a gap that grew ever larger with my death. He was some brainy, nerdy guy and I was a gorgeous, fashion conscious dead girl. How could we ever hope to make something work?

People said opposites attract. I supposed you couldn't get much more opposite than living him and dead me. Perhaps our souls were entwined in a way neither of us could guess, causing his actions. It seemed fate dealt us a bad hand, not letting us find one another before my untimely demise. If that were the case, at any rate.

His thoughts must have been on the same track as mine. "I'm so sorry, I don't know what came over me. I just wonder... why things happened the way they did..."

It was my turn to cut him off with a nervous shrug. "What do you mean?"

"Just seems that... I wish that... that you'd have not died before I..."

Poor guy looked so uncomfortable. He probably never talked to women like this. What man really did? I'm pretty sure the Testosterone Police would take away his manhood card for being so mushy instead of macho.

"I get it," I agreed. We were silent once more. I don't know what came over me, but in the next second there I was, kissing him. Full on kissing, right on the lips, hard and needy.

He acted surprised for only a few seconds before he embraced me, kissing me back, his mouth just as wanting as mine. I could feel it inside of me, the need for him. The ties that bound us were far more than just one born out of his saving my life. Finally, our lips broke apart.

"I'm, uh, I'm..." What the hell could I say to that? Sorry for jumping you? I didn't normally act like this? Ok, truth be told, I did. Not with those kinds of emotions, but I wasn't a prude. I'd made out with many a hot guy at a club that I didn't know from Adam. A girl needed to kiss a lot of guys before she found Mr. Right. After that kiss, I regretted ever feeling that way. Nothing compared.

"Um...it's..."

Oh good, he was just as dazed and confused as me. Did he feel the same connection? Something in my gut told me he had. There's no way that I was alone in this.

CHAPTER FOURTEEN

Things simmered between us, never fully cooling off. We tried to make the best of it, by ignoring it. Or, at least, I did.

Since there was, yet again, no available seating, we quietly went to work clearing off places where we could rest our butts. Away from each other. No more of that heated kissing, thank you. Though the memory of his warm lips pressing against mine... Oh, the temptation!

Thinking about the warmth of his skin against mine sent tingles along every part of my body, but it also nibbled at a corner of my brain. I didn't feel unnaturally cool, but then again it was Mexico. I thought about my last day on the ship, as we prepared to leave for the day trip. What was that weather report? Something in the 90's? That was awful warm, so why wasn't I hot?

I wasn't cold, but I wasn't hot either. I wasn't sweating. I'd always been sensitive to the heat, so on warm days I always made sure to keep water near me at all times. Nothing spoiled a good time worse than passing out and going to the ER for an IV bag of electrolytes. Wish I could say that was a rare occurrence, but it was guaranteed to happen if I wasn't careful. In the Mexican heat, and no drinks in two days? I should have been so dehydrated that I would probably dry up and blow away at the smallest of breezes. Yet, I felt perfectly comfortable. What did it mean if you never got thirsty even in tropical heat?

This was in no way normal for me. How could I have not noticed that before? Must have been like the breathing thing. We ignored normal biological things until there was a problem. Of course, I knew what to do now. I needed to mention this to Jon, but then he'd want to run some tests. Taking my temperature seemed platonic enough, but the thought of his hands on me? Well, let's just say it made my temperature rise in a whole different way.

Common sense ruled out over my own lust. I needed to tell him. If for no other reason than because I needed to be able to share the weirdness with someone. Who else did I have to tell?

So, I paused in my gathering of papers, and stilled my methodical sorting of them so they'd face the same way. "Um, Jon?"

He cleared his throat before answering. "Yes?"

"Uh... have you noticed... I mean... well... when you touched me... did you feel..." Oh dear Lord, what is wrong with me? I've never been tongue tied around men.

"Feel? Um... uh..."

Oh dear, was he blushing? "Well, it's just that... is it hot?"

Oh man, that sounded like the lamest of pickup lines. He probably expected me to break out in a chorus of It's Getting Hot in Here any second. Yeesh.

"Hot? Um... I suppose." He looked over at me. I noticed a bead of sweat on his brow. Normally sweat made me feel beyond grossed out, but somehow on him I just wanted to wipe it away. Kiss it away.

I needed to derail the kissing train right now. I might forget what I wanted to tell him if I didn't change my thought patterns. Which was? Oh right, heat. Heat not between us.

"I mean, is it hot? Do you know how hot it is supposed to be? I just... I'm not hot. Shouldn't I be?"

He looked confused and I wasn't surprised. I was babbling and not making a whole lot of sense. Frustrated, I threw up my arms. "I'm sorry, Jon. I just don't know what's come over me. It's just that I thought I should feel hot. But I don't. And usually heat bothers me. I feel hot before anyone else."

He put down the book he'd been trying to place when I'd opened my mouth and spouted utter verbal diarrhea. He crossed the room and knelt in front of me.

"I think it does. I'm sorry. Just... this whole situation... it's got me a bit out of sorts, too. As far as your temperature, well, I didn't notice. I was..."

"Distracted?" Uh oh. What did it mean when you started finishing someone's sentences?

He cleared his throat and pushed his glasses up his nose. Nerves in a bunch? I guessed so.

"Uh, yeah. Distracted..."

"Um, do you think that there's something in that? That I don't feel hot?"

"Probably. The body cools postmortem..." He paused and I knew it was because of me. I didn't need a mirror; I could feel the color leaving my face. "You okay?"

Concern edged his words and that touched me. I didn't know how to answer him so I remained quiet while he stared at me intently.

"I'm sorry... I just... to hear you say that. I really am dead, aren't I?"

It was his turn to pale. "I'm so sorry. I should have thought more about what I was saying. Um..."

The fact I was still walking and talking held little comfort. Talking about all these differences made my condition even more real. Couldn't I just pretend this was some sort of crazy nightmare?

I sighed, a longing and dejected sound. I wanted to plan a major sob fest, but instead I fought back tears. I needed to be strong. No one liked a girl that burst into tears at the drop of a hat. Sure, my death probably wasn't so "drop of the hat," but still.

"It's fine. It sucks, but I guess I've just gotta deal. I'm too young to be dead. I was on vacation. Who dies on vacation?" I was being a bit whiny. Maybe he'd offer me cheese.

"Let's not think about it. I'm really sorry. I didn't think about it. Really." Well, at least he had the decency to look like he felt bad.

"It's all right. I know. Let's get back to it... I need to focus on... anything."

He looked at me and I really hoped that wasn't pity in his eyes. I didn't want his pity or anyone else's. At least he seemed fine with that. He picked up pretty much where he left off.

"The body cools, so I bet that your body temperature is running low. The question is, how low and will it go lower?"

"What happens if my body temperature gets too low?"

"No idea, really. I know what happens when a person – um, so, I just don't know. Guess we'll find out? We should probably monitor your temperature. But I don't know if I have a thermometer."

Who had a thermometer? Parents with babies that get ear infections? I sure didn't have one back home. "If you don't have one, how will we monitor me?"

"Got me. But we probably should. We'll have to figure it out. I'll go check; you never know what could be laying around here."

Really? No kidding? I started to snicker, but it turned into a roar of laughter. Must have been caused by the nerves. I just started laughing and couldn't stop. Deep belly laughs that made my sides hurt. My laughter became infectious. He joined in. In between chortles, I managed to work in, "You don't say?"

"I know, it's a wreck. You don't have to say it again. Who knows what I have here. Let me know if you see Jimmy Hoffa."

"That could be interesting. We should try to find him."

It felt good to just joke around, even for a few moments. To pretend I was a normal, living, warm blooded, American girl. Maybe that was why I enjoyed that kiss earlier and longed for another. You don't get more normal and warm blooded than a good passionate kiss.

"I don't have any ideas. But, hey, I'll check the bathroom. Maybe there's something in there."

If he came out of that nasty bathroom with a thermometer, there was no way he'd get it near my person. Lord only knew what diseases grew in the shadows of that hole. I shivered. And he noticed.

"Cold?"

"Uh, no. Just thinking of that bathroom. Are you growing toxic mold in there? The cure to cancer? It's foul!"

Yeah, it was rude. But there was no way to politely explain that the room was beyond absolutely and positively disgusting.

"I suppose it is. I keep some of my artifacts in there as I clean them, and it gets filthy."

So that was it? He used it to clean dirty artifacts from

the ground? I didn't know if I believed that was an excuse or not. Especially since I was sure that thing in the corner was not only alive but sure to rise and kill people in their sleep.

"Uh-huh." Still wouldn't want something found in that room near me. I had better things to do with my second chance at life than end it in that way.

"I'm pretty sure there's nothing there. I wonder if Lea-honia would have a thermometer?"

"Maybe. I dunno," I shrugged. At least if it came from her, I knew it would have been cleaned and disinfected. Not carrying 2000-year-old cooties or something. Something killed off these people that Jon liked to dig up and learn about. I'd rather not meet whatever it was that did the killing.

Dying once on vacation was one time too many. And if he died, well goodness knows there'd be no way I could haul his corpse to some ancient temple to perform witch doctor magic on him.

"Maybe we can ask her?" Jon suggested.

"And how, pray tell, do you plan to do that? 'Have you met my friend, the dead girl? We just wanted to make sure that her body temperature wasn't like... dead.'"

"Good point. We'll figure it out."

"Yeah? Cuz I'm also thinking going to a doctor might not be in my best interest. Do you know what doctors like to do to dead people? I'd like my insides to remain firmly attached to the inside of my body, thank you very much."

"You'd definitely become a science experiment then. I would hate to see you locked up somewhere and treated like a lab rat."

So, he could understand my peevishness of earlier. That was nice. Who knew what they would do to him if he could do this again? Well, that was an awful lot of power and people coveted power more than anything else.

"Yeah. So... doctors bad. Fine by me. I never really liked doctors anyway," I agreed.

"So, this works for you?"

"Of course, it works for me. I'm not... you know... dead. Well, technically I am, but I'm not. If it means avoiding doctors, I'm okay with that. I would like to remain... well... not six feet under. Now, can we find something else to talk about?"

"Let's talk about Day of the Dead," Jon said, changing the subject for me. "I'm not sure what this will mean for you, but it's a huge holiday here. Like, really huge. Halloween has nothing on Day of the Dead. I think because so many around here are like Leahonia, they have ancestors that go back thousands of years on this continent."

"So why is that? In the US it's not so much like that. The Indians keep to themselves."

"I guess it's just a difference of settlements at the time. The English didn't want to mix with the Indians, and so they constantly fought. Here, the Spanish wanted to bring the locals into their faith of Catholicism. Of course, they weren't so nice about it."

"No religious freedom. People in the States now would flip."

"Christianity became the dominant religion, but you see a lot of the original pagan leanings in areas like this one. Sure, it's all said to be legend now, but the stories remain. It's like Bigfoot and Nessie. The stories are there, but no one believes the creatures exist."

"I got all that. What's your point?" I asked.

"My point is that with Day of the Dead, it's such a huge holiday. But here, they believe it more than they observe it. It's like Halloween. What is Halloween to you?"

"You get dressed up, you party, there's loads of free

candy," I shrugged. Easy, peasy.

"Right, it's all fun. But why do you dress up?"

"Because... it's fun? Who doesn't like to pretend they are a princess or a superhero or something?"

"Why did the tradition to dress up start?" he persisted.

"Hell if I know. Does it matter?" Seriously, it seemed to me like this conversation was pointless. Where was he going with all this?

"It does. See, it started out for wholly other reasons. Some people thought if they dressed up like a ghoul, it would scare real ones away."

"No kidding? That's the stupidest thing I've ever heard!"

"Yeah, if I were a ghoul, surely I'd have some kind of great ghoul-like power. So why would I be afraid of a human dressed up like me?"

He had a point. "Or what if they thought I was one of them. Would I get an invite to go terrorize humans? Not so sure I wanna do that. Seems like it could go bad. Like gangs kicking you out bad."

"You said princesses... how are they scary? That's fun. Nothing but fun," he pointed out.

"Right. So, you are saying that some of these people really do this stuff because of like, believing it? Not just out of habit or because of society?"

"Yeah, this isn't like non-Christians celebrating Christmas. They aren't just doing it because everyone else does. There really is a deep-seated belief. Some might not admit it, but it's there."

"Like throwing salt over your shoulder?"

"Exactly. So, because of that, I think we need tread carefully. But at the same time, I'm hoping maybe we can get some more information. We just need to find the right people."

"Who's the right people?"

"That, I don't know."

I thought it might be a pretty bad idea to just go wandering about telling people about how I was really a dead girl walking. Tell the wrong person and whammo. Bad things happened. Like lab rat cages. Or people thinking they needed to return you to the land of the dead. Not that I knew how that would happen, but I'm sure it was possible. You died once, you could die again, right? Even vampires could die if you stuck a stake through their heart.

Were there vampires? If so, I wanted them to keep to their own fangs. That's right. I could easily bust outta legend and start the party of the undead. But I was fairly harmless. Right? The thought of the scary things that go bump in the night, not so much.

"Well, I don't know anyone here. You know anyone there that might know who fits the bill?" I asked.

"As you heard, I went with Leahonia and her family last year. I met a few people. None that I could say for sure would be helpful to us. But you never know. They know me. They think I'm interesting."

They do? He must not come off near as geeky to them. "Interesting..."

"To them, this is just their life. They don't think anything of living so close to Chichen Itza. Or the fact that there's a giant temple there or that the people who built the temple were geniuses. Their legends are just everyday life to them. They are amused that my whole job is to learn about these things."

"And that is interesting? Really?"

"I guess so," Jon shrugged. "To me it's work. It's different. It's not what I grew up with. I guess it would be like someone coming to your work and watching what you do. It's normal to you, but not to them."

"Hmmm, I could see that." I loved my job. But to study

someone doing it? That was kind of weird.

"On a bright note, everyone is really friendly and open to talking to me. It helps a lot to have a good rapport with the people who can help you most in your research."

"I bet. Do you think maybe we can figure out how to get the people to open up and talk about raising the dead? 'Cause, I know it's like spooky time and all, but still. That might be a bit... much."

"Judging by Leahonia's reaction, yes. But, I'm hopeful. Maybe one of the teenagers. They tend to be the most open. In today's world, they think everything is just bunk. If they can't see it, they don't believe it."

"Sounds rather... American..."

"Maybe that's the nature of today's world. Everything is so global. It may be rural and a different country, but with movies and television and tourism? The world is a much smaller place today than it was before."

I hadn't really thought about it. With people able to easily come and go from just about anywhere, and the news reporters not afraid to use that ability... there was nothing we didn't know. Or at least, that was what we thought. People tended to get a bit pissy if they thought they were uninformed.

Look at me, I watched the Travel Channel. There were people who watched documentaries on just about anything and everything on Discovery or History channels. Everything got covered eventually. It sure looked like people had the same concerns, the same interests, the same clothes. Leahonia wore a pair of blue jeans today, yet here I was wearing something more traditionally Mexican.

"You are right. People don't just take things on blind faith anymore. They want proof. The whole need to see it before they believe it thing."

"Right. The youth think because they have a little more

education in them, that they know everything. You remember being a kid."

Did I ever. I was the biggest know-it-all.

We devised a game plan. Namely, I'd be quiet, and he'd talk. He was more the expert than me and would hopefully find a way to talk to people so that they didn't go all nuts on him. Meanwhile, we'd stick to the story of me getting stranded during the earthquake. Jon was being a good fellow American. After the holiday we were planning to take a trip to try to get me back home.

Which brought me back to another concern.

"Jon?"

"Yeah?"

"I'm kind of worried. There's going to be eating at this festival, right? How bad is it going to look if I don't accept food?"

People heard about it all the time: Someone goes to some foreign country. They get offered food. They don't eat it. Then the people would kill them from the rudeness of not eating food. I didn't want to make any enemies, especially if I would be sticking around this area for any length of time. Not that I wanted to, but we had to work out some serious issues in order to get me out of here.

"There will be food. But it will probably be okay. You still not hungry?"

"No. And the last time I ate was the morning on the ship before coming to land. I didn't even really eat then. I was in too much of a rush."

"Your last meal was light?"

"Yeah. Regretting it. Guess it was the time to eat copious amounts of chocolate cake or something and it is too late now!"

He grinned. "I miss chocolate cake. I haven't had any for so long. I need to get back to America more."

"No one makes chocolate cake in Mexico?"

"Well, sure. But my mother has the most divine recipe. I can almost taste it now." He licked his lips.

"Yeah, it's been a couple of days or more, and I haven't eaten anything," I explained.

"Or drank?"

"Nope."

"Hmm," he looked thoughtful for a moment. He studied me intently before continuing. "Well, you don't look like you are getting dehydrated or anything. Do you feel OK?"

"See, that's just it. I feel great. I'm kind of concerned because Leahonia is already questioning it. She offered me food at her house earlier. What am I supposed to do if I'm not hungry, thirsty, or sleepy?"

"That could be problematic."

"Indeed. I tried to brush it off. But I know she's coming back. She wants me to go over there tonight. What am I supposed to do all night long if I don't need to sleep?"

"Read? I have plenty of books. I would say do something to bring as little attention to yourself as possible. Other than that, just lay there?"

I could tell he was stumped like me. It could go very wrong if I wasn't careful. How would I blend in with living folks if I didn't do basic things? Getting a cup of coffee or a bite to eat? Those were normal everyday tasks for the living.

But, read one of his books? The one snoozefest book came immediately to my mind. Well, if I wanted to sleep, that was the right one. I'd sleep like the dead – pun very much intended. "Got anything a bit lighter?"

Anything? Cozy mystery? Latest issue of Cosmo? Anything? Yeah, like a brainiac and a guy would have anything like that? Not likely.

Given Leahonia's decent, but broken English, I was

guessing not a lot would be at her house. It was probably all in Spanish. If those words weren't related to food, I'd be lost.

"Probably not. We'll figure it out. Let's tackle the food. I could really go for a snack. Actually, I'm really hungry."

He waded through his notes and books to the little kitchen area. Only reason you could see anything was thanks to Leahonia's hard work. He picked up two pieces of fruit from a bowl resting by the sink and bit into one. I could tell he liked it from the way he devoured it and moved to the second piece. Within a few minutes, he was done and there was some nice food trash created.

"What purpose did that serve? Other than to help with your hunger issues?"

"Now there's sign of two pieces of fruit being eaten. There are two of us."

Seemed a little too easy. "You think that she's going to buy I ate a piece of fruit here and that's all I need?"

"Maybe. Everyone knows that American women don't eat anything. They are always watching their weight, their carbs, their whatever." He winked at me.

This was his plan? To let her think I eat like one fruit a day? I suppose it was better than no plan at all, but still! It seemed rather thin to me.

"Well, sure. If she notices that. But, I'm a horrible liar. What do I do if she doesn't notice?"

"Got me. We'll figure out a way to make sure she notices. Try to move food around on your plate so it looks like you are eating. Just keep up with the watching your weight thing and maybe it'll work out."

I was skeptical. Leahonia didn't seem that stupid to me. No way she'd buy one piece of fruit. Maybe I was wrong. It was worth a shot if nothing else. It would have been nice if I had some guidance. I was never one for being a loner and now here I was a lonely dead girl. I tried to take comfort in the fact that Jon didn't seem to mind my differences, but it didn't mean a whole lot right then.

Perhaps it would be good to stay here. Not many people, less of a chance of being found out, that sort of a thing. Could I really go forever without designer labels and good stores? We went back to straightening things up quietly. There didn't seem much more to talk about at this point. I did manage to convince Jon to let me organize his books a bit. By the time Leahonia returned, two shelves of his bookcase actually held books.

To give her credit, Leahonia took in the sight without much more than a double take. I'm sure she could have said so many snarky comments. I know I would have. Instead she took it all in stride.

Jon came with us to Leahonia's. Just my luck, as we walked, she informed us she would make us a wonderful dinner. I bet it would be wonderful, but how was I going to get through it? In the end, I did get through it. Like Jon said, I pushed food around on my plate.

I didn't take much to begin with. I just hoped that she bought it. Later that night, I couldn't sleep. I looked at every photograph of Leahonia's family, I leafed through pictures drawn by her kids.

I made it through the night, and I got out of breakfast, offering to take something to Jon. She prepared food for both of us and sent me on my way. I even found my way without getting lost.

And that was it. We piled into Jon's truck, Leahonia and her family in the bed and me in the cab with Jon. We bumped along what could barely be called roads. Jon knew the way and we rode mostly in silence, listening to the noise from Leahonia's family in the back.

Juan of the Dead

I didn't know where we were going or what would happen when we got there. If I had, I might have chosen to just hide from reality back at Jon's place a while longer.

CHAPTER FIFTEEN

How I survived the bumpy ride in a beater truck along roads resembling a post- apocalyptic nightmare, I'd never know. We got to our destination and that's all that mattered. I suffered no broken bones, and a quick inspection showed no bruising. I considered myself lucky. As we helped Leahonia and her family down out of the bed of the truck, I noticed they seemed none the worse for wear, either.

I wasn't sure what I expected, other than some juxtaposition of my American view of Halloween with a Mexican backdrop. It wasn't like that, but it was interesting.

We parked on the outskirts of a rundown town and walked in. I looked at my feet, thankful for the sandals that Leahonia found me that morning. There's no way I could've handled all that walking in my one and only pair of Choos. Lesson learned- next time you go off for the back end of nowhere, wear a trusty pair of sneakers. You never knew when you were going to die and get stranded. But I wasn't going all sensible. Oh no. I could get a pair of sneakers and still look good. Wait till I figured out how to replace my Amex. My credit card was going to get a workout.

It was still early in the day, so the festivities weren't in full bloom yet. I was assured that as the day progressed, the excitement would truly begin. Fine by me. It may have been called Day of the Dead, but who wanted to do spooky stuff in the middle of the day? Bring on the night! Besides, I lived for the nightlife!

I was able to watch people set up tables with displays as I quietly walked through the small town. The splash of color and cheerful laughter filled my heart with joy. These people knew how to make the best of death- they celebrated!

Finally, my curiosity got the better of me. "Jon, what are they doing to their doors?"

"It's for the Altar Contest." As usual, his answer didn't hold a lot of information.

"New girl. No clue. Altar for what?" The thought of an altar didn't fill me with a lot of good memories. Not after that gross cootie one from the temple.

"The locals have this contest. It's pretty cool. The winners in each little area actually travel to Merida. Anyway, the altars they decorate by their doors are for the dead."

"And just why do they have an altar for the dead? What do they plan to do with the altar?" My mind flashed back to the one that Jon so recently used for a dead person – me!

"Oh, they are for show. It is the place they use to honor their loved ones. See, like this one," he gestured to one before us.

I looked at the altar, little more than a small table. Covering it was a handmade cloth with exquisite detail work. Along the edge of the cloth, forming a circle, were embroidered yellow and pink flowers. As I looked at the various pictures resting on top of the table, I saw a young woman, maybe five or six years younger than myself. She looked so full of life in the portraits, but I knew she was gone from this earth. How sad that she died young, like me. Before she really got a chance to live.

"She was so young..." If my voice sounded sad, it was. I felt such sadness for both of us. This girl probably would have done more with that second chance than I had.

"Si, Señorita." Leahonia's quiet words startled me.

"What happened?"

"She die of sickness. There no money for good doctor. She stay here and she die. Six month ago. She made this cloth. It for her marriage home. She to marry... maybe one month ago?"

"She made this?" I look back at the tablecloth. I couldn't imagine the hours she put into it. When I moved out of my parents' place, I just went to the local store for my linens.

"Si, Senorita."

"Leahonia, I told you. Bea. Please. Call me Bea."

Leahonia blushed. She was so polite and kind. I don't know if she would ever call me Bea, but I hoped so. Feeling awkward myself, I turned back to the altar.

Jon pointed at a plate. It held some sort of food. "This is a special chicken meal they make, just for this day."

Why did all holidays have traditional foods? Wasn't it weird that we always had things revolve around food? I never noticed it until I died, and it seemed like my appetite mostly vanished.

I looked at the various crosses and rosaries spread on the table. There was one that drew my eye. I had no idea what the stones were for the rosary, but they were a lovely shade of rose. The cross that hung from the bottom was silver toned and quite ornate. The picture in front of it showed an older woman wearing the rosary kissing a young girl.

"Wow. That's just lovely." My voice barely a breath.

"Si. That grandma and she gave this rosary before she die. It very special."

"Thanks, Leahonia." It was nice to have her along for the local information. She filled us in on several other altars as we walked around. She knew many of the people from this village.

We drew close to the last little home with an altar out front. The altar combined simplicity and elegance at the same time. That was a knack I'd never managed to perfect, but definitely admired in others. The frames all matched, and the photographs were in black and white. A gentleman well into his sixties stared back at me from the black and white photographs. The table bore items I assumed were his. A hand carved pipe, a cane, a key chain. Signs of things he used often, I was sure. The amount of love that went into this project was endearing. I wondered how anyone could feel that way about someone else.

"Mama!" Leahonia cried to the woman behind the altar. A short yet stout woman stood up from where she was kneeling."Lea!" A sea of Spanish followed as the two women embraced. I gave up trying to understand the flurry of words traveling between the two.

"This is Leahonia's mother. They do this every time they get together. Be thankful that's not real often. Neither really have the money to be traveling back and forth a lot."

My parents lived less than two miles away. Maybe. I didn't know, I'd never been good with distances. It took me no time to get to them. I definitely enjoyed living close enough to my parents that we could see each other often. Though sometimes I wondered if it was too often.

We stood by quietly while Leahonia's mother embraced

Leahonia's two sons and one daughter. She then came and gave Jon a tight hug. She was a tiny woman; she only came about halfway up his chest.

"Señor Juan! Good to see you! And this? Who this? Girl-friend?" She came towards me with open arms.

I thought he might choke. Geez, was I so bad? "Um no, Mama Camila."

"No? You good together!" She hugged me tight anyway. Uncomfortable in her embrace, I tried to put my arms around her. Good thing I didn't need to breathe as much as regular folk, I'd have suffocated on the spot. How could one tiny woman harness that sort of power?

"No, I'm just a friend." I tried to tell her, though where I found the air to get it out would probably stump the most famous of detectives.

"Bah friend!" She dismissed the thought with a wave of her hand.

"No, just a friend, Mama." He didn't sound too convincing and I could tell she wasn't about to buy that. This woman was a tough cookie. No fooling her, which made me all the more uncomfortable in her arms.

I tried to wrestle away, but that was hard. She must have realized how tight she was squeezing me because her embrace loosened. I managed to win my freedom, but I still worried. Could she tell if my skin was too cold? Or that I hadn't slept or eaten in days? That I was something more than what I looked like outside? I fretted over her randomly guessing I was dead.

What would I do if she started questioning things? I took a few steps back, hoping that if I was further away, she might not embrace me again. I've never been much of the huggie sort, anyway. Now that I was dead, I had a secret that I really didn't want to have take me to the grave.

So, I tried to back up Jon. "Yes, we're friends. It's been a crazy few days. He and Leahonia have been so kind to me."

Yes, backing Jon up seemed good.

"I see more. Welcome! Any friend Señor Juan, friend us. Come around. I make lunch. You hungry?"

Well crap. This was going to go over like a ton of bricks. Maybe that old cliché wasn't even good. What was worse than a ton of bricks? I couldn't think of anything so decided ton of bricks would have to work. I wished to be said ton of bricks right now though, since bricks didn't need to deal with offers of food.

Jon's stomach grumbled. Thanks for the moral support, buddy.

Okay, so that was rude. What was he supposed to do? Abstain from food as long as I did as some sort of wacky solidarity thing? I don't think that's quite what anyone would expect. I know, whine, whine, whine. Oh, I have no appetite. Blah blah blah. But really.? I knew it was yummy. People didn't make those kinds of sounds deep in their throats if the food was gross. and I was kind of missing that experience.

Jon followed Leahonia and Camila around the altar to enter the humble home. The inside looked much like Leahonia's: neat as a pin and homey with the flair of their native country. I instantly felt welcome. Until we reached the kitchen and I saw the feast before us. Queue discomfort to re-take the stage.

"I think I want to go for a walk. Look at more of the altars and stuff." I edged back the way that we'd come. "We don't do anything like this in America."

Going for a walk on my own probably wasn't such a good idea, but I didn't think I could stand there while everyone ate. It was hard enough last night at the dinner Leahonia prepared for her family. This looked like the sort of thing you'd see at Thanksgiving or Christmas. Huge. Massive. More food than an army could eat.

I saw steaming refried beans and rice. Chips. Salsa. More rice. Chicken. Beef. Tortilla shells. Corn. You name it. It was here. Somewhere, a grocery store's shelves were bare. If I didn't eat or tried to fake eating, I knew it would end badly. Feelings would be hurt. I needed to find a way to avoid this mess in the making. Feigning distraction from the festival had to buy me some time.

"No, no, eat. Wait. We go out later." Leahonia's look worried me. If she had suspicions, they would be warranted. I really needed to get out of there. The walls felt like they were closing in on me.

"Maybe I should go with her. She is really excited about this."

Oh, good. Jon read my mind. I could kiss him. Wait, I didn't want to do that again, no matter how much I enjoyed it.

"Here, take this with you." Camila shoved chicken legs at us.

Food to go? You betcha. I took the offered food and wondered what I'd do with it. Smelling it made me feel a bit nauseous. I better get out of there before I turned green. What would happen if I threw up? I hadn't eaten anything in forever. There couldn't be anything to throw up. Gross. I didn't want to find out. I moved as fast as Jon would let me. Escaping into the fresh air outside I shoved the chicken leg at him.

"Take this. Please. It's making me sick."

He looked startled but took it. As we walked, he tore into the chicken legs. One in each hand. He looked all the part of a kid at the county fair. As long as I didn't have to see the chicken, that was fine by me. He could have at it. I, meanwhile, tried to wipe every trace of the chicken from my hand. If I wasn't careful, I'd rub my hand raw on my pants.

Through his chicken he asked, "Really? Sick? This is so delicious!"

Like I wanted to hear that? No. Uncool. My temper flared. "What the hell? That stuff is nasty. I want nothing to do with it so you can keep your peanut gallery comments to yourself."

It didn't faze him. He kept right on chewing. Gross. I swear he was eating as noisily as possible just to annoy me.

"You should try it. You might like it."

My stomach rolled. "I don't want it. Leave me alone. I don't need you to follow me either. You can go be a schmuck on your own time."

I tried to distance myself from him, but at that moment something whizzed by my ear. Jon stopped. I kept walking. "What was that?"

I turned to look at him. "I don't care what that was. I'm getting away from you and your food."

Something else came through the air at me. I ducked just before it would have hit me in the eye.

Then again, maybe I didn't want to get away from Jon. What the hell was that and why was it aimed at me? There's no way something came at a person like that without intentional aim.

"Um, Bea?"

"Yeah, I know. Let's get out of here together." I took off running and I heard him following right behind. He shoved me to the right, and we ducked around the side of a house.

"Let's turn back around this way. Maybe we can get back to Camila's."

Whatever his plan was, I didn't care. I knew we would never make it back to his truck. And then as I took another hard right, something whizzed through the air where I stood moments before. I picked up the pace and so did Jon.

Juan of the Dead

Had no one taken notice of things flying through the air willy nilly? What about the crazy Americans running for their lives? What the hell kind of country was this? And people said New Yorkers were blind to that which went on around them? Welcome to Mexico.

Then again, I didn't see anyone. When we went inside Camila's home, the streets were alive with people. Now I couldn't see anyone. Had they really all retired to eat? Collectively into their homes at the same time? That seemed odd. Then again, with the spread at Camila's, maybe they all went to her house. We could barrel right into a giant town meet and greet. I didn't think that sounded like a good idea at all.

I could see it now. The town, all chilling and doing their Day of the Dead thing. Telling stories, watching football, or something; I don't know. Whatever it was people did on big holidays in Mexico. And I run in with crazy people chucking who knows what left and right. Half the town gets bashed in the head and I'm proclaimed the town doomsday girl. Talk about a way to get invited back to parties.

Yeah, they'd like me then. I'd be banished like the boy with halitosis. No one wanted someone with bad breath around. It was why God invented Altoids. I knew I always kept a tin in my purse. You never knew when a quick suck on an Altoid would freshen your breath after pizza. A girl had to be prepared for any hottie that wanted to lay their lips on hers. Damn. My Altoids were in my Coach handbag. Under who knew how much rubble. Stupid Mexico. All I could score here was crappy Chicklets.

We kept running for Camila's with little missiles of whatever flying past us. Somehow, we managed to escape injury from the flying debris or from falling. Thank goodness for these sandals being flat. If I'd had to run in my Choos, these crazies chasing us would have caught me ages ago. I'd have thrown my ankle after three steps and ended up face planted and butt in the air. On a bright note, maybe Jon would have ended up on top of me.

I could see Camila's home ahead. I kept my eyes on the goal and hoped I could hold out. I never was the most athletic sort. While I had some good super strength going on with my un-dead powers, I didn't get any sort of cool super speed. Forget that faster than a locomotive thing – that would stay in the realm of Superman for now. Shucks. That could turn out way useful in a chase.

The altar stood between us and the front door. How would we get around it? I didn't want to just go lunging over it and destroy Camila's hard work. Seemed a bit sacrilegious.

We never got a chance to find out. About forty feet from the door, something plowed into my side. I flew into Jon and the two of us tumbled into a scraggly bush. Entangled in a mess of Jon's limbs, I tried to get up, to no avail. Rough hands grabbed me by my shoulders and hauled me to my feet. I flailed as I was thrown over this person's shoulder.

What the hell kind of caveman treatment was that? I knew that there was like this whole economic divide between those in Mexico and say, where I came from. But near as I could tell that didn't hinder attractive women from being here. Of course, with treatment like this, who would give this brute the time of day? It's called R-E-S-P-E-C-T. Hello? Women were now equals and all we asked for was a polite invitation.

If I needed to breathe, he'd have knocked the air out of me. Lucky me. I started to kick. He could think I was easy to nab, but I wasn't going down without a fight. I was talking basic self-defense here. Obviously, there was a pack of psychos in this town. Goodness knows what kind of gang initiation they had in store for me. What if he was taking me to be gang raped? I didn't think so.

I thrashed and his grip tightened on me. He grunted something but I couldn't make it out. Wish I'd studied more in Spanish classes. Right now, I was wishing I knew how to say "Let me down you crazy person." I guess we can't have everything.

I tried to look up, but my hair fell in my eyes. I wondered if Jon was coming along for this joy ride. Was he getting his own trip via shoulder throw?

The footfalls of my captor were heavy, but fast. Within a very short period of time he stopped and threw me off of him with as little care as his previous handling.

I better not bruise. If he bruised me, what would happen with my slower metabolism? I didn't want to find out how injuries would affect me. I considered myself lucky that my death inflicted injuries were healed. I wasn't going to count on that nice perk to continue.

I wish I knew what perks would continue. Like walking. Time to exercise that one. I struggled to get up and instead found myself rolling to the side as Jon's body flew towards me. Oh good, he came along for the joyride. Bet he's thrilled.

I pushed myself up and noticed that I was in a bed of hay. Or maybe straw. Was there a difference? Not much, as far as I was concerned. Just as I got to my knees we started moving. Nice, a truck filled with hay was just waiting around for us to be thrown into? I thought not. This smacked of abduction.

I debated throwing myself from the side of the truck but thought twice as I gazed at the hard ground. Once more back to the whole what would happen to any injuries I endured? I didn't want to go tempting fate. Jon groaned beside me. I turned to him, looking for anything wrong. His lip was bleeding. It looked like he may have bitten it while being tossed about, but nothing more sinister than that. He clutched at his side with one hand and moaned again.

"Jon?"

He opened his eyes and looked at me. "What?"

"You okay?" You're laying here moaning like you're gonna die. What do you think I want when I say your name?

"I think those guys cracked my ribs in all of that. What the hell was all of that anyway?"

"You're asking me? You live here. Or near here. I'm just the chick from America lost without her passport."

Like what? I planned for all this to happen? Oh yes, that was right at the top of my 'to do while on vacation' list. First, get killed. Second, get raised from the dead by Jon. Third, lose all my ID and whatnot. Fourth, get kidnapped from a Day of the Dead celebration. Yup, that sounded about right. Everyone planned a vacation like that, right? It's all the rage. Who said Disney World was the dream vacation?

He winced and tried to sit up. "So, they didn't say anything to you, either?"

"Just some grunting like a caveman. So nope, I'm clueless. Still. Did you see anything? I couldn't." Dumb long hair was a pain sometimes. Though I should be thankful caveman dude didn't grab me and drag me by my tresses.

"That's a shame. I didn't see much either. It happened too fast."

I looked at his hair. It was long, for a man. Long enough for my fingers to run through nicely. It did kind of fall in front of his eyes a bit. Not much, and in a kind of sexy way. What the hell was wrong with me? We'd been abducted and I was thinking that his hair was sexy? My hormones were definitely out of control. I knew I liked to party like the next girl, but good grief. Nothing like this. Seemed that whenever I was alone with Jon my mind hit the gutters and took off running a marathon.

Did I really want to stop it? Maybe Jon could rock my undead world. Why not? Brainy guys could be quite the tigers sometimes, right? Still, this was probably not the place to go throwing myself in his arms.

I tore my eyes away from him and looked out of the truck as the Mexican countryside rolled by. We weren't going exceptionally fast, probably due to the bumpy road. Hadn't this country ever heard of asphalt? Good grief. How hard was it to make a decent road that didn't have eight gazillion pits in it? I bet half this country suffered from motion sickness due to the hot mess they called roadways.

I couldn't handle it on my knees. The ride was just far too rough. I turned myself over and laid back into the hay. It seemed to help the jostling not be so bad and spread it out over my whole body. Lying beside Jon was a really nice perk.

This couldn't be so bad, right? I was a nobody dead girl from America. Jon was a science nerd. How high up on someone's wish list could we really be? Once these people realized that I was not so good for the whole ransom thing, they'd let us go. Right? Or maybe they'd realize they had a bad case of mistaken identity.

As we lay there in silence, I also wondered where they were taking us. Was this going to be one of those stories you heard about on the news? American tourist kidnapped by the drug cartel and forced to become a heroin mule? My thoughts went in all kinds of directions, and none ended anywhere pleasant.

"Jon?"

"Yes, Bea?" I could tell from his voice that he was hurting. "Got a plan to get us out of this mess?"

"No. You?"

"Something tells me running's not gonna cut it this time." It didn't work so well last time, after all. This time we wouldn't know where we were, and the only method of escape was our feet. It didn't seem likely that we'd get real far. Goons with trucks would win.

"Probably not. Maybe we should just find out what they want. You know, show them we mean no harm. Do whatever they want." He winced but managed to sit up.

If he was injured, we would definitely be screwed. No way could I hope to escape with him being at subpar levels. As it was, neither of us were contenders for the Olympics. Our "good" was most people's bad day. Maybe if you put the two of us together, you'd have someone actually equipped to deal with this sort of thing. Physically at least.

The truck made a hard turn and Jon fell towards me. He managed to catch himself before landing on me, but still his face was awfully close to mine. Neither of us could move, so drawn were we to each other. Neither seemed to care about the inappropriateness of the timing. It was like the truck vanished from our perception. All we saw was the other. All we knew was that the other was so close. I felt the connection between us, like electricity crackling in the mere inches between our faces.

And the truck turned again. Just like that Jon was thrown in the other direction and the world rushed back in on us again. The truck screeched to a halt.

I didn't have time to wonder where we were. I only had enough time to acknowledge the truck's lack of momentum when I heard voices. I didn't know the language and a quick look at Jon was all I needed. This was nothing he could translate quickly. I only hoped they could speak English or Jon could muddle his way through it.

Juan of the Dead

CHAPTER
SIXTEEN

The back of the truck opened, and three men stood there. Ahh, our abductors showed their faces at last. They dressed in little more than rags and looked like they hadn't taken a bath in months.

One attempted to speak to us, but it was more of that language I didn't recognize. He was an obvious leader, though his good buddies, Thing One and Thing Two, threw in a few thoughts here and there. Not that I knew what their thoughts were. We didn't respond to anything the men said.

These guys just kept spewing verbal nonsense at us. The words came so fast that I could hardly even make out sylla-bles. Jon's eyes were closed. I figured he must be trying to concentrate hard to pick up anything he could work with. The men stopped talking and looked at us.

Uh oh. Was he waiting for us to say something? I don't even think what he'd said resembled any sort of Spanish. I thought Mexico was all Spanish speaking. Except the few that learned English of course. English was just a given any-where. Mostly because Americans like me were too snotty to learn any other language. But hey, when you lived in the best country on the planet, why bother learning another language?

Another barrage of words, though this one was shorter. The sounds came from deep in the throat, more guttural than most languages I was familiar with.

It was worth a shot. "I don't understand you. No hablo your language." Maybe living here, this guy would at least recognize the bad Spanglish.

The man looked at me, and away he went again with whatever dialect of gibberish he spoke before. This time, however, he directed his verbiage to one of the men beside him. I really wished I knew what he was saying. For all I knew he was telling this guy, "That's it, grab the machete, they are dead!"

I noticed Jon muttering under his breath beside me. I couldn't make out most of it, not because I couldn't hear him, but because it didn't make much sense. Maybe he was working on a way to talk to these rejects.

The little group of kidnappers grew. Lovely, reinforce-ments back at HQ. Just what we needed. We were up to six and I idly wondered if the new super strength granted in resurrection would allow me to take on all six. Theoretically, I bet I could take out these six loons, steal the truck, and Jon and I could be on our merry little way.

Theoretical only, because I had no clue how to fight. I was no Buffy the Vampire Slayer. I suppose these guys weren't vampires so it would be more along the lines of Bea the Kidnapper Beater. That just didn't have the same ring to it. I kind of liked vampire slayer. I needed to come up with some sort of nifty cool name for myself.

Juan of the Dead

Bea the Undead. Okay, so my brain fizzled at that point. Too bad. Maybe I should have enrolled in one of those self-defense classes for women. You know, where you learn how to beat the snot out of a would-be-attacker, so you don't get dragged into the bushes by a rapist murderer scary dude? Yeah. Half my friends had done those sorts of things, but not me. Best I had was some yoga. While Downward Facing Dog might give these creeps a cheap thrill, I didn't think that it would do a whole lot to intimidate them. I had a fierce Warrior pose, but that wouldn't do a whole lot for knocking kidnappers upside the head.

So, what did I do? I just sat there like a lump. What was the use of uber undead powers if I didn't have the skills to use them? What a loser I was turning out to be. I couldn't even give these guys a proper tongue lashing since we didn't speak the same language. It's just not the same to snark at someone if they don't understand what you are saying.

Jon's head popped up and he stumbled through something that might be in the same language these dudes spoke. The leader of the pack turned his attention back to us, dismissing the guy he'd been talking to.

Lackey Numero Uno walked off, obviously on some mission from Bossman. Oh, goodie. Here was hoping Uno didn't show back up with a machete or something. Bossman looked at Jon for a moment before speaking more guttural garbage.

Jon closed his eyes and repeated the sounds that Bossman had uttered. I listened as he mumbled some more, before he replied. I sure hoped that whatever he was saying resembled a resounding "Who the crud do you think you are, buttmunch; let us go!"

Maybe not the brightest thing to say to someone holding you hostage in the back of a truck filled with hay in who-knows-where Mexico. Did I care? Not really. Maybe I was just cranky since a couple days ago I like totally died. Tends to make you even less excited about more crap being thrown into your life.

These fools messed with the wrong undead chick. I felt like knocking some heads together and if I could figure out a way to do it successfully, these guys were going down. Given my strength, I may forget not to go easy on them. Kidnapper creeps could end up with bashed in skulls.

They better not think Jon's going to go all raise the dead on them like he did me, either. They were filthy savages whose hot factor was nowhere near my own and they kidnapped us. Jon wouldn't be so nice to freaks like them, I wouldn't let him.

Bossman looked at Jon and said something else. At least Bossman seemed to slow down his speech. Hope that helped Jon. I hated being left in the dark about what the two were saying, but I was too afraid to disturb Jon's concentration. Instead, I got to just sit and twiddle my thumbs during the snail's pace of hostage conversation.

Wasn't I lucky?

I stifled a yawn. Which was nice in distracting me from the whole people talking a language I was unfamiliar with thing. I wondered what it meant that I yawned. Wasn't yawning some sort of breathing thing. Like trying to get in more oxygen? Why on earth was I yawning if I didn't need to breathe like normal folk? It was probably boredom. Which explained thinking about yawning so much.

I moved on to inspecting my manicure. Like the earthquake hadn't done enough damage? What on earth would getting knocked over by a human cannonball and lugged around on someone's shoulder do to me? Lucky for these guys, my manicure didn't look any worse off than yesterday. If it was even possible to get worse.

Juan of the Dead

Where was a good drug store when you needed one? An emergency bottle of nail polish and a file would do wonders for my hands. I never left home without a file, but I never planned to lose my purse under a building, either.

The more I stared at my fingers, the more incensed I became. Where was Fate? I wanted to give her an earful. I didn't do anything to make my karma tank like this. First I die, then I get kidnapped? Best of all, I couldn't communicate with the freaks kidnapping me. If I were in an action movie, right about now is where I'd spring into action. My arms and legs a flurry as my kidnappers fell to the ground one by one, unable to keep up with my awesome action hero antics. I'd kick that one in the gut, I'd knock the heads of those two together. I'd punch Bossman in the nose and laugh as blood gushed everywhere.

Bossman and Jon were still picking their way through lame language negotiations, when the lackey came back with a young girl, no more than sixteen. At least she was acquainted with what we civilized people referred to as cleanliness. Her clothes were simple, but well cared for.

Best of all, she spoke Spanish. Score. Having lived in Mexico for a while now, Jon was fairly fluent in Spanish. The two took off like horses at the races. It all still sounded like gibberish to me, but I felt hopeful that things would move along now.

Thank goodness, no telling how crazy I would have become if things had lasted much longer.

Jon broke off speaking to the girl and turned to me. "You aren't going to like this."

"No kidding? These freaks abduct us, and you think I'm not going to like what they have to say? What clued you into that?" Like it was his fault we were in this mess? I didn't care. I could be pissy with him and know that my anger was understood.

"It's a bit worse than that."

"What the hell could be worse than being abducted by a bunch of wackos? Did they seriously want to boil us and eat us for dinner? Seems rather unlikely they'd tell you those plans."

Hey, I'd heard about cannibals in the world. Was it so farfetched to think maybe some made their way to Mexico?

"They know what you are." That was it. Plain and simple. But how could they know? Heck, we didn't even really know what I was.

"I take it that is bad?" If they thought it didn't matter, then who cared, but if they wanted to do unspeakable things to me, that was a whole other matter. Me and unspeakable things didn't sound like fun.

"Not as bad as the fact that they weren't the ones chasing us to begin with."

Well, crap. Need I say that one again? Crap on a crap-stick. I'd kind of just assumed these were the freaks chasing us to begin with. That left me with only one thought.

"So, who was chasing us?" ·

"I don't know. But it seems you are pretty popular."

Of course, I was popular. I'd always been popular, so why would things change in the wake of my untimely demise? Then again, I'd always been popular with people who were normal, not those wanting to commit various criminal acts like assault and kidnapping. I didn't know if I liked the idea of popularity with criminals.

"Great. So, my popularity with the felonious has increased. I'm oh so lucky." I pursed my lips and looked at the girl Jon spoke with. "Think you can find out what that means?"

Jon turned his attention back to the girl and they spoke again. Him. Her. Him. Her. I really hoped he was getting usable information this time. Not the standard half information to taunt me with. Seriously, if he came back with next to nothing, I'd have to think about coaching him some more in how to get information from someone.

They spoke for longer this time before Jon stopped to talk to me again. "Okay, so here's the deal," he sighed heavily. "This would be so cool if not for, well, the circumstances."

"You mean like being the victims of kidnapping from psychos?"

"They aren't psychos. And really, you should be thankful. They saved you."

"How is this saving? Seems to me abduction is abduction. Any way you want to spin it, it's still a federal crime. At least it is in America. I don't know what passes for law down here." I'd sure hope that attacking someone and dragging them off without permission was still against the law here.

"Because, if those other people had caught us, you'd be in pieces."

Like what? They'd have beat me up and broken my bones? "Say what?"

"As in, that's what they think needs to be done to those with your... condition. Dismember and behead you."

What the hell? Chop me up? Okay, so that did sound bad. I was only kidding when I thought about becoming Bea Soup for these dudes. Now I found out that there were people who really did want to turn me into little tiny pieces?

"Uh, why?" I wasn't really sure I wanted to know what went through the minds of crazy people, but at the same time if someone wanted to do that sort of thing to me, I supposed I should know the reasons.

"I guess because they think that way you can't come back again."

"Come back? From where?"

"Death."

Oh. That. Erm, did that mean I could die again? I didn't want to think about that.

"Uh, so they wanted to kill me? Uh, kill me again?" Yeesh. Definitely glad we got away, though I wasn't ready to become best buds with this pack of people quite yet. Saving my life was nice and all, but wouldn't it have been better to take out my assailants instead? Near as I could tell, just dragging me off meant that the would-be murderers were still around to try again.

"Something about you being an abomination to the laws of nature."

Abomination? They better not have said abomination. No way was I an abomination! Then again, I didn't like him thinking that about me, so maybe I did hope they were the ones that called me that.

"Well, they can law-of-nature themselves away. I'm here and they can deal with it."

I was graced with a second chance at life. What did they want me to do, say no thanks? How about instead I take the chance since it was too unfair to die so young or while on vacation, let alone both!

"That's the problem. Seems they do want to deal with it. By ending your life."

Now I had some pack of crazies hot for my bod and wanting me six feet under. Glorious. But we were away from them for now. What about the matter at hand?

"And these guys? What do they want?"

He hesitated. Uh oh. That can't be good.

"To worship you."

Wait, maybe it could be good. Worship me? I was finally noticed for my awesome fashion sense and drop-dead good looks? I can easily get behind that.

"Nice. I like the idea of worship."

He rolled his eyes while pushing up his glasses. Did he think I wouldn't notice? I glared at him. He continued anyway. "Yeah, I guess that's the best translation. They said they are at your disposal and they've waited for your arrival."

They've waited for me? How did they know I was coming? If I'd gotten an invitation to this party, I would have RSVP'ed in the negative and run like hell in the other direction. As would any sensible person.

"Uh... just what does that mean?"

"I can't believe this. I guess there's some sort of a prophecy."

Now, that was cool. A prophecy of me? This I had to hear. "Share more," I prompted.

"They can't really, it doesn't translate out well. But basically, there's a tradition passed down through their tribe about... well... you."

Nice! I liked this. Maybe these people weren't so bad after all. First, they had a prophecy about me and then they saved me from my second death. Maybe I could warm up to them after all.

I look at the people before me. None looked like they were ready to bow to Goddess Bea, so I wasn't sure that Jon was right on this whole worship thing. At the same time, they didn't look ready to chop me up to feed me to the fish or whatever you did with a chopped up hot girl. Really, I figured I could live without the worship so long as it also meant living without people trying to turn me into Fillet o' Bea.

However, if they did choose to worship me, first command would be to find some better clothes. I liked the idea of minions, but I had standards. I really just couldn't look like I'd just walked out of the Amazon rain forest. Hmmm, maybe they did just walk out of the Amazon rain forest.

"Where are they from?"

"I didn't ask. Mostly I got that much and figured I was doing good and I better let you know."

Eh, good point. Sitting around while others were prattling on about the price of tea in China in a foreign language was not high on the entertainment factor.

"Humph." Could he tell I was grumpy? Well the way my life was going lately, who could blame me? "So, what's next?"

Bossman came towards me and held out his hand. I stared at him for a few minutes before Jon spoke up. "He is wanting to give you a hand out of the truck."

How gentlemanly of Bossman. Where was that chivalry when I was being treated like a sack of potatoes? I suppose the imminent danger of the other crazy people probably knocked politeness aside, but still. I didn't need some man to help me out of a truck.

I gracelessly stood in the back of the hay filled truck and stumbled to the edge where I jumped down. Bossman turned his hand to Jon, who did take advantage of the kindness. I tried to stand a little taller. I am woman, hear me roar. I didn't need no stinking help. So there.

Juan of the Dead

CHAPTER SEVENTEEN

Bossman turned to our young translator and said something to her in the guttural language. If he was here, you'd think he could say something in the native language. Nope, not this guy. I wondered about that. Lucky for me my questions were about to be answered. The girl turned and spoke to Jon in Spanish. Going through so many people was a real pain in the ass.

"They want us to follow them. We're going somewhere we can really talk in comfort as well as privacy. Things are pretty safe here, for now, I guess."

I nodded and we took off walking. Bossman and the girl led us while Thing One and Thing Two took up the rear. I wondered just what was going to be more comfortable than the back of the luxurious hay truck.

The thing that surprised me about this whole trip was that I'd always pictured Mexico as this giant dust bowl. Nothing but sand and flatness and little adobe houses.

Here in the Yucatan, I found myself bushwhacking through forests. If you were really into the wilderness, this would be your ideal spot.

If anything, this seemed to be the exact opposite of the path towards civilization. Which was why after a few minutes, when we came to a gathering of tents, I was not surprised.

Now, don't think these things were your average camping tents. You'd not find these things in the local Walmart. These looked homemade. They were large enough that the men could easily stand inside. I had to admit, if one was going camping in the middle of nowhere, this was the way to do it.

We entered the largest tent, which stood in the middle of the cluster. I realized this was the main gathering place. I took that to mean the other tents were private. Inside, the ground was covered with a large woven rug. Pillows rested on top of the rug for people to sit on. I knew that because there were two men already sitting inside.

The men made no motions or attempts to stand upon our entrance. Instead, Bossman waved us to some pillows of our own. I sat on one and decided these people were pretty slick. With nothing but the rug between us and the jungle ground, the pillow made all the difference. I liked it, but I wasn't a roughin' it kind of gal.

The girl grabbed a pillow from the circle around the edge of the rug. She took it into the center of the great tent and set it down. She knelt and looked towards Bossman for direction which he happily gave. I sure hoped somewhere in all those growls he gave her, she got a "Good job, sistah". She really was working hard just because these guys didn't know how to speak.

"Think we could get some introductions?" I didn't think it too much to ask the names of my saviors and abductors.

Unless they really wanted me to refer to them is Frick, Frack, and whatever else I could come up with. For that matter, knowing who was hot for Sliced and Diced Bea would be awful nice. What was that adage about holding enemies close? Exactly.

Jon nodded and whispered to me, "I think we'll get a lot of answers now. I just hope they'll be good."

Me too. What if these people wanted to worship me by all manner of creepiness? You never knew what worship could be. I didn't want to be bronzed or stuffed or find myself married to an entire village of skeevy men. The ick factor on all three? Through the roof.

"Why are you whispering?" If they couldn't understand English did it matter if he spoke loudly or not? This seemed like the case of where someone shouts thinking that loudness will conquer a language barrier.

"Dunno. I guess I just didn't want to draw attention to myself. You never know what might be considered rude."

Oh, yeah. Blasted cultural divides. I really didn't like this part of traveling. If you were so stressed about offending a native, could you ever really relax? On vacation you should be able to let your hair down. Be footloose and fancy free. Not so worried you might end up burned at the stake.

I simply nodded. Things looked like they might be happening. Somehow our numbers grew to almost fifteen in the tent. All of them sat down, loosely forming a circle along the wall of the tent.

Looking around I saw that the congregation was comprised of only men. What was the deal with that? Chicks were good enough to translate for these guys but not much else?

Note to self: If that was the case, I needed to use my awesome powers as She-Who-Must-Be-Worshipped to bring in some woman's lib.

Boggs

Bossman said something to the two original inhabitants of the tent. No more Bossman for him, he looked like middle management. Hope he didn't mind the demotion. I watched the exchange between him and the Head Honcho Duo. It really only took a few minutes and then he retreated to the outskirts of the circle. With a few words to our translator, she began her work; that entailed talking to Jon in Spanish. This time, however, she paused frequently so he could bring me up to speed. Thank goodness because it made the whole procedure far less frustrating.

No introductions yet. Instead, it was Story Time at Tent Chalet. Since it appeared my job was to merely sit back and enjoy the ride, I tried to do just that. Luckily, we did get her name, Anna-Lucia, before she set off in the tale of these people.

Turns out they weren't from here. That explained the tent action as well as the language barrier. Who knew there were still basically undiscovered people in the world? What else hid in the darkest corners of our world?

Jon didn't say where our new friends came from. It didn't matter to me unless they decided it was time for another road trip. I was in enough of a pickle having no papers in Mexico. I didn't want to consider the nightmare if they snuck me across country lines. Now if they wanted to hook me up by sneaking across the Mexico- America border, I'd think about it. That didn't seem high on the likely, however, and the idea of skirting Border Control didn't thrill me.

Anna-Lucia's tale ended up fascinating me. Either she and Jon made a good pair for storytelling, or this was just interesting. Or maybe a combination of the two. For generations longer than they could count, the elders recited prophecy of one who would come. Lucky duck me, I was the one. How I pulled that card from the poker game of life,

I'll never know.

I'd happily be the life of the party, but I wasn't so sure about being "The One".

Wasn't Jesus the last to bear that honor? We saw how well that worked out for him. Brutal death? No thank you! Then again, he did get to come back from that death. As it happened, I also came back from death. Hmmm, maybe there was something to this? Still, he was like all wise and powerful. I was all... well, I was not that stuff.

Fancy that – little old me was destined to usher in great changes. The whole Age of Aquarius shindig. What did I know about that? I knew it was a groovy song from the '60's. The Head Honcho Duo were like my very own wisemen, sans gifts. They watched for the signs of the times, so to speak. They saw them, packed up their little party, and made their way here. I could forgive the no frankincense, myrrh, or gold since their buddies saved me and Jon.

They even knew everything would go down in or near Chichen Itza. Go figure. Me? I'd never heard of this place. They not only knew where it was, but they revered the ancient culture that once lived here.

Maybe I should take some time and learn more about this area. I decided I'd give Jon some more time to further my new education in ancient American people. After the crazy people were dealt with, that was.

They weren't alone in their foreknowledge of my inevitable untimely demise and subsequent return from the dead. A neighboring tribe, for lack of a better word, held the same knowledge. They feared what I would do and what that might mean for their way of life. Stupid superstitions. They thought just because some crazy people created mass destruction by raising the dead, the same would happen this time. That meant that Jon was naughty, and I was about to cause massive destruction.

Boggs

I supposed, mostly because Jon mentioned it as a possibility, that the two people were once one. Nations split over less than different visions of the future. Politics was stupid.

What was I left with? One group wanted me to bring free love and berries. The other thought I'd bring utter annihilation to their way of life and would stop at nothing to ensure that did not come to pass.

Top on my To Do list? Make sure the efforts of the latter did not come to pass. Nothing was more fearsome than a woman on a mission. Ever seen a salvage sale? When there's only one designer item left and three women set their sights on it, things got brutal fast. Yours truly held a pretty high success rate in such circumstances.

These crazy guys wanting to do a hatchet job on me didn't stand a chance. Where there's a will, there's more than a way.

If all these people knew I was going to die and be raised from the dead, why the heck didn't anyone tell me? Was it so hard to send someone a telegram anymore? Text my phone? Email me? How about this low-tech plan: Push me out from underneath the giant freaking calendar! I could still have a normal heartbeat, my Coach purse and, best of all, no one would need to resort to violence.

Was I the only one who did things the easy way? If you didn't want me to defy the laws of nature by being the walking dead, then ensure I didn't croak. You couldn't get more basic than that.

Did these guys have any real plans for saving my skin? Not really. They wanted us to come up with something. I had to say, this perturbed me. They actually knew of those who opened hunting season on Bea. What did I know? Nothing.

Dealing with those hellbent on returning me to the fully

deceased status was probably the more prudent route, but it didn't sound too healthy for my stress levels. I didn't like the idea of going around looking for trouble; it found me easily enough.

Anyone know how to get off Trouble's radar?

I kind of liked the idea of cutting out of here and heading for greener pastures. Sure, the runaway plan probably wasn't the best idea, but it worked for me. Got me away from people that might like to do unkind things to me and maybe we could find a nice hotel. Something with multiple stars. At this point, I'd even take three stars over a tent in the back end of nowhere with a price tag on my head.

Surely, there was someplace we could go hide out where we could also drink something fruity and cold while basking on the beach. The longer I was dead, the paler I got. I wanted my tan, so I favored the beach plan. Funny enough, they didn't like my plan.

If you aren't going to like the plan of the one who's going to bring you enlightenment, then maybe you weren't worthy of said enlightenment.

They should've taken my advice, if you asked me. Let's go to the beach. Maybe Jon didn't explain it right. Then again, given the way the Head Honcho Duo were clutching their bellies while laughing, I bet he did. Punk. I bet he editorialized it with some such garbage about how my idea was lame. My idea would lead to relaxing and sunbathing. Neither of which could ever be bad.

When the Head Honcho Duo stopped their rather raucous laughter, I glared at Jon. What a traitor. I'd get him later. He would beg me for mercy.

Jon's translation of these guys' answer didn't thrill me any. They wanted to keep me here under lock and key. With tents, it's not so much real lock and key. Mostly just big burly bodyguard types. So, me hanging in a tent doing nothing, especially not working on my tan. A few body-guards, and the rest would go off hunting the creepers wanting to turn me into a human puzzle.

Now, I knew that I should be grateful that they cared. That's a whole mess of caring that I couldn't imagine. I didn't think I'd kill for anyone. In fact, I knew I wouldn't kill for anyone. Nobody is worth a lifetime in prison or the death sentence. I'm sorry, that's just how it was. So, it kind of bothered me that they wanted to kill for me. Frick and Frack, bless their souls, offered to bodyguard me.

Why did I have a feeling they thought it was babysitting duty? Probably because I felt like it was babysitting duty. Oh, we gotta watch the poor little woman with homicidal maniacs after her.

I wasn't so sure I liked the idea of having keepers, but then again, I did like breathing. Or at least breathing to appear normal. I could learn to deal with keepers.

Juan of the Dead

CHAPTER EIGHTEEN

I left the boys to do their thing and went on a mental walkabout. They could dish out plans themselves. It wasn't like I had any sort of marketable skills to solve this problem. What was I going to do, Amex my hunters to death?

The problem with letting others make the decisions for your life was that you then had to put up with what they chose, while getting bored. No Vogue to read, no one to talk to, nothing.

It was amazing what you'd think about when you ran out of real things. I hadn't slept since Jon awoke me from the eternal dirt nap. Not sleeping meant I was going to now have twenty-four hours a day to fill. Neverwish for more hours in a day, trust me, you could totally have too many. I needed to take up a hobby.

Jon interrupted my thoughts. "Bea, we think we have a workable solution."

I hoped it was better than just ruthlessly killing people. I really didn't do well with death. Ironic, right?

"Okies. Shoot."

"You're going to stay here." He motioned for my good buddies, Frick and Frack.

Oh good, I wanted more bonding time with the wonder twins.

"You've got someone to watch over you. There's some good information I can get here, so I'm staying, too. Seems the Elders have more legends. Meanwhile they'll send out scouts and see if we can at least determine where this other tribe's staying. We'll try to determine what kind of threat they pose and see if we can grab someone to bring back here and prove you are all right."

"That sounds far more reasonable."

At least give them the chance to talk. Shouldn't they have the right to at least defend themselves?

If we didn't at least try, I'd have one massive guilt trip to process. Worst that could happen was we'd find they were completely unrelenting.

"With a smaller crowd, we can have more of a dialogue. I'm hoping for some real information. Maybe we can even get some answers."

"Think there is a 'So You Wanna Be the Undead' resource book out there? I can't imagine it to be a popular wiki hit on the net."

I didn't have many questions, but the ones I did have consisted of: "Will I ever die now?" and "Where was the dang light?" Okay, so the last one they probably couldn't answer, and I needed to figure it out on my own. I'd never been one to be all Bible thumping and whatnot, but it wasn't like I didn't believe in it. The thought that there was definitely nothing out there kind of made me sad. Maybe you just had to wait a while before you saw the light. I liked to hope so.

Then again, these people probably didn't know if I was immortal, either. Barring psychos chopping me up, of course. I mean, if my new friends did know, wouldn't they have their own undead people to worry about, and they could hoist this whole chosen one shtick onto one of them?

Many of the men stood and left the tent, off to be good little hunter boys.

Find me a crazy person so we can find out just how off their rocker they are! Soon there were only five of us left in the tent: Jon, me, Anna-Lucia, and the Duo. Frick and Frack stood just outside.

"I'm hoping we can find what other legends there may have been and if there's ever been another like you."

I felt testy. It was nice to be unique, but there came a point where you didn't want to be that unique. Not that I wanted to know that there were more like me. A brain could only wrap itself around so much at one time.

"Whatever."

If I learned I was not alone, was I supposed to go romping off to meet up with other undead people? Yay, a conclave of undead sorts. They could help me learn to live in society with my new issues. If I never aged, I was going to need to figure out how to fake people out. At the same time, what kind of people would they be? The legends I'd heard weren't very promising. Let's not even talk pop culture.

"There's nothing? Come on," he nudged me. I hated his nagging.

"This is just all a lot to deal with. It's kind of bringing me down, the fact I can't talk to anyone but you and I've got some crazy people chasing me and..." I trailed off and bit my lip.

He put his hand on my arm. "I'm really sorry... I..."

I wasn't really paying attention to his words though I

was glad for the empathy. Glad, but kind of tired. He'd done what he'd done, and it was over. No going back now. But, that's not why I wasn't paying attention. It was the electric sizzle zinging up and down my arm from his touch.

Lucky for both of us, we had the Head Honcho Duo and Anna-Lucia, so we were able to escape the touch vortex. He removed his hand from my arm, with what I hoped was, re-luctance.

I tried to brush off his apology. "This is my... life now. Whatever. I'll just learn to deal."

Maybe I was too harsh. He looked upset and his hand dropped limply to his side.

"I never meant for this. You have to know that."

I tried to soften my tone. I suppose he didn't think raising me from the dead would make people hot to trot to undo his work. "I know, Jon. A lots happened in the last couple of days."

"It sure has. Who knew?"

"Apparently they did." The acid was back. "Rather rude of them not to fill us in, don't ya think?"

His eyes brightened. "I can't believe I had no idea that these people even existed."

Uh oh...

We had ourselves a case of job-crush right here. He wasn't kidding when he told me about his job. He really did like this stuff. It was awful dang cute to watch him get so excited.

"That would have been some good knowledge to have." Thinking about things like that made my brain hurt. Kinda moot anyway since I didn't see any wild haired mad scientists with a DeLorean hanging around. No chance to go back in time and fix things.

"Maybe." He looked thoughtful for just a second. "I can't wait to see what more I can learn from them. Their language is very interesting."

"How much of that do you really understand?" I asked.

"You don't want to know. It's pretty tough. What little I understand sounds like a mash up of what's supposed to be two different dead languages. That could be part of the problem. Maybe we've learned mispronunciations since we thought they were dead."

Hmm, a linguistics for dummies lesson. Fascinating. A simple "not much" would have sufficed. I could lock the useless trivia away in the back of my head. Never know when I might be on a trivia game show.

"How many languages do you know?"

"Really just English and Spanish. I know some bits and pieces to several dead languages, but they aren't really useful in the modern world."

"Like Latin? Isn't that a dead language?" For brainiacs, I mentally added.

"Exactly. Languages that are no longer spoken are hard to learn. You can't really know for sure if you are pronouncing it right and there's no one to really practice on."

"I see. So that's why you said it's hard with these guys?"

"Pretty much. Think about our language and how many different sounds a letter can make," Jon explained.

"For real. Why do we have letters that have five sounds?" I groaned. What is the point of that? For that matter why did we have words that sounded the same, but were spelled differently?

"Exactly. We may think we have the right sound, but we could be wrong. It's kind of like how people say the same word different in the north and in the south. Same words, different sounds."

"Big time. I've traveled to Boston and New Orleans. It's almost like they're speaking two different languages!"

"So, you get it. Maybe there's a little of that sort of thing going on. My sounds are off."

"Crap, how do you deal with that? Can't you totally mis-interpret words?"

"Yes, that's what makes it so hard. I'm really trying to concentrate."

"I saw you. It was pretty impressive though. It sounded like a bunch of growling to me."

"I bet it did. Their language is very guttural," he chuck-led.

"It was almost more so than German. I knew some Ger-man kids in high school. Student exchanges and stuff."

"Yeah, in that way it is like German."

I realized then we were being rude. Here we were yam-mering away in English and our would-be good friends were just sitting there patiently. While a portion of me felt it served them right to deal with waiting around for a while, I also knew it wasn't nice.

"We should probably get back to the task at hand." I kind of nodded my head towards Anna-Lucia and the two guys.

"You're right," he agreed, clearing his throat. He turned to Anna-Lucia himself and said something in Spanish. I'm sure it was probably a brief explanation of what we'd been discussing. She replied and he nodded toward her. She then turned to the guys behind her and said something.

"What do you plan to ask, Jon?" Maybe I could get some ideas to help.

"I've got some things I want to see if they can translate for me. From where I found the instructions dealing with how to..."

"Make me what I am? Do you really think they'll know how to translate that?" I was skeptical. These guys were from South America and I wondered how similar the lan-guages could be with that kind of mileage between the two areas. Then again, these people spoke some ancient mix up of dialects, so I guess anything was possible.

"I don't know. Maybe not. It's not the same language. Well, there are roots that are similar. I don't know if it's something like how languages like French, Spanish, and Italian are similar because of their Latin roots."

"Okay. My big question, do these people have names?"

"Do you think that's important?"

"I can't be calling them 'hey you' now can I?" Okay, I suppose since I couldn't talk to them at all, I wouldn't be calling them anything. But that's a moot point. I wanted something better in my head.

"Good point," Jon said. He went out and a few minutes later he came back with names. Thank goodness.

Turns out the Duo Lefty was Mac, or at least that's what it sounded like to me. Good enough. Duo Righty was Glen. That seemed normal enough. Frick and Frack, wherever they'd vanished to, were names so unpronounceable that I decided I had to shorten them. I got Raul and Don in my attempt. There were some other sounds in there, but Raul and Don would work just fine.

At least now if I needed something, I could call for them. Surely, they could understand simple pantomimes. No clue which was which, but there'd be plenty of time for that later. Jon was still speaking with Anna-Lucia. He looked rather animated and I figured that meant he must be talking geek with her. He stopped in what sounded like the middle of a sentence. After a brief moment, he started back up waving his hands like a loon. I watched with an arched eyebrow mildly amused.

He turned back to me, his face a flush.

Oh dear, this was going to be interesting.

"You aren't going to believe this!"

"My belief system is changing," I stated. "You'd be surprised what I believe in now." Like death is not the end? That's one.

"These people want to take us back to South America."

I cut him off before he could start another nerd ramble. "I don't know about that. Seems kind of problematic."

Besides, what were they planning to do? These are people who abducted us in the first place. What if they were lying about the other people? Maybe there were no other people hunting me. It could all be a ploy to get me back to their village and... I don't know. Whatever people like them would do to people like me.

"No, not right now," Jon clarified. "Later. Once we've straightened out the mess we're in."

"I'd like to point out that there's an even bigger mess. Like the fact I have no ID. No ID means no crossing borders. Just how do they plan to smuggle me through without a passport?"

"I don't think they have passports, Bea."

Oh great, now he was going to treat me like I was stupid. "But wouldn't it be better for me to try to get some sort of identification? If they take me elsewhere, how am I going to explain my presence there? Won't it make it worse for me to go home?"

He thought for a moment. "I don't know. We're going to have to make something up anyway. Here or there."

"What's there to make up here. I was on a cruise, there was an earthquake, I missed my ride. That's easy enough to track. Why do you want to go so bad?" I asked. My eyes narrowed as I looked at him.

Me playing hopscotch through various countries could not have been what got him all excited. Men like that get excited at one of two things: Naked women and whatever their sicko obsession might be.

"They have records, it's how they knew to come here.

They have ancient sites and artifacts. That's what I do. I can use all of that to learn from."

Why was I not surprised? He could go to another country and dig around with the stuff of people long dead. He did love the dusty and the musty.

"Yeah, but I say we just stay here. Or at least head to some major city where maybe I can find some help to get back home." Call me Dorothy. There's no place like home. It's not just where the heart is. It's where a girl belongs.

"But this is the opportunity of a lifetime. And they really want you. I don't think you have anything back home that can compare with what they want to give you."

Goes to show what he knew. I had a closet of beautiful clothes bearing the names of my most favorite people like Christian Louboutin, Oscar de la Renta, and Dooney & Burke. Scores of beautiful shoes and handbags. My job, my friends, my family. My Caribou Coffee, where I could get all manner of yummy drinks. Television, movies, my car.

"Humph." I crossed my arms. "I highly doubt it."

"They will take care of your every need. They were not kidding about that whole worshipping you and thinking that you will do so many great things for them. You're gonna blow that off?"

I had a higher standard of living than him. He obviously didn't mind living in squalor in the back end of nowhere. I needed to live somewhere where people lived, and things were close at hand and I could have my creature comforts.

I liked where I lived. I wanted nothing more than to stay there. Moving wasn't really in my plans, and especially not to someplace like this. I'm sure where they wanted to take me wasn't much different. This wasn't even a nice place to visit, I didn't want to live here.

"No, I want to go home. Get on with my life," I insisted.

"We might be able to make that happen," Jon sighed.

"But this is the opportunity of a lifetime to learn more about what's happened with you. How it works, and why you are so special."

I didn't like it. Seemed like it was going to cause more trouble. Story of my life these days. I stepped foot in Mexico and lost control of my life. "Okay, I'll think about it."

"I'll let them know we're going."

The hell? What was that? "I didn't say that!" I barked.

"You can think about it while we travel. It'll be fine," he shrugged.

"You can go dig in your artifacts and ancient whatever. How about you text me when you figure it all out? See this could easily work with me going home."

"Not really. You should stay with us. What if we find out we need to do something and you aren't around?"

"Like what?" I knew he was pretty vague on what really happened, a fact that still bugged me. How can someone do something like this without knowing what was going on? But still, surely, he should have known something. Didn't stuff like this come with disclaimers like, "Batteries not included" and "Don't feed after midnight"? Turned out, no. A testament to the need for keeping good records.

Frick came into the tent. I wondered which one he was, Raul or Don? He held a tray made of rough wood. While it was simple in design, it was beautiful. You just didn't get craftsmanship like that anymore. Forget slave labor in China, we just discovered the new place for American goods to come from. I'd love to order up a few of those trays for Christmas gifts.

On top of the tray was sliced fruit. They'd be mouthwatering if I had an appetite. Too bad I didn't, they smelled wonderful. Along with the fruit, I saw some bowls. Interestingly enough, there was one for everyone except for me, if we counted Raul and Don. Frak followed right behind with bread.

I felt a little envious at that moment. The delightful aromas of the food almost tempted me to try eating. I really needed to figure out what was going on with that. I gave it a shot.

"Jon? Do you think they know what the deal is with my whole lack of hunger and thirst thing? Or any of the other things going on with me?"

Maybe they were witchdoctors, but I didn't think a standard MD could really know what to do with a case like mine. Anything that I could get from them would be helpful in this regard.

"Sure, looks like they expected it. I'm not sure what that means exactly. Give me a moment."

I watched as Anna-Lucia spoke with Jon and the Elders. Within a few minutes she'd replied to Jon. I recognized one word, "No."

No, what? No, I don't eat? No, I don't eat a lot? No, I don't want to scream at the frustrations of it all?

"They assumed you wouldn't eat, at least not like the rest of us. They are fine with that."

I figured that had to make it easier when they planned to abduct two unsuspecting people. They wanted some sort of prophecy-fulfillment from me; to join forces with them to fight for Truth, Justice, and the Hispanic way. It was probably good for them to know they didn't need to pack for me.

One less thing to plague my mind. "Thank goodness. It's really annoying to try to come up with ways to fake eat."

Jon moved closer to the others as they tore into the food. It must have been good. If only I'd met up with these people before I died. I tried to blend into the background while they all ate. They allowed me to be myself and not eat, but I didn't want them to be uncomfortable, either.

Boggs

I laid back, stretching over several pillows. Looking up, I noticed a circular hole in the top of the roof. I wondered what that was and how this tent we'd entered managed to stay up in the extreme weather.

Closing my eyes, I thought about the tasks at hand. Without any sort of identification, I didn't know of any way to fix things for me. At least if I went along with these ya-hoos I'd get a good adventure to tell people whenever I went back home. Where was this kind of vacation when I was in school and had to write stupid essays entitled, "What I did last summer"? I always hated those.

Juan of the Dead

Boggs

CHAPTER NINETEEN

When I'd heard nothing but silence for far too long, I opened my eyes and sat up. Everyone was passed out around me. If they were all passed out, who was minding the store? I felt the panic rise within me.

As I took in the slumped bodies, I knew something was amiss. It wasn't like they were all laid out like I'd been, indicating a choice to rest their eyes. Jon was slumped over where he sat with his legs folded under him. It was the most uncomfortable position I'd ever seen. One of the Head Honcho Duo, maybe Mac, had fallen into the other who then fell backwards.

Something was not right, and I didn't like the looks of things one bit. Turns out my reservations came with good reason.

That moment, someone grabbed me from behind and threw something over my head. Blinded, I tried to kick my assailant, but that didn't work too well. Mostly it led to me getting jerked around.

They better not leave any bruises on me.

"What the hell are you doing? Get off me!" My cry was ignored as whomever it was dragged me backwards. I thrashed against their hold, but the grip only tightened. Man, that hurt.

If only I could see. Here I'd thought that the rough treatment was over. When would people learn respect? You could just ask someone to come with you. What was with all the trying to force things?

Here I was, 33, and I'd never been banged up or shoved around like in this last week. No bully issues growing up, nothing more than the cramped jostling on the Metro or whatever. Understandable and normal stuff.

I squirmed more, but it didn't do anything to help free me. I threw my head about hoping that whatever was over it would come off. Anything so I could see those who were hauling me out of the tent.

It was easy to tell when we'd left the tent, I could feel the breeze on my arms. Too bad everyone was unconscious inside the tent. I didn't think my good buddies would take too kindly to this poor treatment of me. These new people would pay heavily.

There was backup outside, and this guy didn't like my attempts to get away. Someone grabbed my feet out from under me and I could tell I was being hoisted along by two people. I stopped my efforts to escape. Between being blind and held aloft, I figured my chances were negligible for success. If I could just wait this out, they'd put me down eventually. My problem was that I wanted to be free.

It wasn't long before they put me down. In a way. I felt like they were attempting to turn me into the human un-dead pretzel. Ick. Unfortunately, they continued to hold me tight. I couldn't really move a whole lot, but it felt like they were sitting with me thrown over their laps. What was this? They had better not get any wise ideas. I heard an engine start up. What was it with people and abducting me? Since when did I come with my very own ransom note?

"Where do you think you're taking me? Let me go!" I knew these guys could hear me, but I heard no response.

I tried a different tactic. "Hey, you know, all you had to do was ask. I might have come along if you'd acted like civilized people. Ever hear of an invitation? Think you could let me sit up?"

Nothing.

This was way past getting on my nerves. First, there was the whole killing me thing. Sure, that was fate, but still. Then the raising me from the dead. Okay, I could deal with that one. After all, it meant I was still able to do stuff. The loss of my personal items was tough, even if I could eventually replace those things. But then you threw in the chasing me, attacking me, and making me run in shoes definitely not meant for such action. And now, two abductions in one day?

Enough was enough. I wanted someone to ask for my approval before things started happening. It wasn't so much to ask. I had rights and freedoms and liberties.

"Hello? People? Anyone there? Think you can remove this thing from my head?" I pleaded.

At least the last people who pulled the kidnapping action on me didn't try to blind me. We were in the middle of nowhere. What on earth was the purpose of covering my eyes? So I couldn't see the big fat lot of nothing as we drove?

The vehicle bumped along, and I didn't care too much for the comfort level of two large people holding me tight across themselves.

"How about just letting me sit up? Is that too much to

ask?" I persisted. Really, sitting between two brutes in a moving vehicle couldn't offer me chance to get away, could it? I didn't think so. They must have disagreed with that because my pleas were met with staunch silence and absolutely no action to help me out.

The vehicle swerved around a corner and I felt my stomach lurch. Without being able to see, everything seemed more intense. I was so glad these guys drove like wild maniacs down the piss poor roads of Mexico. It was beginning to feel like the time I went on Space Mountain after eating two corn dogs and a whole churro.

How fast was this guy driving? We slammed around again, and I started to slip, but my captors pulled me closer. On the bright note, they were keeping their hands in socially accepted places, but I knew in my heart I'd have bruises from their rough handling.

Time had no meaning when you couldn't see anything, and you were being held prisoner by brutes while bouncing around the countryside at Mach 3. Then again, speed didn't have much meaning either. Maybe it was only twenty miles per hour, but it sure felt like Mach 3. I was about sick of the world right now and just wanted some answers. Like who had me now? I sure hoped these guys weren't the slice-n-dicers. When at last we came to a stop, I thought I might fly off the laps of those holding me.

"Hey, ever hear of brakes? They are your friend; you don't have to be so cruel to them! How about easing into a stop?"

And still, silence. Were these guys a bunch of mutes or what? How hard was it to

answer a stinking question? Even if they didn't know what I was saying, they could at least grunt out whatever so I could know they didn't understand something. I'd never thought myself to be all that high maintenance or demanding till I died.

Don't get me wrong, I was very particular. I liked things to go a certain way and whatnot, just like everyone else. But this bordered on ridiculous. I just wanted people to act normal without me having to practically force it out of them.

The goon holding my ankles slid off the seat. As I felt his lap slip from under me, I knew it was time for the Wrestle Bea Out of the Car game. This could go one of two ways: a huge pain or a nightmare. I chose huge pain and tried to work as best I could with my detainers. I was so thankful that getting out was so much less trouble than getting in. I also found myself put on my feet again, with a meaty brute hand gripping each of my arms.

"Did you decide to let me walk like I actually have a choice in what's going on? Gee, thanks, creeps," I grumbled.

Someone shoved me in my back to start me moving forward and I walked, being steered by my captors. I followed as best I could, tripping over unseen obstacles. It was almost like they wanted me to fall.

"Hey, think you could help me not trip and kill myself?" How hard was it to steer me away from a root or whatever that thing was I just stumbled on? My toe smarted from where it got caught because no one had the curtesy to tell me I needed to lift my foot higher.

I heard a terrible creaking, squealing sound. Someone could have been murdering a car, it sounded so bad. I winced at the high decibel shriek of metal on metal, not that anyone could tell since my face was covered.

"What the hell was that?" Why I bothered asking, I'd never know. It wasn't like I even expected an answer at that point. It just seemed the only way for me to let them know how unhappy I was by this situation. Surely, they could hear my displeasure in my tone. Instead of words, I was shoved forward once more. I banged my other foot on something hard. What was wrong with these people?

"That's it, you guys want me to go somewhere you gotta help me actually get there or let me see. Duh!"

Nothing really changed so I took my throbbing foot and felt my way up to the top of what turned out to be a step. It was far too smooth as I dragged the toe of my sandal along it. When I found the top, it leveled out. Thinking it was a step, I took care with my other foot to do the same thing. Four steps later, there was only a bump of an inch or two, a door jamb. That horrible sound must have been a door in dire need of an oil can.

I could hear our footfalls echoing, the building was that large and empty. Well, how predictable was this? I got kidnapped and taken to some sort of abandoned building. Five pesos to anyone that got me out of this nightmare that this place turned out to be a warehouse. Was five pesos the same as like betting someone ten bucks in America?

More pushing me along until we ended up by a chair. I knew this because I was forced down to sit in it, which was very disconcerting. Having someone shove you from a standing to a sitting position felt like you were going to fall to the ground.

The chair wasn't particularly comfortable, but I didn't expect any less. These people didn't care about my comfort in any way. I wanted to be in on their agenda, maybe I could save myself some injury if we moved again. They finally tore the thing off of my head. I could feel my hair fly in every direction. I bet I looked just dandy. Guess these people didn't care about how much time and work went into doing my hair in the morning. I shook my head to get my tresses to at least get back into some semblance of order and out of my eyes.

As my eyes adjusted to the light, I grunted. Yup, a warehouse. How original were these people? They watched way too many bad movies. I took in the motley crew that made up my new captors. These guys weren't much better off than the last. If they wanted to go about kidnapping random Americans, they should try for going elsewhere and finding someone with money to pay a ransom. So, they could be less... motley.

They stood in a line in front of where I sat. Five people. Just staring at me. I stared back. They didn't move or say anything. It was like second grade all over again.

"This is going somewhere fast. You guys have me, now what do you want to do with me?"

Nothing like cutting to the chase. They didn't move, though. Not even a blink.

I heard a sound from behind me, shoes on the floor of the warehouse. You could tell they were the footfalls of a woman. Even with that warning, I didn't expect what happened next.

CHAPTER TWENTY

What to my wondering eyes should appear, but Leahonia. My kind hostess with the mostest from last night.

"Hello, Bea." Short and sweet, huh?

"Leahonia?" I arched an eyebrow at her.

"You left my mother's dinner," she scolded lightly.

"I don't think that's cause for this sort of treatment. Your goons were a little... rough."

"I'm very sorry, but you went off with the wrong sort of crowd. You really should have stayed for dinner, Bea."

"I didn't have much choice in that, either. Your country is very rude. No one extends a simple invitation. I'd gladly RSVP to a Save the Date. It's not that hard. You just ask. Say please. It's what's socially acceptable."

"We did ask for you to stay. You didn't have to go for a walk."

Why bother with the pretense? Obviously Leahonia knew more than she'd originally let on. "I think you and I both know why I didn't want to stay."

"Oh yes, your condition. I figured that out easily enough. You really should learn some discretion if you want to survive in this world."

When did her English get so good? She really played us the fool. Was she spying on Jon all along? Had she figured out when he came to Mexico what he'd one day do?

"Thanks for the helpful hints. You did who knows what to Jon and the others. Why should I trust you?"

I hoped that Jon was okay. The others... well sure I wanted them to be fine, but they abducted me too. I had no interest in getting involved in their crazy ideas or petty squabbles. I just wanted to get back to my own life.

"They'll be fine. We just drugged them. A little something in their food to take a nice long nap. I assure, all is well. Meanwhile, you and I can have a chat."

"Uh huh. And if you wanted to talk, you know we could have. I was in your home last night. We travelled up to your mother's together. We walked through town. Any old time you wanted; you could have struck up a conversation."

"True. But I needed time..."

I cut her off coldly. "Time to what? To have your goons truss me up and drag me all over? Isn't this all a bit dramatic? Especially since, once more, you had me right where you could chat. Just tell me you want a sit down and hey, there you go. One talk with me coming right up."

"That's nice for you to say, but we both know it wouldn't have happened that way. Are you really this stupid or is it all an act?"

What the-? "Hey, I'm reasonable. I'll talk to anyone." Well, almost anyone. "So, you got me here. After all this trouble, don't you think we should just get on with it. You really went to a lot of effort so it must be important."

"Indeed. Let's get on with this. I think we can both cut

to the chase. We know what you are."

"Smokin' hot? Fashionable? I'm a lot of things, Leahonia. I think you should be clearer." Now who's being stupid? She wants to cut to the chase, she can put things out there.

We all knew she was referring to my recently deceased status in life, but I was still in the dark as to what that meant. Clarity was not really a strong point in Nowhere, Mexico.

"Bea, really. I'm trying to be nice. Do you really want me to say it?" she asked, voice just as sweet as could be.

Yes. Answer my five-billion-dollar question, please. What the hell am I?

"You and I have a different opinion of nice," I grumbled. "My nice is a simple please, yours is roughing people up and taking them from their friends."

"You are reanimated. We all know what that means."

That I no longer craved chocolate or a good dim sum place? Gee, glad we're all on the same page here.

"How about you tell me what you think that means, Leahonia. Seems to me there's a lot of different ideas floating around out there."

"There can be only one idea. Everyone knows the Reanimated have but one goal."

"Hey, I do have only one goal! To leave your Godforsaken country and get back to civilization. I just wanna go home and get on with my life. It's not so much to ask, don't you think?"

"I'm sure you would like to get back there. Much easier to feed your hunger that way."

Wow, I could feel the icicles in her voice. Where had the sweet gone?

My eyebrow curved up. "I have no idea what hunger you speak of. In case you hadn't noticed, I don't really want much to do with food these days. I'm kind of hoping it'll help me lose those last pesky five pounds."

"Don't play innocent with me. You may have Jon conned, but we know what your kind eats. We also know what you do. We can't let that happen."

"Are you brain damaged? How many times do I have to tell you, I have no idea what you are talking about? You and your goons are going to what? Make sure I don't what? Scare kids on Halloween?"

She never took her eyes off of me, while she spoke to the goons behind her. The language didn't sound Spanish. One of her goons answered and I thought I noticed some similar sounds to the language spoken by the group I'd just left.

"We'll admit we don't know how long it takes for the hunger to get in. We try not to let things get that far. But we also know you are special. The prophecies spoken of are rather detailed in that."

Seriously, what was this hunger? I was feeling some hunger for sure. Hunger for freedom, for home, for that which I used to call normal. But those weren't the sort of hunger that would fix the cries of a stomach. I shrugged at her.

"Still don't know what you mean. The thought of food makes me sick," I said. It did.

"It'll come up sooner or later," she dismissed. "But we're all attached to our brains. We are off limits."

Ick. Wouldn't that be kind of slimy? And really, the thought of digging around in someone's cranium? I shuddered. Blood and I didn't mix.

"Gross! Look, I sat out of biology dissection because the thought of cutting up and looking inside dead critters was icky enough to make my skin crawl. No way do I want to eat your brains. You've watched one too many horror movies. Do I really look like a shuffling zombie?"

So, what, she's used to people like me going all homicidal for brains on people? I got news for her, shuffling was distasteful and drooling was simply out of the question. No way was anyone going to call me a zombie, anyway. Living challenged I'd take. Zombie, well, I may have to rethink the murder thing.

"You are reanimated. That is what Reanimated Ones do. Your purpose is to murder. Your food is brains."

"Okay, so I guess you haven't gotten it through your brain. Makes me think that even if I was in the mood, your brains might not give me enough vitamins and minerals." How's that for slick. I called her stupid and said her brain wouldn't be nutritious enough all at the same time. Now that's what I call style. "I really am no different from you. I just happen to have died a couple of days ago."

"You haven't noticed anything unusual about yourself since then? I highly doubt that. Besides I heard your conversation with Señor Juan." Her tone turned frostier. I rubbed my arms from the psychosomatic cold I felt.

"Sure. I don't seem tired, hungry, or any of that. I think we may have mentioned the whole eating thing already. Really, it seems like a win-win situation to me."

"It will come. But we're going to take care of that, so I suppose you won't see," she shrugged.

She was real adamant. She just would not leave it alone, would she? Give her an A in Beating A Dead Horse 101.

"What if I give you my word. No dining on yummy human brains?" I made a face to show her just how non-yummy I thought that might be.

"The Reanimated Ones cannot be trusted. The hunger consumes," Leahonia insisted.

"Maybe I'm different. I hear there's some prophecy or something. Maybe I don't need to lurch around the countryside feasting on the brains of those I murder." See, I know stuff, too.

"I see our mutual... friends... have told you much. They should have left well enough alone." The dramatic pauses were obnoxious. Could she be more over the top?

"So, you say. Do you know how hard it is to get information flowing through so many translations? I hate foreign countries. All I know is they said they wanted me to just be cool and hang out with them. You, they claim, want to end my life. Now that's just not nice and definitely puts a cramp in my style. I like the hanging out idea more."

"Yes, I suppose that their language barrier would be a problem. They didn't see the wisdom in meshing more with the global world. Their loss."

Oh, goodie. Looks like we had some sort of high school rivalry going on. What next? Can her dad beat up their dad?

She continued, "This is not your world anymore. Your very presence defies the laws of nature."

"I'm kind of liking the not dead thing. Really, is it so fair for me to die? Why me? I didn't ask for all of this. I was minding my own business."

"That is hardly my concern. I didn't make the rules."

"You expect me to believe you are what? Just a do-gooder? You going to go all 'I am the law' on me? I didn't break any laws that I know about. I'm just the victim of unfortunate circumstances."

"You can't play the victim forever. You make your own decisions, Bea."

"Maybe the universe decided it wasn't done with me after all. Did you ever think about that? What if the Universe made a big fat oops in knocking me off and now it wants to rectify things?"

"I don't think that's the way it works, Bea. You should have moved on. Death is a steppingstone in your progression."

"Move on to what, though? You forget. I've died. There wasn't anything. One minute I was standing in a tourist trap shop looking at the various blah-de-blah souvenir stuff. Then there's a whole lot of earth shaking going on. Next thing I know, there I am waking up on a stone slab inside Temple Creepville. Jon's there saying I'd met my end. Well, I may have met my end, but there sure was no maker hanging around to shake my hand. So, you tell me, exactly what 'continue' do you have in mind for me if there's nothing but a vast black nothing?"

She was unwavering. "It is all a part of you being here unnaturally. You obviously didn't have enough time to make the move from this life to the next, so you didn't advance your soul."

This was her plan? I should die so I could what? Go up the enlightenment chain? How very Buddhist. Was that Buddhist? I didn't know or particularly care.

"I'm all about advancing. But, seems to me that maybe I need to do some more advancing in this form. I wasn't a bad person before I died. I gave to charity. I paid my taxes. I minded my own business and kept my nose clean. But I could do better."

Okay, so I kept my nose fairly clean. There was nothing wrong with having fun in life as long as you didn't break any laws.

"It doesn't matter how much of a saint you were in life, Bea. Things are different now. Stop hanging on."

"Is that what you think this is? I'm hanging on?" Like life was a shirt from high school you just can't think of throwing away no matter how wash worn and threadbare it is? I don't think so. Life is... well it is life. How does one hang on to life, exactly?

"Yes, I do. You say you want to go back to your home. Return to your life. It's no longer your home anymore. It's no longer your life. After you die, you have no claim on anything here anymore. Let it free you. You can move on from all the troubles and pains of this life."

"Seems to me like even if I do move on to the next stage of whatever, wouldn't there be troubles and pains there? I vote for the troubles and pains I know, thank you very much. I know what life is like here. Really, I don't find it that bad. Except for right now because I have a great big huge pain in the..."

"Now that's just really impolite, Bea. Every major world religion believes in a rewarding afterlife for the good. If you were as good as you say, you should be getting that eternal reward."

It's funny how much your beliefs get called into question after something major like dying happens. She was right, but I just wasn't buying the product anymore.

"What if there's no eternal reward? What if this is it? I always figured there'd be something on the other side, Leahonia. I did. I don't know that I expected clouds and harps and halos. Or St Peter and some pearly gates. I didn't know what to expect to see. It wasn't emptiness though. That was the biggest disappointment in my life. Learning there was no Santa Claus was less traumatic."

"There is an eternal reward. Maybe you weren't good enough to earn it."

"Then let me try to do better. I can go save kittens, feed the homeless, and do more good deeds. If I had remained dead, I'd have no chance to improve myself."

"I don't believe it works that way," she said, shaking her head. I didn't think she'd change that belief no matter how long we talked in circles. I needed a new plan, but this was the kind of thinking on my feet I'd never been good at. Circles it was!

"Maybe it does. How do you know? Do you have insider information that I don't know about? Did the Big Guy Upstairs tell you something he's not letting me in on? Share with the class, maybe I'll change my mind."

It was a chance, and a big one. But really? How likely was it that any god would come down and tell her all sorts of inside god-secrets? 'Oh here, let me tell you how the universe works with a surety.' Not very probably, so chance taken.

"No, that hasn't happened. But how can you not believe the words of our ancestors. Of those that did receive enlightenment?"

"Really, did your ancestors experience that? Are you descended from Moses? Noah? Whomever?" So, that would be kind of cool. But did it really make her any more correct? I didn't think so.

"Well, it all depends on what you think. If Noah's story was true, aren't we all descended from him?'

Dear me, it was philosophy time. I could not believe my ears. She said I was all unnatural and breaking the laws of all that she held dear, yet she wanted to take the time to debate philosophy? Good grief.

But, as long as she was doing that, I was staying in the very much not chopped up state I pretty much liked more than anything on this planet. Yeah, I liked being intact even more than my MIA Coach handbag. Imagine that one.

"I dunno. I really don't know how that all works. It's outta my league. I only went to Sunday School, I didn't go study this stuff or anything." I didn't even go to Sunday School regularly. We weren't a particularly faithful family. We were more holidays, major events, and whenever-we-actually-remembered sort of worshipers.

"Maybe you should have taken more time to learn your own beliefs. Look at the punishment you have been doled out!" she said, holding her arms out toward me.

"You see this as punishment? I'm alive! I was dead! How is this a punishment? I stand by my second chance reward idea. If you see living as a punishment, that's very sad. And you need help before you try to do something drastic. Like hurt yourself or someone else."

She seriously was beginning to sound like someone in desperate need of the suicide hot line. Life was not a punishment; it was a gift. She wanted me to move on so much, what did that say about her?

"I don't see life as a punishment. But you are not alive."

And back we came. Her reminding me I was very much not alive no matter how much I could walk and talk. Pretty callous if you ask me. It was like telling the person with the humped back they had a giant hump sitting back there, as if they didn't even know? If I ever saw Leahonia's mother again, I wanted to ask why she didn't teach Leahonia better manners. What happened to the whole 'if you can't say something nice' rule?

"But I'm here. And this is some semblance of life. Maybe you need to become more enlightened. I think, therefore I am. So, there was a bit of a hiccup in my life plan. Who made you God and judge over all?"

She bristled. She stood a little straighter and her face turned hard. "I've never put out there that I was God. How dare you make such accusations!"

"Well, you want to run around determining what is and isn't alive. Making calls that are so far out of your jurisdiction as to be in another time zone. I don't see the accusation as falling too far from the tree."

"That is the most ridiculous thing I've heard. I think our discussion is almost over." She slit her eyes at me.

"Wait, are you kidding me? You are going to end this just because you don't like the way it is going? And people think I'm spoiled. Geez. I've got nothing on you. If this is the way you treat me, I'd hate to see what you do to friends. Friends sometimes disagree, too. Do you knock them off as well? Or is that just saved for me?"

She was flustered now. You could see it in the way she fumed. Through clenched teeth she said, "I would never kill someone. You don't know me."

She was right, I didn't know her. Yesterday I would have liked the chance to get to know her. Today I wasn't so sure. This took 'frenemy' to a whole new level.

"I'll give you that. I don't know you. You don't know me, either. How can you judge me?"

"Because you are a monster. You are unnatural. I've already told you that!" she barked back. Was she getting frustrated? I know I was.

"Monster? There's no need for name calling. I'm just a victim of bad luck. Maybe my luck is changing. Why can't you give me the benefit of the doubt? It's all I've been asking for."

"Because you need to die. You need to go back to the way you were," Leahonia insisted. More circles.

"But you welcomed me into your home. Did I do anything so bad there? If I'm the monster you say I am, why would you do that? If I'm so bad, wouldn't I have done whatever you are afraid of last night while you slept?"

For someone claiming I needed to go back to being deceased in the classical sense, she wasn't really moving things along. It seemed to me like she was trying to justify her own actions to make herself feel better.

"You are right. I did welcome you into my home. I needed to prove you were what you are, and to keep an eye on you. I was right. So now I need to do what it is I am supposed to do."

"Kill me? I don't think you want to. Why do you think

that is, Leahonia?"

"You are mistaken. I want to put things right and return order to the universe."

What a noble cause. Who could fault her? Oh yeah, me.

"You could have easily done it last night. On the way to the festival. At your mother's house. When your goons kidnapped me. What's really happening? We're sitting here having a little chat. I ask you again, why do you think that is?"

"I just want you to understand that it isn't personal."

"You say you want to kill me. You can't get much more personal than that."

"It's only because of what you are. If you were alive, then I'd happily leave you

alone. But you aren't."

Something dinged in my head. I felt like the proverbial light bulb just flipped on over top of me. "Semantics. I say I am alive. I have a heartbeat. We checked."

That made her pause. She looked at me without blinking before asking, "A heartbeat?"

"Yup. And since I'm not hooked up to machines or anything, I'd say that makes me alive. I'm talking. I have a heartbeat. These are usual things that one checks to determine if a person is living or dead right?"

It was dicey chance and I left her to balance the scales. I had died and I should be worm food. Yet, I was most obviously not. She turned to her goons. I guessed my sitting here without trying to escape wasn't good enough. Leanhonia pointed, "You two, hold her down."

Two broke away and came and grabbed me, each grasping an arm. I sure hoped they weren't going to treat me like the Thanksgiving wishbone. That would be most unpleasant as they were beefy enough to succeed in ripping me apart. Gruesome thought.

"What are you doing?" I tried to struggle, but their grip was sure. Leahonia grabbed my wrist. I guess she was better at taking a pulse than I was. She concentrated and I could see when she felt the first beat. And the second. Her eyes grew large and her mouth formed an 'o'. Take that!

"You do have a pulse." Her voice was soft, and she backed away. Her goons didn't let go of me and I couldn't see their expressions. I didn't try to look at anyone else, choosing to keep my gaze leveled on her. I forced myself to blink like a normal living person, even though I didn't need to. Anything to help her see that there was nothing out of the ordinary with me.

Yes, that's me. Living girl, not dead. Living. Yes, you want to believe it... living. "You really shouldn't jump to conclusions about people." I lowered my gaze away from hers. Could you blame me for trying to play her? If she thought I was being demure or humble or whatever, I might stand a chance at saving myself from becoming Bea Nuggets.

"I...I...I...I..." She was stammering now, and I knew the last thing expected was a pulse from yours truly.

What else would surprise her? Would the goons follow her if she swayed to my side? They seemed to be perfectly happy letting her run the show right now, but she obviously had some serious indoctrination to work through. It's how these cult types were.

I gave her a few minutes to stammer while trying to put her thoughts together. I still had to mentally slap myself in order to remember all of this was real and not some sort of crazy nightmare or a weird movie on late night TV. There's no way I could expect less of her. Things were pretty bad when you had a hard time accepting the bizarre world that was your own life.

Once she quieted down, she began to pace in front of me. Her goons stared straight ahead like good little soldiers. She'd taught them well. They could keep their cool. She, however, was another case all together. She slowed her pacing until she was once more in front of me. With a finger to her mouth she turned towards me.

"How is that possible?" One simple question. One very complicated answer that I didn't even know.

"You think I know?" I laughed. "This is your world, not mine. In my world people who die, they really do stay dead. I've been clueless since I woke up after that earthquake. Best I can say is this is me. Jon and I were hoping to get some answers when we came for the Day of the Dead celebration. Maybe it's just like, some sort of crazy fancy CPR."

"How can you not know? How can..."

"How can I not know? Are you kidding me? I'm just a tenant in this body. Along for the wild ride. All I know is that I'm here. I'm, for lack of a better word, alive. My pulse is still active, but way the heck slow. Some other various things. Unless you have a copy of 'Undead for Dummies' then you're barking up the wrong tree if you want information"

"How can you know so little?"

Is she kidding me? "Do I really look like I'm from around here, Leahonia? Again, I was just an innocent bystander. It's not like I put out an ad asking for this. 'Desperately seeking nerd boy hottie to raise me from the dead.' It just happened."

She began to rant. "Juan should have done more research before running off without thinking. He has a scientific mind, so I can't believe he'd do something like this."

I couldn't believe she was blaming him! Like he'd planned the whole thing, himself? It was all just an accident! I couldn't help myself, I needed to defend poor Juan, er Jon. Even if I had similar thoughts after waking up undead.

"Hey now, Jon's great. He may not have put a lot of fore-thought into all of this nonsense, but I think he sees more than people realize. I don't think that he's ever been any-thing but a genius."

Oh no. I sounded like a twelve-year-old with a crush. Now I would admit, there was obviously some chemistry there. Some sort of biological attraction. But come on. This was just disturbed.

Yet, I couldn't stop. My mouth kept moving, the words kept coming. It was official. I was gushing.

"I believe him when he says he didn't even think about it. He's a good guy that likes to help people. You can't get more needing medical attention than crushed in a building by an earthquake. So, you know what? You can take what you think you know about Jon and stuff it."

Defensive much? Get over it. Not like he could hear me anyway. So, he'd never know. How obnoxious for a guy to know you were off gushing over him like a preteen loser.

"He should not mess with things that were outside his realm of knowledge. It's reckless," Leahonia said.

His actions were reckless, but since they worked well for me, I could look the other way. I might agree, but she wasn't going to know that.

"I am choosing to look at this like a happy mistake. Sure, he probably could have known more about what he was doing, but it worked out well. Maybe you should do the same. Look at me. Do I look scary? Do I look like a mon-ster? Way I see it is this: I used to be a real bear before my morning cup of coffee. But, now? I don't seem to need to sleep. Not a problem anymore. Trust me. People will line up to thank Jon for that gift. Well, except the girl who works at my local coffee shop. I bet they're going to miss me."

"You might be missed. But don't you think your family should get the chance to mourn you properly? You are dead."

"Back to that? How would you like it if I kept pointing out that you had a great big zit on your nose? Pretty rude, right?"

Was I going to have to keep that battle going? Maybe we could get something tattooed to my forehead stating that I knew I was dead and please don't bring it up. I needed a t-shirt for crying out loud.

"Touchy?" Now she looked smug. I guess the surprise at the revelation I had a pulse had totally worn off. Shame. I needed to milk that for what it was worth.

"You know, since I do have a pulse and all, maybe it's not so much that I am dead, but that I was dead. You know, medical science is something these days. People are brought back thanks to doctors all the time." Okay, so I don't know how often that happened or why it happened for some and not others. Did it matter? It did happen, and that was an argument in my favor.

"We know that's not the case, now don't we?" Well, rats. It was worth a shot. Too bad she wasn't buying.

"I know I want to go home and get on with my life. I know I'm trapped here, and I haven't a clue how to get home because I've lost my ID and my passport and stuff. Everything else? Clueless."

Her voice creeped up an octave. "You do so know. You know you are unnatural. Enough. We've talked enough."

Oh dear. Leahonia realized that for all our talking, it meant nothing. We were always going to end up here. I sighed.

"I'd say so. Now, if I could take my leave?" Hey, I wasn't going to totally give up.

"No, you may not leave. You really are stupid." Her gaze hard, she pressed her lips together and pinched the skin between both eyes. Good, she was giving me a headache, too. Turnabout was only fair play, right?

"Look, how about we just part ways. You keep your opinion, I keep mine. We can agree to disagree. If I leave here, you don't have to worry about me being whatever it is you think I am. Even if it's true, your people will be safe. Near as I can tell, this is a win-win situation."

"How is it win-win if I allow you to fall victim to your nature? You might win, but what about your victims?"

"So far the only victims to my anything that I know about is some people who I totally beat grabbing for good deals. You learn to be fast, that's for sure. If you want the good bargains, you have to be ready to fight."

"The victims to your hunger." Leahonia glared at me with the stupid-girl look.

"You've mentioned that before. I'm telling you, I'm not hungry. I haven't been hungry. It's why I didn't eat at your house. The oh so big clue as to what I was or whatever."

"The hunger will come. My people, we're told from early on how bad it is. It will engulf you, consume you, that you will lose all of yourself to it. The first few days? Not so bad. Then, the hunger."

"Just what is this hunger? You make it sound like its freaking crack. I'm no drug addict."

"You don't need to be a drug addict before. We have the stories."

I was glad I managed to distract her again. I didn't expect it to last long. "If it's the same ones you told Jon and me, then that was so long ago. Mere legends are what you are basing this off of? Don't you think your stories have maybe kind of grown or something after all this time? Made things sound worse than they actually are?"

"You don't understand. We have the prophecies. And we know what happened before. That's enough to know that you are a threat to not only us but to the rest of mankind."

"But I'm no boogeyman. I'm normal. Okay, except for the not eating or sleeping thing. But, come on. Is that really so bad? Haven't you always wanted more hours in a day? Think of what you could do if you needed less sleep! The eating thing is really a shame because I gotta admit, I do like good food. I kind of miss eating."

"Miss it enough to think you are ready to see what it is your body needs to survive on? Your body needs something. I know you've already died, but it doesn't mean you can't starve."

She turned away from me at this point. It was almost like she couldn't bear to look me in the eyes anymore. Was it the fact that I was fighting for my life? Or the fact that I brought up good points? Just what was she so afraid that I could or would do?

I kept my voice soft. "Leahonia, why you? Look at you, I don't think you want to do this anymore than I want you to. Why are you here trying to convince yourself this is the right thing to do?"

She looked over her shoulder at me. "It is the right thing to do. One of your kind killed my father before we could stop it. I can't let you do that sort of thing to someone else. Some other little girl who has to grow up like I did."

A vendetta? While I could hear the hurt in her voice, something wasn't quite right. If she was so bent on revenge, why hadn't she done something right away? No. There was more to that and I needed to find out what it was.

Juan of the Dead

CHAPTER
TWENTY-ONE

"That's very noble of you, Leahonia. I can't imagine. But I didn't do that to your father. Someone else did. Don't take it out on me."

Her hands clenched by her side, the strain on her palpable. Her voice struggled to get through clenched teeth. "You may not have done it, but you will. He was my Papa. And that... that... monster... killed him. Destroyed everything that was good about him. Devoured his soul. I was only five. I couldn't do anything to stop it. I screamed and I screamed. I couldn't even run away."

My heart nearly broke and I wanted to choke. No wonder she got roped into this sort of thing. She watched her father's murder? Though her back was still to me, I looked away. The shame that anyone, like me or no, could do that to someone else was just too awful to bear.

"Then how... you... you're here. Something happened..."

"My screams brought people, it's the only reason I'm

still alive. They killed that creature, but it was too late for my father. I knew then that the stories we have are true. I've seen it firsthand and I have vowed to never let that happen again. To never let another monster go free."

"So, what am I then? Your play-toy? You want me to suffer like you did? You were a little girl. I can't imagine what you went through. But that was not me. I'm not like that person that killed your father. I'm not trying to kill any-one. I don't want to kill anyone. Why can't you believe that?"

"I wish I could. I'm done. I just... I thought that it would be courteous to try to explain to you why we have to do what we have to do. You do seem... well... normal. I had a hard time believing that you were the one that we'd been waiting for all this time. But you are, and now we must do what we must do."

She turned back to me. I saw tears in her eyes. I wished there was some way I could change what she had to go through, but there wasn't. No one can bring back a little girl's father.

"Can you just tell me one thing?" I just needed to know, before I resigned myself to inevitable death.

"I think I've wasted enough time already."

"Please, Leahonia. I just don't understand what the hell is up with this prophecy. What are you so afraid of?"

She looked at me and I met her gaze with my own. There had to be a reason one group of people thought I was the greatest thing since sample sales, and another group was convinced I was the greatest abomination since duct taped clothes.

"The prophecy. Didn't they tell you it all?"

"I was going through three different people. Those guys thought I was some kind of returning queen or goddess or something that I know for sure I'm not. I'm just me. I can't help anyone rise to greatness or whatever. What else is going on here?"

"I don't know how to translate it into English very well. Why do you want to know, anyway? It won't matter much.. ."

I suppose it wouldn't matter if they killed me. She had to know I'd try everything to stop that, though. Didn't she? "I don't need it verbatim. If I gotta die, I should at least know why. It's only fair. You said so yourself." And it buys me time to plan my next move. Maybe she won't think about

that.

She sighed, a weary sound. "I suppose you are right."

Cheer! I tried to focus on what she said, while I also tried to plan a way to escape the furious five. Too bad dying didn't open up the infinite knowledge of the universe. Or at least the infinite knowledge of Jackie Chan or Bruce Lee. Those guys would laugh off these odds and ask for another thirty goons.

"Thank you. This has all been shoved on me and I really have no clue what is going on. Or what it means. Do you know what it feels like to be the bystander and seeing your life being driven by forces way beyond your control?"

"I said I'd tell you."

Oh, now she's impatient? She didn't need to snap at me. Geez. Testy, testy.

And so, she started. I really wasn't ready for what she had to say, but she went all in.

"The prophecies are old. They come from the time I already told you about. No one was safe from the wars of the undead that raged. The beings were uncontrollable. Then one tribe claimed to have 'mastered' this so-called art. They knew how to raise someone without all the dire consequences of mindless murderous tendencies. You'd think this would be good, but it wasn't. The killing didn't stop.

"Those that were raised, they could think and reason. But still the hunger that set in... they couldn't fight it. We found their writings; it drove them near mad. They were men and women who were good and wanted to remain that way. Just as you claim to be. But they couldn't fight the hunger. At first, they didn't know what it was for. They tried everything. Once they gave in, they could not stop. Some tried to be kind, taking the old or infirm. It was a different time, there weren't many of the weak.

"And so, these beings became murderers just like their feral wild cousins from before. The only way to stop them was to dismember them. Some didn't want to be that way; they took their own lives. How noble of them, but a shame they couldn't have taken matters into their own hands before murdering so many innocent people in the name of the hunger. Those supposedly good few wrote of a time they foresaw. No one knew exactly how they came about receiving these prophecies. For a long time, they were probably just fantastical tales. How do you explain the things we have today to a people over a thousand years ago? A car? Telephones? Light bulbs? You can't. But the legends came down anyway. More a tale of caution so no one would try to embrace these dark arts again.

"Some think the legends are nothing more than tales their grandfathers told. That they don't mean anything other than people being scared of the night. Those people scoff. But then there's some of us who look at the world and we see the things we cannot understand... things from the stories.

"These stories are more than legends, so we vowed to watch and wait. And now here you are. You who was prophesied about. You who will change everything. I cannot begin to recite it word for word in English so you can understand. But the prophecy tells of one who will be risen. She will not be from our people, but from a gleaming country of gold. She will die in a great earthquake and a stranger to her and to the arts will raise her in Chichen Itza."

Okay, I had to give it to her. That sure sounded like me. Well, I didn't know about that country of gold thing, but wasn't that what everyone seemed to think about America? We were all rich and the streets were lined with gold? Yeah, well whatever they wanted to believe. We had our poor and our needy and if you knew where the gold paved streets were, let me know.

"This is nice to hear Leahonia, and I gotta admit, that sure sounds like me. But I see nothing that makes me out to be all scary."

"I wasn't done. You will unite the forces of those who have risen from death. Those who are like you. You will bring them from where they hide, scattered around the world. Banding together, you will usher in an age for your kind like no other. You will rule from the great mountains and peace will reign."

Humph. Peace sounded good. Ruling sounded like a nightmare. Don't get me wrong, I liked the idea of bossing people around. But, let's get real, leadership was nothing but a great big royal pain in the rump. Leaders didn't get credit for the good things they did and got blamed for all the crap that happened. No, thank you. The stress alone aged you. Wrinkles became no one. Especially me. I didn't need the headache.

"Maybe I'll abdicate. I don't wanna rule anything. All in all, though, is peace that bad? It doesn't seem that way to me. What's so wrong with peace?" I shrugged.

"It's not the peace, but the price it comes by. For you to

bring your people together, that is a threat to those of us who are living. Frankly, the thought that we haven't hunted you all to extinction is a threat to those of us who are living. Each one of you that survives means people who are dying to feed you."

"Just what is it I'm supposed to eat? Cause you make it sound like I'm now going to be some kind of cannibal. Gross. You aren't looking like a giant ham bone or donut. I told you, I'm no different than I was before I was alive." More circles.

"Your kind eats brains. And haven't we been over this already? The hunger will come."

I gagged; again. The thought was so far beyond disgusting that I didn't know how to get back. I suppose that was considered a delicacy in some places, but guess what? Not for me. I sure hoped it never became one.

"No, thank you. You can keep that to yourself. I'm not coming at your frontal lobe with a spork. Gross."

"What about when you are so wracked with hunger you cannot control it any longer?"

"If I get hungry, drive me to a McDonald's for a cheeseburger. That's my idea of living on the edge of cuisine." I liked good food. If I was going to eat anything disgusting it would come from the fast food joints that sold things that only halfway passed for food.

"I don't think it would satisfy the hunger." She didn't need to sound so sure of herself.

"Hey, I'm willing to give it a shot. I still want my Coach handbag back. I want to know what's going to come out from Ralph Lauren next year. If I can keep my fashion sense, I bet I can keep my taste for good food. Throw me a lobster, I bet I'll be fine."

I wasn't stupid. If I was going to ask for something to eat, I was going all in. I'd ask for the good stuff. I figured caviar was fairly hard to come by in these parts, and maybe even lobster. What's the worse that would happen? She'd say no and make me choose something else? Eh, fine. Best that would happen was I'd be served one very scrumptious lobster.

"Why should I 'give it a shot' as you say? If I'm right, it's our lives at risk. Why should I be so willing to sacrifice ourselves?"

I snorted. "I think you've got some pretty good odds. Five goons plus you against little-old me. And you have the home field advantage. I see this as a situation for you to do the right thing. Give me a chance to prove myself. Otherwise, you are really no better than what you claim me to be - a murderer."

I watched as she digested that. It was a low blow calling her a murderer. But she did the same to me. I hadn't harmed anyone. I didn't know about her. If she and her friends hunted "my kind", couldn't that be considered murder?

My head hurt. This was way too much deep thinking for me. I liked my life to be simple. Wake up, make myself gorgeous, go to work, hang out with friends. That's it. How had my life veered off into all this complicated mumbo jumbo?

Ah, the good old days. How I wished they were still here. Bring on the pool boys and the fruity drinks. Go away prophecies and scientific magic crap and people wanting to debate the philosophies of life.

"You make a point. I would be no better than you. But I don't think you are human anymore, so then it's not murder. You Americans hunt to maintain the animal population from growing out of control. We do the same."

Did she just call me an animal? First, I'm a murderer and now, I'm an animal? "Excuse me? Your people must think they are so great if you can be so judgmental. I am not an animal. You may focus on my differences, but I'm still human. No matter what you and your bigoted friends may think."

The time passed. I was done. I needed to find my way out of here and leave.

"You call us judgmental? Your kind consider us as lambs to the slaughter!" she retorted.

"You have no way to know what my kind or I think. Is there any more to your little prophecy, or have you just blown things way out of proportion? Maybe my so-called-people just want to be left alone by the likes of you."

I wanted to spit at her but controlled myself. Barely. The audacity. Next thing I knew, she'd try to justify enslavement. If there really was an 'us' to speak of. Since I hadn't run into any other un-dead people, let alone anyone jonesing for a good taste of cranium soup, I wasn't so ready to buy in to her far-out theories.

"You really aren't taking this seriously. If your kind tries to gather, there will be bloodshed."

"See, I don't like bloodshed, I'm more the free nuts and berries sort. So maybe that's the benefit of me leading the way. I'll do it with peace and harmony. "

It could happen. Growing pains to reach peace and harmony tend to ripple out, touching all. But, did that mean it would be blood running the walls and misery for all? I didn't think so.

"You say that now. Wait for the hunger. You'll change your mind."

"That's it!" I was done with her and her 'blah-blah wait for the hunger' junk. "Enough with the hunger. It's not bothering me now and I say we cross that bridge when we come to it. You need to not be so prejudiced. Maybe this so-called hunger you are worried about isn't so bad with me. Back off!"

Could she tell I was angry? I really did like peace and went out of my way to avoid outright conflict. Barbed words were one thing, but violence didn't do anyone any good. Even so, I felt an increasingly strong urge to punch her in the face. Break her nose to match her broken record of brain-eating garbage.

She looked at me in silence for a few minutes. If I was lucky, she was thinking twice about what I said and the fact I wasn't running through the countryside killing and maiming all I came in contact with.

I wasn't lucky, so she was probably considering what part of me to cut off first. Just where do you start when you make julienne fries out of another person? Are you kind and kill them first or do you make them suffer and start at the toes? I didn't particularly want to find out.

"You make a good argument, but I live with facts. You are what you are. At some point, you'll realize it, too."

"I'm doing just dandy, and you seem to think I should be off killing everyone. You think if I wanted people dead, I'd just be sitting here?" She looked like she wanted to say something, but I wouldn't let her. I plowed on. "And this prophecy... Come on. It's a prophecy. Do you really expect me to believe that something someone said so many years ago is really going to happen? Like Nostradamus? End of the world? Four horsemen? All that stuff? I find that ridiculous. What kind of a hold do people have over you that they can pony around some old wives' tale to get you to agree to go murder someone? Someone who's done absolutely nothing wrong? You seemed so kind yesterday, what changed?"

Okay, it was over. And by over, I meant over. There would be no more verbal ping pong. Either she'd tell me what the prophecy said that had her running scared or she'd move the events of our little meeting forward. I was stronger than them and had a pretty strong desire to live. No matter how you looked at it, there was a fight brewing and it was just a matter of when.

After a moment of my silence, she spoke. "You done?"

I just nodded and waited. My mad fighting skills were about-30 on a scale from one to ten. Didn't bode well for me versus Leahonia and the Five Thugs. I would have to count on sheer brute strength. Funny to think of me and 'sheer brute strength' in the same context.

"Don't mock us. The prophecy foretold of your rising from the dead. Shouldn't that be proof enough to you?"

"Seems to me you could have saved us all a lot of trouble by I don't know... preventing my death? Instead, you sat around twiddling your thumbs. I didn't ask for any of this, it just happened and if you knew it would happen and did absolutely nothing... then I say you deal with those consequences."

She could have ended this in ways that didn't involve me becoming worm food throughout the Mexican countryside.

"We couldn't do that. You can't mess with fate that way." Her voice grew shrill but her statement just made my argument easier.

"Wait. So, you gotta let the prophecy fulfill itself by letting me die and get brought back? Just to re-kill me so I don't like, take over the world or something? How does that even make sense? Either way you are making this prophecy null and void!"

A girl could get a migraine from that sort of thinking. Migraines only brought that little crease in your forehead between your eyes. Eh, who wanted that? No thank you.

At least it got her to stop and think. Maybe more about that than anything else I said today. I suppose at some point someone had to listen to reason. Or not.

"If it wasn't you, it would be someone. Better to let

events play out to be sure. Let's get on with things. I think I've been more than fair talking to you about why we have to do this."

Fair would be listening to reason and letting me go. Fair would be apologizing for not stopping me from croaking and helping me get at least partway home for the trouble you caused me.

"Nothing will change your mind? It's time for Whack-a-Bea?" I just had to be sure before I went tearing up my manicure and mussing my hair.

"I'm really sorry. If it makes you feel better, I think we could have been friends if things had been different."

She wanted to kill me...chop me up...scatter my remains! With friends like that... "You often kidnap and kill your friends? Must make for a lonely life."

The humor was lost on her. I gotta say, maybe if she took a lighter view on life we wouldn't be in this sort of predicament. Seems when you are a happy person you don't run around killing innocent earthquake victims.

I prepared myself. It all came down to this moment. Time almost slowed down for me. None of that life flashing before your eyes sort of thing. I'd already died once this week. I suppose that I didn't need to have that whole stereotypical thing going on.

Leahonia's gang of thugs didn't even flinch a collective muscle. They stood rock still, waiting for her orders. She came towards me, but she held no weapon. I couldn't guess her plan; I could only watch and wait.

Would the goon squad all jump to action and descend on me at once? Did the team of brutes hide knives in their pants? Would they turn on me like rabid dogs? Or would they attempt to be more humane and try to kill me before going about their gruesome task?

Leahonia stood right beside me, bent so her mouth was

at my ear. Her hot breath made me want to pull away, but instead I listened. "I really am sorry. They'll make it quick."

With that she walked away, her footfalls on the hard floor receding. Chicken. She could order my death and dismemberment, but she couldn't witness it?

The gaggle of goons looked at me as though they were a hive mind working together as one in five separate bodies. Hello, creepy? Damn, these cult-like people. They really were mindless sheep. If only I had some red Kool-Aid to ply them with.

Let them drink and then wait for them to drop. No, I'd have to rely on myself instead. Not really a concept I trusted enough to put a lot of faith into. With as little movement as possible, I prepared myself. With my hands tied behind me, there wasn't a lot to try, but my legs were mostly free. It wasn't much of a plan, but I could kick, scream, and bite. If these mindless fools were dumb enough to give me more leverage by cutting me loose, all the better. I might fight like a girl, but I would fight. Or run. Really, it didn't matter so long as I saved my skin.

I had some superhuman strength, and despite the extreme disadvantage I was currently at, I could still make something work. Five to one were not favorable odds, but hey... I had to try

As the first reached me, I went for the psych out stare down. Lucky me, I didn't need to blink like normal people. Yay for being not-quite-dead girl! I refused to turn away and he began blinking and couldn't stop. Blinkie got a little too close and I kicked him. Hard. I didn't get more than kneecap high, but kneecap was all it took to get him to back off. Super powered super kick resulted in a nasty crunching sound moments before Blinkie hit the floor. I flashed his buddies a friendly smile.

Dead Girl 1- Cult Brutes 0.

Juan of the Dead

I knew better than to let my attention stay on Blinkie. I ignored him as he clutched his knee. He wasn't totally out of commission, but less of a worry for the moment. Even stuck in a chair, I could probably get away faster than he could crawl after me.

His four buddies knew I wasn't totally on board with the whole "let's kill Bea" bandwagon and planned to fight to live. Sure, they had the advantage, but they were smart enough to realize that a caged animal can still cause some damage.

I was never very good at strategy games like chess. I stunk at guessing what someone else would do. My planning abilities were sorely lacking. I flexed my arms, hoping to see if I could bust through whatever they bound me with. It would be a phenomenal time to discover I could bust free like Superman in handcuffs.

I could bust a kneecap without breaking a sweat but forget the ties that bind. I was stuck with them, at least for now. That's fine, I'd keep with my kicking and biting plan until something better came up. They might win, but they would have to work for it.

The four finally encircled me. Keeping pace with one another, they approached me. Four brutes versus me. The angles would make it difficult for me to do a lot, but I would do what I could.

Muscles tensed again, I tried my best at a poker face. A flirty and cute poker face. All smiles and big innocent eyes. After all, I was sitting in a chair with my arms tied behind me. How much damage could I really do? I hoped that these impressions I wanted them to get would flow right out of me and to them. Sure, I hurt their buddy, but there's no way I would hurt them.

My right leg shot out and whacked another guy. It knocked him to the side and he fell into one of his buddies.

Boggs

As quick as my leg had gone out it was back under me and I hoisted myself up, chair and all. I heard the cry of a brute as I hit him with the chair leg.

I'm sure I looked quite the site, rather hunched with the chair on me. I was ready to rumble, as much as anyone could in such a situation. Lucky for me, the cavalry showed up.

Juan of the Dead

CHAPTER
TWENTY-TWO

Looking at the brutes, I weighed my options. Slim. None. Got anything for me? Nope? That's what I thought. I opened my mouth, not really sure what I was going to say, when the most horrible sound I'd ever heard came from outside.

Just in time, too. Could they have waited any longer? I think not. But hey, I wasn't chopped into little pieces and dumped into some kind of pit yet, so I was all good with them showing up. Anything to help me stay in the land of the living. Or I suppose that's really the land of the not-quite-living-but-still-intact.

I really needed to figure out what the heck to call myself. If I spent any more time fiddling around with my state of being, I would develop worry lines. I decided that as soon as I got out of this predicament, I'd figure that one out. A name for myself, not wrinkles.

The sound was more than a rumble. There was the distinct sound of metal rubbing against metal that set your teeth on edge. I didn't have time to guess what the sound was before the sound of gunfire started.

Leahonia's voice reached us from the far side of the warehouse. "Get out there and see what is going on!" Her barking tone made Hefty, Beefy, and Brutey hustle their buns.

Mmm, rather nice buns, too. Scratch that tThese are the dudes who want to kill me!

"Not some of yours then?" I let the acid drip from my words. I didn't really care who was out there so long as they took care of Leahonia and her band of crazies. If they wanted a piece of me, well they'd at least knock out some-one in the line. While they did that, maybe I could figure out how to get free and run. Run and not stop till I got out of this godforsaken country.

Who cared about passports anymore? I was willing to attempt to swim across the Rio. I just wanted to go home. And once I got there, I was never going to leave again. For-get this traveling crap. I just wanted to get back to normal.

Leahonia and I stood there, engaged in our own little stare off. It felt like that moment before the shootout at the O.K. Corral where the two cowboys' hands hovered over their pistols, just staring at one another. Daring the other to move. What was Leahonia thinking? Was she going to try to take care of me herself?

Maybe I could distract her with that whole catching more flies with honey thing. "It's not too late. Why don't we just get out of here. I'll go home and get back to my life. You can do whatever it is you do when you aren't harassing innocent tourists. Pick on small kids and stuff."

I might not be so good with the sweet. Ooops. My bad. Like she was going to buy it anyway? Right. I couldn't get that lucky. someone with good luck doesn't go on a cruise to Mexico, die, and get raised from the dead, right?

"I think not," she said. "Only one of us walks out of here."

"Well, I am sorry that you feel that way. I thought maybe we could be friends.

Exchange Christmas cards and all that. Sorry, you don't want to leave here." She could say only one of us was going to walk out, but I swore it would be me. I died once already. I didn't plan to do it again anytime soon, thank you very much.

"I'm leaving here. And so are you. But you are leaving in pieces."

"You and what army are going to stop me?" I snarked at her. "Cuz it seems to me as though your little army of brutes might be otherwise engaged. So, I thought I'd just high tail it outta here. You can stay and hang with them or you can let me by."

"Not a chance. I already told you. I'm not going to let you harm any innocent people."

"You never give up! I haven't hurt anyone. Maybe over there in Crazy Town you have people who are awful, but over here in Sanityville we don't roll that way."

"You really think that your life is sane?" Her condescending tone annoyed me. Maybe that was because coming back from the dead was a little insane to begin with, but we could wrestle that one out later- after I was away and safe and not risking my ability to walk and talk anymore.

"It's saner than yours. Don't you see how crazy it is to punish me for someone else's mistakes?"

While engaged in the hideous conversation with Leahonia, I inched my way towards the door- not the door the brutes headed out of, but another door I'd spied. Leahonia matched me step for hobble.

"I don't think that you would mean to. Maybe you were a nice person. But that's all changed now."

Who do I report Undead Discrimination to? I bet the Board of Tourism for Mexico wouldn't really care or do anything for me.

"Excuse me? I am a nice person." Okay, sometimes I was a nice person. Maybe I hadn't been at my best since the accident, but could you blame me? I died! That's enough to cause anyone to get a wee bit cranky.

"You say that now. But you are an abomination!" Her voice pierced my ears. I rubbed my ears with my finger. I tried to keep my voice calm when I replied. "What happened to two wrongs don't make a right?"

Leahonia didn't care. "It is forgivable to rid the world of the tools of the Devil. Someone's gotta do it."

"Really? Tools of the Devil? So, it better be you? Look, I am not a tool of anyone. I think you really need to get out more."

"Yes, you are his tool. You leave death and destruction in your wake. That furthers his plan, not the plan of God."

Egads. I hated religious zealots, even before all this went down. You just couldn't reason with them. I lived too close to the Bible Belt. Don't get me wrong. I felt like God and I were okay and all that, but I wasn't about to go around thumping on any Bibles. I'll leave that to the J Dubs and those cute guys on bikes.

I knew that she wasn't completely stupid, so she had to know what I was going for, but I still didn't look at the door for risk of giving myself away. With my peripheral vision I judged the distance to the doorknob and lunged, not sure how I'd open it while tied to the chair. I had to try something, this conversation was old, and like something from a bad horror movie. Who knew bad guys really carried on conversations like that?

I lunged a half second before her, but she was closer to the door than me when it flew open. Jon stood on the other side and I'd never been so glad to see a man before in my life. Jon looked fierce and I was glad he came ready to rumble. I ducked behind him as he leveled a pipe. I thought about sticking around to watch him deal a beating on Leahonia, but I just wasn't interested. More than ready to kiss this mess goodbye, my plan was to hoof it out of there while she was otherwise engaged.

I ran as best I could with the chair tied to me. Behind me, I heard Jon grunt and the sound of the pipe hitting what I could only imagine was Leahonia. I wasn't gonna look behind me to make sure. I was maybe only halfway down the hallway on the other side of my exit door, when I heard Jon calling my name.

"Bea, wait up!" Jon called out.

Wait up, my ass. No way. After I got out of here, I still had to get past the Brute Squad, and I wanted all the momentum I could get. He could just catch up.

If he couldn't keep up with one girl tied to a chair, then what kind of man was he, anyway? Okay, so I was an undead superhuman kinda girl with uber mad-dog fighting skills, but that was no excuse.

You know what they needed in Mexico? They needed their buildings to have proper electricity and an exit sign. I had no idea what the Spanish word for exit was, but all I needed was a large, glowing red sign. The hallway was pretty dim, but luckily, I had my new awesome night vision to help me see better.

I finally spied a door and I plowed into it. I probably could have used a doorknob, but that's totally too much effort when running for your life. Super strength deployed, and I busted the door right in two. Go me. It opened to stairs and I flew down them at a breakneck pace. Didn't really worry since I'd already broken my neck once this week and hey look, I survived it. Right?

"Bea!" He was huffing now and I could tell it cost him to cry my name. I looked up and saw he was coming down the stairs after me.

"Catch up, but I'm not stopping! That chick is psycho and so are her friends!" I tossed the words over my shoulder and didn't slow down my momentum. Chair hunchback helped gravity move me along. Reaching the bottom of the stairs I kicked at the next door and it also broke in two.

Super strength rocks my socks. I'm just saying. Lucky for me, I was now within a few feet of the door outta this hellhole. The door in front of me looked like it was made out of some sort of rusty metal. Deciding that might tax my new-found strength too much, I debated what to do which gave Jon time to catch up to me.

"Bea, she's down," he panted in an effort to get the words out. "I think you are okay. You can slow down."

I kicked the door, but nothing happened. "Yeah well, she might wake up or her goons might show up. I just wanna get out of here. And then I don't care. If I gotta get in a rowboat with some illegals, I'm outta this godforsaken hellhole of a country. I wish I'd never come here."

He looked a little sad. I tried to care, but in that moment I just wanted to wallow. I kept on. "All I wanted was a nice little vacation. A relaxing cruise. Is that too much to ask? Oh no, I am the person who goes to Mexico, gets killed, brought back from the dead, and then I have psycho freaks chasing after me wanting to hack me up and return me to the dead! I'm too young to die! This is just too much!"

"Bea, I'm so sorry," he said again for the zillionth. He was still panting, though not as hard. His eyes turned to the floor, I really thought he meant it. I bet he was sorry. I don't think he ever planned for my life to go down the toilet with one quick flush. It just happened.

I kicked the door again, though not as hard, in frustration. "Look, I get it. Whatever. I just want to get out of here."

I looked around. Where was I gonna go? Hell if I knew, but I chose a direction and stomped off. Yeah, I was displeased. Jon followed.

"Bea, we'll get you out. I brought backup. They're taking care of the goons. Don't you hear? It's gotten quiet."

So it had. I hadn't even noticed. No gunfire or anything.

"Um, yeah, you are right." I stopped and looked at Jon. I didn't want to let the meaning sink in. If I did, well I don't know what would happen. I'd grown up in Virginia. I lived a peaceful life. I hadn't even run over a squirrel. Okay, well there was that one time the possum ran out into the middle of the road, but it crawled away. Suddenly, I wasn't so sure I wanted to go outside. What would I see? I shuddered.

"We'll take you back. We'll find a way to get you home. I promise. I'm so sorry."

He sounded so earnest- and that's when I felt the tear. One led to another and then another. Jon shifted his weight on his feet and just looked at me. I tried, but I just couldn't hold it in anymore. The tears came and the next thing I knew I was sobbing.

"I don't know how..." They were the last words I could even say before I was crying so hard I could no longer speak.

Jon moved forward, "Let me cut you free from this chair." Ever the boy scout, he pulled a pocketknife from his pocket and freed me from the chair while I continued to sob. After the chair clattered to the floor, he drew me into him, and I cried relentlessly on his shoulder.

When the tears stopped, I looked up at him. Our eyes

met and first one hand and then the other cupped my face. His thumbs wiped the moisture from my cheeks. I don't re-member what happened next, except that we were kissing with increasing passion.

At last we broke apart and he took one of my hands in his. "This way. I'll get you out of here."

I was more than happy to let him come to my rescue again.

CHAPTER
TWENTY-THREE

I followed Jon from the warehouse of doom, thankful I could do so fully upright. Hey, you try running for any length of time while strapped to a chair and you'll debate burning all chairs, too. I was going to thank my new status as not-so-alive for the fact I could even accomplish escape at all while tied to that thing.

Lucky for us, no brute squad lay in wait on this side of the warehouse. They must have all been focused on wherever the ruckus came from. Glancing behind me, I saw the warehouse sat on a hill just steep enough that we came out of a partially subterranean floor- that explained the stairs and hallways.

Jon ran for the end of the building and around the corner. I followed suit. Sometime during our escape from Leahonia, the gunfire had ceased, and I hoped that meant good things for the Pro Bea team. He slowed to a stop as we reached the next corner. I tried not to plow into him in my haste.

"What are we--" I tried to ask but he put up a silencing hand. A hand? Really?

"Just checking to make sure everything was taken care of. I wouldn't want to startle anyone," he explained.

Good point.

I could forgive the hand. Swiss cheese Bea didn't sound any more preferable than sliced and diced Bea. I could wait for him to finish peering around the corner if it meant no one shot at me.

"Who are you here with and-" Again the hand.

"There will be time for that. Later. Let's just get out of here."

I was more than down with the 'get out of here' plan. Taking out a few of the anti-Bea crowd along the way wasn't going to make me lose any sleep. Then again, I supposed it helped that I wasn't sleeping any more, but still. I was always so popular; how could someone want me dead now? Worse, dead and in pieces?

He motioned me forward as he took a few tentative steps around the side of the building. I still didn't hear anything, which gave me hope for a clean escape. After the first few steps, when nothing happened, he picked up the pace. Trotting to keep up, I saw a beat-up truck in front of us.

We reached the dusty vehicle and he boosted me into the back before scrambling in beside me.

"Lay down and let's hope if Leahonia has any people left, they didn't see us."

"And what is this going to get us?" I asked, annoyed and tired of this circus. If her people didn't see us, how would the people that came with Jon know we were there? I was all for keeping a low profile, but I was more for getting the hell out of dodge.

"We wait. This was the plan," Jon said. I stared at him.

" Hide in a truck? Some plan. I'd rather take off and get out of here. Like now."

Who wouldn't?

"We'll leave shortly. Just...be quiet!" I gave him points for exclaiming while keeping his voice low. That's a talent.

As it happened, that was also when I heard the sound of footsteps. Not a lot of footsteps, one set, and it came our way. I bit my lip but followed Jon's advice to remain quiet. I felt my body tense and went with it. I knew it was my own fight or flight instincts kicking in and I'm not too proud to admit that flight sounded pretty darn good when faced with fighting someone wanting a duel to the death.

"I saw you come this way, Bea. Just give in. It's time to call it a day."

Oh, hell. It was Leahonia and she sounded pissed. Maybe from the headache I'm sure that Jon left her with? Served her right.

My head instinctively turned towards her voice and I spied a metal rod laying in the bed of the truck beside me. I slowly reached over and grasped it in my hand as I listened to Leahonia.

"It's better this way, Bea. Think of your family. Think of your friends. They don't need to see you when things get bad."

Sadly, new life-status changes did not come with cool x-ray vision, so I couldn't tell where she was. Did she know we werein the bed of this beater truck? No way we could get the drop on her, and as far as I knew, whomever Jon came with remained occupied elsewhere.

This time, I wasn't going to let Leahonia get the drop on me. No way did I want a replay of chair-restraint or any chance for her to prattle on any more about her duty to rid the world of me. A girl could only take so much, and I was through. Dying could make a girl cranky.

"I know you think you can get away. You are only delay-ing the inevitable. Even if you think things are okay now, how are you going to deal with it when everyone you care about turns against you? Do you really want to see your family coming after you to do this?"

As if.

My family would take me as I am. Always had. Always will. That's why families rocked. Didn't Leahonia get that memo? What were they teaching her in the hellhole she called home? I clamped my mouth shut, not wanting a re-ply to give away our location.

The tone of her voice went up, maybe she was reaching that frantic point that all evil bad guys in movies reached. You know, the one right before the hero swooped in for the take down, like with a handy dandy metal bar?

"You might as well come out. We can do this with honor. Isn't that the legacy you want to leave on this earth? You aren't going to escape. My people are currently finishing off the last of the rag tag band of misfits that came to try to save you. Poor misguided miscreants."

Did she say misguided miscreants? Who talks like that? The crazier she got, the more her English seemed to im-prove. It was time to deal with this, but was she close enough?

"Oh, Bea. You know, I didn't peg you for such a coward. Vain and lazy? Well, that was evident fairly quickly. But this cowardice? Aren't Americans supposed to be better than all this?"

Her voice definitely sounded closer. I just hoped she was close enough that I wouldn't lose my element of surprise.

That might have been my last coherent thought as I leapt from the bed of the truck waving the metal pipe and shrieking. I really don't remember much else other than leaping from the back of that truck like a crazed action movie star and bearing down on Leahonia.

I must have blacked out. Could stress make you pull a blacked out beat down on someone? Maybe. If by blacked out, you mean all I saw was the red of my anger and a giant bulls-eye target on Leahonia, then yes.

Coming out of my haze of anger, I heard Jon's voice. Like it was really far away or in a tunnel. Why was his voice all weird sounding?

Things came into focus around me, sound returned, and I peered up at Jon with blinking eyes. When had the sound gone away from the world? And what was he saying? I blinked a few more times, and he repeated what he said. I shook my head, it felt full of cobwebs. I still didn't understand what he was saying.

"Bea. Bea. Put down the crowbar."

Crowbar? What's a crowbar? Oh. He must mean this metal rod thing. Really? That's what a crowbar looks like? I looked at the metal in my hand, slick with blood. "Ewwwwwww!"

The shriek as I dropped the offensive bit of metal probably wasn't the bravest or coolest thing to do in such a situation. I'm also pretty sure the scrabbling across the grass to distance myself from it wasn't really attractive.

When I saw that the crowbar fell onto the prone and bloodied body of Leahonia, I shrieked again.

"Bea. Bea. I need you to calm down." Jon took a few steps towards me. I screamed again.

"Bea..."

I managed to gasp for some air before yelling an answer back at him. "Calm? Calm! What? What? How? But..."

I might not quite be put together yet. Can you blame me?

I might make a killing at the salvage sales, but that's all

figurative. I wouldn't literally harm anyone, not like what the prone body of Leahonia evidenced. Hell, I dodged out of the way of suicidal squirrels when driving. Pesky rodents should not try to throw themselves onto a moving car, but they couldn't help it if their brain was the size of a lima bean. I pointed at Leahonia's body.

"Is? What? She? Jon!"

He took a few more steps toward me and knelt down. "It's okay. Bea, it's okay. You really just need to calm down and then..."

"But...I... I... did I?" The rush in my head and the panic in my chest was very slowly abating as I looked into Jon's eyes. I tried to focus on him and not the prone body of Leahonia.

"Bea, it's Okay. Shhh. I don't think she'll be a problem but let me look at you."

Look at me? What?

We needed to get out of here. It looked like I just killed Leahonia and there were wacky people wanting to kill me and I really just hated Mexico. What did Jon want to do? Apparently get frisky. I glared at the hand that he reached towards my chest.

"But, Jon! We-"

"Stop!" The forceful tone of his voice made me snap my mouth shut. "Let me see what she did to you!"

What she did to me? I looked down and saw his hand wasn't actually reaching towards my chest. It was reaching towards...That's when I passed out.

Juan of the Dead

CHAPTER
TWENTY-FOUR

I came to lying on the ground, a shirt pillowing my head. I cracked open my eyes and saw Jon sitting beside me.

"What happened?" I groaned.

"You fainted," Jon said.

No, duh.

"Yeah, but what happened?" I repeated.

"I couldn't find any evidence that the bullet-"

Bullet? The memory flooded my mind of a gaping hole in my chest near my right shoulder, making me woozy. Leahonia actually shot me. I felt faint again.

"Where is that b-"

Jon put his hand out to stop me as I tried to sit up. "Just stay down for a while. I think you've been through enough.."

I batted his hand away and managed to scoot myself into a seated position. Putting any weight on my right arm sent a raging fire storming through to my chest.

"Augh."

"Yeah," Jon started. "Like I said. We didn't find any sign of the bullet but..."

"Getting shot sucks? Yeah I'm getting that." I winced and my left hand reached towards that right shoulder. "What the hell am I supposed to do about this?"

I looked down and while I saw the tattered hole in my shirt, I didn't see any evidence of a wound. I looked back up and met Jon's eyes as he shrugged. "Yeah, it healed. I don't have an explanation."

I sure didn't have an explanation, but speed healing could come in handy. Totally didn't want the need of it, but sometimes you ran into psychos in Mexico thinking they needed Swiss Cheese Bea. Too bad the nifty ability didn't super heal my clothes. My blouse was ruined by a bullet hole. Nice.

Then I remembered what else happened and I chewed on a nail. My manicure was toast already so what did it matter? All I could think about was how I apparently killed Leahonia, brutally. Would I end up in Mexican prison for that? Would they sentence me to die? Again? Could they sentence me to die again?

The thoughts raced through my head, but all I wanted to do was burst into tears. Truly, this was the worst vacation in the history of bad vacations. What more could go wrong?

"Uh, Bea?" The voice sounded tentative and I looked up, blinking. John slowly reached his hand to remove my hand from my mouth. "You might want to stop..."

Again, I batted his hand away and the words exploded from my mouth. "What? You think sometimes a girl can't freak out? We can't be perfect all the time! So what? I bite my nails? Okay, sometimes I do that. Sometimes I also burp or wear sweats or..."

I noticed he was staring, not at my face but at my hands. I looked down and saw them speckled with blood and gore. Except where I'd been chewing on my nails.

"Bea, you weren't chewing on your nails..."

Except where I'd been licking my fingertips. They were clean. I hadn't even noticed, which should probably have freaked me out more, but instead I just stared at my hands. I turned my right hand over to look at the palm, filthy from ravaging Leahonia.

I don't know what came over me next. Instead of trying to find some way to clean it off, begging for water or a bathroom or a real honest to goodness working shower with heat, I took that hand and licked it. The blood was dry, and whatever the rest of the matter stuck to my hands as well, but I didn't care.

I also didn't care that Jon looked on, horrified as my taste buds reveled in the act of cleaning the gore from my hands. Under my ragged fingernails my tongue found the tiniest shreds of what I can only imagine consisted of Leahonia's flesh. Never had anything tasted so good that should taste so wrong.

Standing, I lifted my eyes to greet Jon's as he stood frozen in place. Behind him, I saw those men that came to my rescue, the people that helped to save me from Leahonia and her henchmen. All stood still, looking at me. Were they afraid? Disgusted? Did they think maybe Leahonia, in the end, was correct about my nature?

A man standing about ten feet behind Jon spoke first, his voice quite calm given the nature of his words. "We have saved for you the heart of your foe."

I looked over Jon's shoulder at the man offering me the heart of Leahonia. My enemy's heart. I know what you are thinking- I'm a sane girl and would obviously avoid such brutality. Decent people just didn't go around eating people's hearts.

Well some did, I guess. There was that Dahmer guy. And the Donner party probably ate the hearts of people when they went all cannibal-like on the trek west. So maybe it was an American thing and no one wanted to admit it.

Of course, this man didn't actually say anything about eating the heart either. Maybe he meant for me to take it as a trophy. I suppose a normal person might consider stuffing the heart or bronzing it. Mounting it on the wall like the head of a deer in some creepy act of pride. None of this mattered, my brain just went straight to eating. Or maybe it was my stomach?

That's when I first noticed the hunger. Maybe I hadn't wanted to eat before now, but hearing about the heart changed that. I suddenly felt very ravenous and nothing sounded tastier than a heart. Even a heart that was cold from death instead of warm and still pumping its final beats.

I stood, quick as the blink of an eye, and pushed past Jon. Sure enough, there stood the man barely taller than myself proffering me the heart. It looked so weak in his hands, and I found it hard to believe that not long ago it beat inside the chest of a human just as healthy as anyone could want. I didn't even think about the fact that the very heart I stared at while licking my lips stopped beating because of something I did. Justified self-defense or not.

Instead I licked my lips again and like a feral beast, I snatched that heart from his hands. I raised it to my mouth and bit into it. Blood trickled down the back of my throat as I chewed on the heart, devouring the organ like anyone else would down a Big Mac.

When it was gone, I again licked my fingers without a care of just how messy or classless that would appear to those standing around me. I ran my tongue over my teeth and my lips, sucking at anything that might remain there from my sloppy eating.

That's when I noticed the faces of everyone standing around me. I suppose that it wasn't every day you saw a woman down an entire human heart raw. Or treat the odd meal as though it were truly finger lickin' good. I turned to look at Jon and felt my face flush for the first real time since he'd worked his voodoo trickery on me after the earth-quake.

"Jon?" I didn't know what to say, the look of horror on his face scared me.

"Bea, I... you... I..." As he stammered, I wondered if I'd lost the only friend I had after everything went all toes up for me. I realized how much that hurt me, and I hoped that he would forget what he just witnessed.

"I'm so... I don't know..." I felt so different all of a sudden, different than I'd ever felt in my life. "I didn't plan for that... I didn't know... Jon? Are you..."

He looked at me, and hesitantly stepped backwards, away from me. Was he afraid of me? Afraid I might do the same thing to him I did to Leahonia?

Oh God, would I if given the chance?

"Bea, I... you... ate... that..."

I hung my head, both confused and ashamed. As the minutes went by, whatever possessed me to eat the heart passed away and I felt more human and horrified at my own behavior. What kind of person just ate a raw heart like that? Maybe I really didn't qualify as a person anymore.

My voice quiet, I looked at Jon hoping he could see the pleading for understanding in my eyes. "I don't know what came over me."

No quips, no edgy wit, just a simple statement of fact. Would he believe it? More importantly, would he accept it? If I were fully alive, this would be where I held my breath in anticipation and fear. Instead, I bit my lip, a nervous habit I hated almost as much as I hated what I'd just done.

I hated it, but it felt just as natural as biting my lip.

"I think I made-" Jon began, but I wouldn't know what he planned to finish that statement with because the man that offered me the heart interrupted and I was just too much of a chicken to ever go back and ask.

"She only did what was natural for her." The man stepped between Jon and me and stated the thing that I felt deep within me about eating the heart. "It is her nature, which is why these people wanted to bring her harm."

His words sounded so formal; I didn't need the accent to tell me that he learned English from a book as opposed to actually speaking it with any sort of regularity. I listened as he continued. "But she is different than what they think. They do not know the true meaning of the prophecies. She's to bring in a new age, and she's to change the fear people have of her kind."

I felt the bristle of anger return, a little more of the usual me. "Excuse me? My kind?" My fists clinched with my words.

"Those like you. I do not know if there are any now, but there have been ages where your kind have walked this earth. Times where your people terrorized those that lived. Your rising changes that. No more shall people need to fear what they do not understand."

"So, what, you think people 'like me' are scary? But I'm not? What are you saying about me?" I could be pretty scary when I wanted, just get between me and a purse sale at the Coach outlet.

"Your people fight with a ruthlessness like no other. The legends speak of massacres at the hands of..."

Jon cut the man off. "So, the legends that we've heard? The walking dead? True?"

The man nodded but I didn't give him a chance to continue.

"You are saying I'm what? The walking dead? But while there's others that are ruthless, I'm not?"

I've definitely acted anything but ruthless since Jon's abracadaba moment back in the Creepazoid Temple of Gross, but why would I be different? And did this man know what I was? Did I dare ask?

"Yes. The prophecies speak of you as a great leader and of bringing peace. We do not know why, it does not say. Only that you will prove different and that you will ensure that the massacres of before never happen again."

"Massacres? But who would be doing this? Wouldn't this be like on the news or whatever? Come on, an army of undead?" This wasn't a zombie movie or anything. "This is real life and that sort of thing doesn't happen in real life."

Then again, babes like me don't die in earthquakes in Mexico and wake up dead in a temple in real life either. I suppose there was a first for everything. Or maybe not a first.

"Let us return to my camp. We can better answer your questions there. The stories are many, the prophecies unclear to those who have not studied them fully."

Oh yeah, the camp that Leahonia and her gang kidnapped me from. Maybe returning was not such a bad idea. At least I could get more comfortable and be away from dead bodies.

"What about Lea-" I began to ask but the man waved his hand to disregard the question. Some hand signs transcend nations.

"Things will be cleaned up here. Let us return."

CHAPTER
TWENTY-FIVE

The trip back to the camp was bumpy, but uneventful outside of a few furtive glances my way from some of those riding in the back of the truck with me. They talked a good game about thinking that I was oh so 'different' or what-ever, but seeing a girl eat a raw human heart had to cause doubts to creep into the mind. I knew I would sure be questioning my sanity for getting in the back of a beat up old pickup truck with a girl that just ate a raw human heart in front of me.

I gave them props for only giving me a few odd glances when they thought I wasn't looking. Anyone else might have done far worse, like jump screaming from the back of the truck or plot my demise like the deceased Leahonia.

I wasn't usually the violent type, so I found it hard to be-lieve that I had so brutally attacked her. I know she attacked me first, planned to re-kill me, and then she actually shot me. That didn't matter, it just seemed wrong that I somehow killed her, and so brutally at that.

If only I knew what had come over me to make me so bloodthirsty. Maybe that was where the aforementioned legends came from. I did know that it sure sounded like Leahonia knew the same legends of terror from whatever "my kind" turned out to be, and it wasn't pretty. Could I escape from that nature? Could I change who people thought I was just because of my status in the living vs dead world? There were plenty of television drama series about just that sort of thing. How many times has the "vampire with a soul" trope played out in America? Exactly. Maybe I could be what I was with a soul.

It could happen.

I didn't want to be bloodthirsty or violent. I definitely didn't want to be part of some perv's weird and creepy undead army. Which made me think: I'd heard from two different sources now about undead army hoards. Who would use the undead as soldiers and why? More importantly, why was none of this mentioned in history lessons?

The whole thing sounded like a bad horror movie you found on cable on a Saturday night. The shady government finds a way to turn soldiers into zombies and unleashes them on the world to obtain supreme world domination. It didn't sound like anything that would actually happen.

Of course, in those movies things would backfire, the zombies would kill their leaders, and suddenly you had the zombie apocalypse going on and people would hole up in the bars and the malls hoping for salvation that would never come.

Thinking about bad zombie horror movies made me wonder something new, something I was afraid to ask. Would Leahonia rise again? Like the victim of a zombie or a vampire? Would she now be undead, the thing she hated most?

A part of me thought that would serve her right. Another part feared that it might be true. I wouldn't want this whole confusing thing to be on anyone else. More than that, I didn't want that to be Leahonia. That woman had some major issues and adding this whole undead thing would probably just make the situation worse.

I decided not to think about Leahonia. After all, what good would that do? The woman was out of my hair for now and I couldn't be happier. She was like a bad case of head lice. Instead I focused on what would happen next.

We drove down the bumpy roads of the middle of nowhere and I thought about what my so-called 'saviors' offered. They didn't really want to let me go, instead wanting to cart me off to South America. What was I going to do in the middle of nowhere South America? Then again, what was I really doing in the middle of nowhere here?

Did these people not understand my intense desire to just go off and be myself, return home, and forget this nightmare of a vacation ever existed? I saw nothing wrong with this plan, and it sure beat whatever expectations they had of me as some 'chosen one'.

Was I curious about the 'other prophecies' they mentioned about me? Okay, I'll admit- I was. Who wouldn't be a little interested to find out what people thought of their future? I still felt a little miffed that no one warned me that my life was going to go all wacky. Even if I couldn't prevent all of this insanity, at least with a little warning I could ensure that I would still have identification. And my Amex.

When we arrived at the secluded camp, I planned to lay down the law. I really didn't want to go live on a mountain top somewhere in South America, even if it meant having adoring fans waiting on me. I really wasn't equipped to live without my gourmet drinks, air conditioning, and Keeping Up with the Kardashians. Too bad I had no idea how to really get that across to these people, even if they had saved my life twice now.

The truck pulled up to the camp and my new buddies hopped out of the back of the truck without even a backward glance in my direction. Nice. Chivalry was truly dead if the chosen one couldn't even get a helping hand out of the back of a truck. Maybe I should ask for a better ride.

I held onto the side of the truck while I lowered myself to the ground with far less grace than I would want to admit to anyone. Face it, there's no way to look good getting out of the back of a beat up pick-up truck in the middle of nowhere. Glad I wasn't going out for Miss America or anything.

Jon exited the cab of the truck and met me just as my feet landed on the ground. Impeccable timing. I wiped my hands on my thighs as he watched in silence. I'm guessing that meant that he was still all weirded out from watching me eat.

Nothing I could do about that. At least I wasn't hungry, and I hoped that meant that there would be no more freaking people out with odd cravings. The bonus meant I wouldn't gross myself out with my odd cravings, either.

In silence we followed the group to the main tent from before. Entering, I looked around but saw that no one was passed out or dead, so I had hopes for their wellbeing. Frick and Frack might have totally failed as bodyguards, but that was hardly their fault. I couldn't blame them for Leahonia slipping them a mickey. Who would have suspected that?

The Head Honcho Duo were also totally missing in action. As was Anna-Lucia. Were they okay? Thank goodness at least one member of the cavalry that rode in to the rescue spoke English. There was something to be said for that, especially if Anna- Lucia was still down for the count. I'm not so sure I trusted Jon's Spanish, especially with his attitude.

"Please, have a seat. I will go and check on our leaders and let them know you have returned." With that, my English-speaking friend ducked out of the tent.

What better choice did I have but to acquiesce? I found the same seat I used before and sank to the floor. I gotta say, if you're going to hang in a tent city, these floor pillows were totally the way to go. If I were the type to get sleepy, I could absolutely see myself curling up on one of these and taking a nap.

That made me wonder, I had recently eaten. Surprise, surprise. Would that mean sleep was in my future once more? The nights got awful long and boring when you didn't sleep and there was no eight hundred channels of television to scroll through.

CHAPTER TWENTY-SIX

We weren't alone for long in the tent, but it was long enough that the silence began to feel uncomfortable. I could feel Jon's eyes on me, even after I turned away, unable to bear his stare. What did he think of me? Who was I fooling anyway? It's not like I expected him to let me hang around him for the rest of time. Nor did I want to. I had a life to get back to. It is what I kept arguing for, a return to my life in Virginia and to all things normal.

I realized that return might never happen, or if it did, it would likely come at a heavy personal cost. Was I ready for that cost? More importantly, was I ready to lose Jon? It was ridiculous that I cared this much for the man I barely knew. Yet his kindness touched me. The sheer magnitude of what he did for me, raising me from the dead, nagged at me. I knew I could never truly be free of him.

I tried not to think about Jon, choosing instead to focus on who came into the tent. It looked like the Head Honcho duo, but no one else that I actively recognized. What happened to Frick and Frack? And what about Anna-Lucia?

It turned out the answers did come. Everyone settled into places, much as before. My new English-speaking friend took the place of Anna-Lucia and turned to look at me.

"Anna-Lucia is very ill. There are people tending to her, however Don and Paulo are resting. They will return to your side soon, but we are hopeful the current threat is over, and you will be safe without their presence until they may return once more to your side."

Really? People speak like this? Only if you were this guy.

Jon looked at the man seated before us. "And what next? It seemed there was some unresolved business before Bea was kidnapped."

"That is what we are here to determine. Our leaders would like to speak with you about that very matter."

One of the men began speaking and our new interpreter turned away to converse in that strange foreign language. I bit my tongue, an attempt at patience.

"The leaders state we will move out in the morning. They do not want to stay here with the camp compromised. We will be returning to..."

"Wait just a minute. I don't know that I want to go with you. Don't get me wrong, I'm thankful that you came rolling in to save the day, but I still want to get back to my own life in America." I really needed to put a halt to any ideas of spiriting me further away from a solution to get back to Virginia.

"Bea, maybe you should hear them out." Jon's voice came out soft, and I sighed.

"Jon, I know you like the idea of running off to the middle of nowhere, away from all things civilized. It's just not my scene. I really don't want to follow them to I don't know where."

"I'm just saying, they think they have ideas that might tell us more about you."

"Look, I know enough about me. I'm me and I am from Virginia and I've had just about enough of all this. This is definitely not the sort of life that I'm cut out for. I just want to be back in the city and blend in with everyone else."

Imagine that. Me, blend in. Who knew that being normal was something I'd desire to be at any point in my life? I had a few friends back home that would laugh at the very idea.

"Bea, I get that. But I still think we need to learn more about, well...about you. Now more than ever."

I glared at Jon. "What does that mean? Now more than ever? What are you trying to say?"

He looked down and I swear he shrank from me. Shrank from me! Probably not a bad idea with the way I was feeling over his comment.

"Well, I just meant, since you know..." he muttered.

"What, Jon? Since I killed someone for shooting me? Self-defense. It's called self-defense. Or what is it, are you afraid because I ate something? You know, I haven't eaten in how many days?"

Who cared that I hadn't been hungry at all until the moment I saw that heart? Who cared that it was a raw dead human heart? Maybe he should just be glad I wasn't looking at him like he was my next meal.

"Well, yes, and you know, other things. We know you're strong and fast. We know you can heal. But will that continue on? Will you have to..." He paused to lick his lips and his voice dropped. "Eat something like that again or will other food suffice?"

"Something else? Like what? Can you take me through the nearest drive through for a hamburger and a milkshake? Who cares? I can figure that out at home just as well as following these guys. I don't care what Leahonia said about these things. I am who I am, and this is not who I am."

I waved at the large tent we sat in. "Don't get me wrong, this is lovely, I've never seen anything like it. But this smacks of camping a little too much and that's just not my scene. Call me when you get proper accommodations. I'll think about joining you then. Maybe."

"Bea, I think you need to hear them out..." Jon glanced at the men before us, who seemed more than willing to let me talk myself out.

"And what? They already said they want me to go back to wherever they are from. But I don't really want to go off to hide in the middle of nowhere. I think the threat is over. Leahonia is gone, I shouldn't have to worry."

Our new translator cleared his throat. Jon and I turned to look at him.

"I do not know that I would be so willing to assume the threat to your life is over. There are more that know the prophecies. There's a long history of your..."

I cut him off. I may not be super academic, and I will even admit to skating by most of my classes in college. Okay, so those classes included history, but I think I would remember if someone said there were hordes of undead ravaging the North and South American countryside. That's just not something you forgot about.

"A history of what? Leahonia already tried that spiel on me and I'm just not buying it. You cannot convince me that raising people from the dead is all that common, especially to use in armies. People would talk about it. Heck, if nothing else, vampires and zombies wouldn't be so popular in the world today. I get that you mean well, but I really am not buying it."

How many times did I have to tell them? Then again, I was still taking my own trip down the great river known as De Nile.

"People do not like what they cannot understand. And not all people employed this method of warfare. It is possible that it was not known or has been purposefully forgotten. Things can get unpleasant and people would rather avoid that which is unpleasant."

He had a point there. How many unpleasant things had I tried to block out of my mind? How about giant calendars falling on my head and killing me? I'd like to have forgotten about that. However, I could believe what he was saying. People tended to rewrite their own history to something that they fancied more; it wasn't so inconceivable that people could have rewritten the history that would involve slobbering zombies killing zillions, leaving legends to build a mythos in the modern age. Tall tales, as it were. No wait, I was starting to come around to all this nonsense.

"You claim it happened here in the Americas in primitive times, at least that's what it sounded like from what I've heard, but it sure doesn't sound modern in any way. So, I don't see how I could be in any danger or how I could be chosen to lead anything. Give me one good reason to believe you."

"I am not a scholar of other cultures, but we are not the only ones to believe this is possible. And given some of the history that I've read, I do believe it is possible that other areas employed the use of the undead as was done here. I believe you can think of times that could fall into that realm yourself if you tried hard enough."

"I don't know about that. War is brutal. People die. It's what happens. Like in the Civil War, that was just so bad. Hundreds of thousands or whatever were killed, and all over slavery. But I don't think anyone was raising the dead or anything."

"Maybe, maybe not. You'd have to take another look at the battles yourself and make that determination. It's not for us to know. The Elders told me that they thought something happened in Italy..."

Italy?

Who would've thought that something like what Leahonia described might have happened in Europe? There were swaths of mass death like in the Black Plague, but that was disease, not the monsters that go bump in the night. And there were wars, but I didn't think anything remotely resembled the descriptions I'd heard.

Jon answered the translator differently, though. "You know, I think there's something there. It was not long after the Spanish Inquisition finally drew to a close-"

"Wait, the Spanish Inquisition? What?" My knowledge of the Spanish Inquisition was not much past comedies from Europe. I knew it happened, it was bad, but I don't remember massive death and mayhem. Of course, I wasn't one to pay attention to history either.

"Well, the Spanish Inquisition was coming to a close in the early part of the 1800's. But it was so long and terrible and some thought it might never end. Yet it did, suddenly. The Roman Catholic Church went through all but a Holy War to try to bring things to an end. Then they had the truth brushed aside for the history books."

"What happened?" Maybe I shouldn't admit to it, but I was intrigued.

"The short story that most people get is that after several hundred years of Spanish terror and religious persecution, the Inquisition ended. Mostly attributed to the French Revolution, which was concurrent, and many stop with that simple answer. But there were some things going across Europe at the time."

"Like what?"

"Well, England fought a losing war in the Americas, bounced back from that to fight with France, some of which did take place in America. Many think that the fighting on the two fronts really caused a lot of failure in England. However, there were signs that they also had ties to what was happening in Spain at the time. Religion played a huge role in the affairs of state at that time, especially in England and Spain."

"Yeah, isn't that why we have the whole separation of church and state in America? People were all fed up with being told who and what to believe so they came to America to hide from it all?"

That's basically what we learned in school, right?

Jon sighed. "Good enough for our purposes at least. The troops that fled from the Americas back to England to help with things there, they brought back things learned in the Americas from the Natives, among other things. England and Spain had ties through their monarchy from time to time- which created uneasy treaties. It is possible if the Native Americans still remembered how to raise the dead, they somehow spread this knowledge to the British who could then take it back to England."

"Okay, but like, we treated the Indians so terribly. If they had that power, why would they not use it to stop the way they were treated? And if the British learned how to do that, it seems to me a great way they could have quickly put an end to the American Revolution. Our troops weren't doing too hot and didn't we only barely win the war?"

"I suppose how you look at it, that is true. Our troops definitely suffered at the hands of the British, but in the end we won. I don't know why the British wouldn't employ the use of such a military measure, unless they were just too concerned about the ceremony. Especially given the beliefs at the time, it would come off as witchcraft and people were burned at the stake for that."

"Hmmm, well I guess you are right. But if they were afraid of the knowledge they learned, why would they share it once they returned home?"

Jon shrugged. "Dunno. Unless maybe they just told the stories. Or maybe someone was too afraid of losing yet another war. The loss of the New World was a bit of a morale hit in England. With the wars that followed in Europe, I could see some people trying desperate things to ensure there would not be another defeat."

Juan of the Dead

CHAPTER TWENTY-SEVEN

We discussed more about the possibility of Europeans using undead warriors.

And by we, Jon and our friendly neighborhood lost civilization types. Me? Not so much. What did I know about the French and the Spanish and the Italians? Let's see, good clothes, hunky men, and sexy shoes.

"There was just so much unrest with the French and the Spanish, but the Roman Catholics didn't like what was going on and they wanted to put an end to it. There was quite the terror at that point as well as bad feelings towards the Church as a whole.

And it would make sense for them to maybe try something that would be a little under the radar. There had been so many rumors of corruption and wrongdoing by that point."

I glanced up from picking at my fingernails. "What, like they have always had problems? I thought maybe it was just now."

Jon looked at me. Maybe he was surprised that I had even been paying attention. Really, I was as well.

"The Church has a long and sordid history. Men are fallible and it just boils down to corruption, plain and simple. For so many centuries, they were the only authority that superseded all else. That sort of power can lead to people making all sorts of bad choices in efforts to maintain control."

"I guess. But why do you believe that they would know anything, let alone would have possibly taken part in something of this magnitude? They are a church and at the end of the day aren't they supposed to espouse things that are good? This seems like it might be, I don't know, not so good? Raising the dead? Wasn't that really just a Jesus thing?"

"Well, that was mainly in the purview of Jesus, but technically he gave that power to the Apostles. But if people didn't know how to do it, then they didn't know how to do it. However, since he gave that power to the leaders of the Catholic Church, it could easily be argued that's how the Church could do such a thing. There's an argument there, especially since most people considered the Church the primary authority on everything. You must remember that at this time, they even controlled the sciences. They didn't like what you said, they branded you a heretic."

"Still, I don't know that I would believe they could do such a thing. And why would you think that was it anyway if there was more stuff going on between France and Spain? Where does Italy fit in?"

"Well, see, most people do think it was just time for the Inquisition to end as people advanced in knowledge and the like. It was a time of great learning and growth and science started to rival God as the Inquisition drew to a close.

The Church wasn't getting away with crying heretic as much. Naturally, that would lead to an end of persecution like seen during the Inquisition.

"Now combine that with all the unrest in the world. You had the American Revolution followed by the French Revolution. Lots of fighting everywhere. People pretty much saying they had enough of the establishment. That would also lead to the end of something such as the Inquisition.

"Why think anything more of it? Most people would stop there. However, there are records of the Vatican communicating with those in Spain and other areas of the world basically saying to cease and desist. But beyond that, there is record of some interesting fighting in Italy, which seemed so far removed from the other altercations."

I really had no idea what he was talking about. Maybe that was the C in World History talking, or my pure disinterest in history as a whole. After all, why should I worry about stuff that happened long before I was born and half a world away? I spent more time partying than caring while I was in school that year.

"I barely remember hearing about the French Revolution. Like, I know that Napoleon wanted like world domination or something, right?"

"Well, yes, and there was a lot of fighting in Europe because of it. Nothing at the level of the World Wars or anything, but there was still a lot of fighting. I'm talking about the Fire of 1817. It burned much of Rome to the ground. The Papal States spent the next 100 years rebuilding their empire."

"Papal States?"

"Italy really wasn't unified until about 50 years later. Rome was part of what was known as the Papal States."

"I guess there really was a lot going on there."

"There was. The 1800s were an interesting time. It

wasn't my focus, but my roommate at college studied military history and really focused on the time period. I picked up a lot of information.

"The world was growing and yet it was shrinking all at the same time. Things were far less localized as technology progressed. We saw trains crisscross continents, allowing for easier travel. Sea travel became easier and safer as well. All these were utilized as people fled their native lands for other places, mostly the Americas. It is only natural that with people looking outside of their borders for more friction and strife to pop up."

"I guess. The French Revolution was after the American Revolution, right?"

"Yeah. I guess the French people thought that since it worked so well for the colonies, why not try it themselves? Things were tough in France. Of course, it ended with Napoleon leading and I'm not so sure that's what they quite expected."

"So, you're saying that Rome burned?" I asked.

"Yes. Just about the whole city burned to the ground. It was devastating for the Church especially. The Pope at the time nearly died. As it was, it took them years to rebuild. But they weren't the only area devastated during the 19th Century. There were issues in France, Spain, England, the Americas. Maybe it was all the fighting that helped propel us forward technologically, but it came at a terrible cost."

"I guess. I really didn't know that about Italy. It's Europe, after all. I just assumed it was always there and the city was really old. It was around like two thousand years ago."

"Really gives all new meaning to the phrase, 'Rome wasn't built in a day', doesn't it? But, here's the thing. The only people who kept any kind of decent records on the world for centuries centered around The Church. And they recorded everything, no matter how trivial it seemed."

"But you said Rome burned."

"Well, yes, but the Catholic Church was able to regroup quickly. And they rarely kept things in one place at that time. There was a lot of corruption and with that came paranoia. If they were to keep functioning as they did, they must have saved a good portion of their records."

"What are you saying? You think maybe Rome might have some answers?"

"Well, they might. But they might also let us know if this is truly something that hasn't been done for a multitude of centuries, but if maybe there are more recent incidents. Which would maybe also tell us if there are more like you. And maybe there will be translations of overheard legends of prophecies. Obviously, there's something out there. I want to know if it's only South American in origin."

I looked at our hosts, who sat just as patient as anything while Jon and I conversed. I noticed that the translator hadn't bothered to tell them what we were saying.

"Do they know anything of that nature? Did this spread from South America? Could people still be creating undead armies?" I didn't think it was too much to ask. Sure, they might not know anything, but who would it hurt to ask?

The man shook his head. "I do not know of any, but this is not my expert study." He turned and began speaking to the Head Honchos.

I looked at Jon, who just shrugged at me. "It is likely they don't know. But maybe they do. I knew I'd found things here, and that it was possible that rumors of legends could get back to the Vatican from missionaries or the Spaniards."

Our translator turned back to us. "They say they know nothing of this sort. There are no stories or prophecies regarding anywhere but here in our lands. That does not mean there aren't stories elsewhere. The world is a large place, but all the people are connected as one."

"What does that mean?" Connected as one? That sounded like some sort of new age enlightenment talk.

"We all come from the same base. We are all connected through the First Parents. We may not know how or how far back we must go, but in the end we all go to the same origins."

Jon looked at me, "Many believe that. There are so many origin tales that show striking similarities. Not everyone had a Garden of Eden, but many believe something of the sort. And there are tales in just about every ancient culture about a flood that covered the entire world. Take it with a grain of salt, but there are those that believe that with so many similar historical accounts, that there must be a shred of truth in them."

I was never crazy religious, but my parents sometimes had me attend the Baptist Church down the street from our home. I knew enough about the Bible to probably make me utterly useless, but I did know about the flood story as well as the Garden of Eden. "I didn't know anyone but Christians believed in those things."

"When you really start to study cultures, you begin to notice similarities. Perhaps it is because our population is ever expanding, but if you go far enough back and there just weren't that many. Or the nomads that traveled would share stories when they met with other nomads. That would spread these tales further and further across the globe. Besides, Christianity takes its origins from the Jews."

"I guess. But, wow, I guess, I feel like my education was lacking. I knew I blew off some classes, but still. Who would have thought any of this was going on?"

Jon looked at our translator and in turn, our hosts. "So, if you think that is possible, maybe we should try to find out. Can you send anyone to research that?"

The translator didn't even bother to ask the Head Honchos. "No. That is not possible. There is still a great fear among our people of that kind of travel. We tend to stay close to home unless there is great need."

I rolled my eyes. "Like coming to find the so-called Chosen One?"

"Exactly. And you see why. We are at odds with others. It makes it very difficult to travel. This is not the first time someone from our people encountered those like we defeated today. We try to keep to ourselves. Those that continue their education at a higher level, do so as close to home as possible. I studied in Brazil for instance."

Figures. What better way to keep people believing how you want than to ensure they are afraid of outsiders? Though, after meeting with Leahonia's band of merry little men, I could see the case for some prudence. That said, I couldn't imagine a life without traveling. I liked to be on the go.

CHAPTER
TWENTY-EIGHT

So, these people didn't travel, they didn't know if any-one else used weird undead armies, and yet they wanted me to frolic with them for the rest of natural or unnatural life? I really liked this plan less and less the more I heard of it.

"I really think that maybe we should try to learn more."

Leave it to Jon to play the academia card. Goodness knew I was fairly useless at it since I could barely remember anything from whatever college classes I took that could possibly pertain to South America or Europe. Don't even get me started on religion. Though after dying and coming back from the dead, I wasn't so sure that religion and I were on good terms anymore.

"Well, here's a question for you, Jon. If they don't travel and we need to find out more, how do you expect to actu-ally make that happen?"

"I guess we need to go if they won't send anyone."

Wait. Go where? Italy?

I was totally down for a trip to Italy. Maybe this was looking up. Go from a cruise to a trip to Italy? Imagine the shopping! Oh wait, my Amex was buried in rubble. Life sucked. Because that reminded me that my passport was also buried in the same rubble pile. With no passport, how was I supposed to get to Italy? The momentary distraction of Italian purses and shoes subsided, and I felt grumpy all over again.

"Great, but uh, remember me? We don't even know how to get me home to Virginia and you're talking about a trip to Italy?"

Jon looked thoughtful. "That would prove problematic-"

Our fearless translator broke in. "Excuse me, but I think we can solve that problem. Just because we don't like to travel doesn't mean that we are without resources. The few we do send out, they travel under false identities. We can get you papers made and if there are any available, they could accompany you."

Fantastic. Now these people are proving useful. Why on earth couldn't they tell me that earlier?

"I thought you just said your people didn't like to travel. Don't get me wrong, I'd love to bounce to Italy and all, and I'd love papers so I can get home. But, if you have travelers, why can't they go get the information we need from Italy?"

"Just because we have them does not mean they are free at the moment. And we do try to reserve the need to travel to only the strictest of emergencies."

"The strictest of emergencies? What do you think this is? I died. I was raised from the dead. At least one person wanted me dead and brought some friends to the party. If this doesn't count for emergency, I don't know what does." Had my voice gotten shriller? Quite possibly.

"Bea, maybe you should calm down," Jon said in that

tone. I glared at Jon for even implying that I needed to show a little more decorum. I'd really had enough.

"Calm down? Did you just tell me to calm down? Maybe you should try going through what I've gone through these last few days. I didn't ask for any of this, but this is what I'm stuck with. And I'm sorry if that seems so mundane to you, but I never planned on dying on a cruise to another country or find myself raised from the dead or hunted by savages. I definitely never planned on becoming anyone's 'chosen one' and I just want to find out if I'm in any more danger and then go home and try to live a normal life. If you don't like that, then stuff it. To top it off, I lost things that I care about so much. And yet you tell me to calm down? I will not calm down!"

I realized that my screeching turned into rambling, but I was about in tears; again! I didn't even care anymore. Let them see me cry. Let them even call me whiny. There's only so much a girl could take, and I was at my limit.

"Bea, we will figure it out. It really will be okay," Jon soothed.

Jon's words really didn't help, but I'd said my fill, so I glared at him. My silence gave the others a chance to converse and before I knew it, our translator spoke once more to us.

"We understand your being upset. We strongly feel that you should stay with us so we can protect you, but you both bring up valid points. If there is a chance to learn more, to better know how The Chosen One can do that which she must do, we need to find that information out. We will travel back to our home. From there we will plan for a departure to Italy for the both of you. Meanwhile we will continue to tap our own resources to prepare for what is to come."

I turned my attention from Jon. "You will help me then?"

Boggs

The man nodded. What a relief. It couldn't be too hard to get something happening for me from an embassy or a consulate or something, if I could prove who I was. Right? But that would involve finding someplace to do that. At this point I didn't even care if they doctored me something to get me across the border. Once back in Virginia, I could easily get replacements for everything I lost in the earthquake.

At least that was what I hoped.

Jon scratched his head with his right hand. "I don't know if I have any contacts in Rome, but if I could get to a computer, I could try. I do believe there's a chance there is something there. The details surrounding the burning of Rome, it was always something that bugged my roommate. Maybe I just picked up on that from him, but then again it could be something."

"Where is your roommate now?" I thought it was a simple enough question.

"I'm not exactly sure. We lost touch a few years ago. It's a little harder for me to keep in touch with a lot of people where I've been working. I haven't had a steady internet connection for three years and no one really uses the postal system anymore. I could find out though. I'd like to start with him."

"What was it that bugged him so much?" Another fairly obvious question in my mind, but I was still curious.

"The timing didn't really match up for all the wars going on, things were actually fairly quiet in Rome at the time of the fire. Yet there were also signs that it was a burning, like you would see in wartime. Most chalk it up to just the time. A simple accidental fire could take down a whole town."

"But they don't think it was an accident?" I asked.

"It all depends on who you talk to. But if you think about the Chicago Fire, that was a tough time in America and especially for Chicago. The supposed story seems fairly accidental enough. A lantern kicked by a cow in a barn. No malice, no forethought, just pure dumb bad luck. Yet the fire raged for several days and destroyed a great deal of the city. I'm sure what happened in Rome could easily be something equally innocent and we just haven't heard of a Roman cow like the O'Leary cow in Chicago. Anything is possible. There's an argument for it coming from some sort of battle."

The translator appeared glued to Jon's words. "There are tales that communities would burn their villages in order to wipe out the undead troops. They knew no other way, and when you are fighting an enemy that would send those that did not care if they took out innocent lives, you get desperate."

I couldn't imagine, even though I lived in an area ravaged by the American Civil War. Northern troops burned enough of our Virginia towns and countryside on their own, why would we need to do the same?

"Do you think that the Roman people set the city on fire to stop some army of dead people from invading?"

Jon shrugged. "Perhaps. I mean, why not? Of course, there's plenty of conspiracy theories out there about the Catholic Church. If they were raising the dead themselves, it is possible that someone attempted to burn records to erase the evidence. Think of it as the shredding of documents in those days. It could be done as a cover up or as a way for someone to stop what they thought was a turn towards wickedness."

Living in Virginia, conspiracy theories were nothing new to me. It seemed like everyone had a pet conspiracy theory, and the closer you got to DC, the wilder the theories got. Considering the amount of government workers where I lived, that tended to get frightening because you wondered how much might actually came from facts.

"People do weird things. I can see that. But I put nothing past politicians. Mostly I just try to ignore them. Unless they come in to where I work. Their money spends just as well as anyone else's."

Jon laughed, his eyes crinkling around the edges. "There is that. This could easily be the same thing. Just without the ease of shredders and a delete key."

"Burning an entire town seems rather extreme though. Like you want to hide something, so you run around throwing Molotov Cocktails into places? That sounds like a bad action movie."

And if that was a bad action movie, what did that make me? Bound for the next plane to Italy, apparently.

ABOUT THE AUTHOR

Jacalyn Boggs lives in Northern Virginia with her chihuahua, Nephi. She loves sunshine, the night sky, traveling the world, and dancing to the music only she hears. Raising two children taught her you never know what's around the next bend.

Always a dreamer, Jacalyn loves reading and watching movies. Her favorite fiction is that which explores the world in some new way. She's currently working on several other writing projects, including the next book in The Reanimated World Tour series.

MORE FROM
ERENDI PUBLISHING

Giant Killer Bats of Alamogordo
Jack Morse

A Collection of Small Endings
JC Rock